SMALL TOWN EMP

Survive the Chaos

Survive the Aftermath

Survive the Conflict

RELAY PUBLISHING EDITION,SEPTEMBER 2019
Copyright © 2019 Relay Publishing Ltd.

Grace Hamilton is a pen name created by Relay Publishing for co-authored Post-Apocalyptic projects. Relay Publishing works with incredible teams of writers and editors to collaboratively create the very best stories for our readers.

Cover Design by LJ Mayhem Covers
www.relaypub.com

SMALL TOWN EMP BOOK THREE

SURVIVE
THE CONFLICT

GRACE HAMILTON

BLURB

The world has descended into a nightmarish hell. Death and destruction reign at every turn. Everywhere Austin Merryman has led his tightknit group of survivors has gone from bad to worse as enemies pursue them for the intelligence he possesses. Yet, his group remains steadfastly together even as the infighting continues.

It's only when the cryptologist traveling with them finally breaks through the last coded barrier, exposing the full extent of the data on the mysterious USB drive, that their luck finally seems to be turning. So many have already given their lives to secure the information, and now they know why.

Now, a small window of opportunity remains for stopping the New World Order from succeeding in their plans, but Austin and his cohorts will have to move fast. Once again, splitting up may be their only option, but at what cost? And can they really launch the countermeasures that could take down the NWO's plan for domination?

But when the enemy closes in and lives of his entire group are threatened, Austin will be forced to choose between his family and the ultimate survival of the entire world...

CONTENTS

1

A ustin Merryman kept his guard up as he headed inside the small convenience store, Amanda Peterson right behind him. The place had been used to serve campers staying in the nearby RV park, and he knew it wasn't likely they'd find any food, but they had to try. Months without any stores and surviving by the seat of his pants meant that just about anything he could loot from the store could be useful— anything they could carry off, anyway.

Austin double-checked behind the store's counter, but the place was empty. Most of the shelves were, too. Off to the side, he saw Amanda pick up some empty boxes from the shelves and then begin rummaging around in the counters beneath the old coffee station, looking for anything that could be useful. They'd learned a lot about improvising and repurposing regular everyday items, all to make living without electricity, running water, and even grocery stores possible.

Leaving her to it, he ducked down to the lower shelves and began searching through the spaces that other scavengers were more likely to have missed. The place was empty enough that he figured that was about their only shot.

"Transmission fluid and some oil," Austin said, standing with the bottles of car fluids that had rolled under a shelving unit.

"Good fuel," she replied. From the look on her face, she hadn't found anything to be excited about.

With their limited loot in plastic bags, they walked back to the door, waiting and listening for any signs that there were other people around. Their scavenging mission was proving to be futile, like the one yesterday and the day before that. They'd hoped the small towns would provide something worthwhile, but destruction had become widespread. The towns had been abandoned for some time, but only after being thoroughly ransacked.

"Clear," Austin finally muttered, stepping outside with the Glock in his right hand, ready for whatever popped up.

He would have killed for one of the ARs or M-4s they'd taken off the NWO back at the house, but their guns had been stolen right out of their hands days ago while they'd still been generally heading west toward a more temperate climate. Without any sure destination, that had been the fallback plan—to keep going and find somewhere they could hole up. They'd landed in an abandoned lodge that had seemed to have a lot of promise, but the nearby scavenging wasn't offering much to live from. Those guns, though—he could still taste the anger over losing them. It was the way of the new world, though. A game of Yankee Swap. They kept their weapons, food, and gear only until someone came along and took it. Then, they in turn did the same thing to another group. It was a revolving door of easy come and easy go with weapons, especially. He was ready for the tide to turn back in their favor and allow them to stumble on more weaponry, but it hadn't happened yet.

Amanda pointed off to the side, away from where they'd come from. "Let's head down that trail and see if we can find anything in the RVs. Maybe we'll get lucky."

He nodded, his eyes scanning the area. "But where is everyone, seriously? Bed, kitchen, shelter, and porta-potties... why wouldn't anyone make this their new home?" he pressed even as he followed her. Maybe this could work for their own needs.

"I don't know, but let's hurry up and get moving. This place is kind of creepy," she answered, her voice low. "Maybe that's reason enough."

The RV park was basically a parking lot with designated spaces. Not many trees, not much natural beauty. Even in the middle of nowhere, it was the park owner's way of packing in as many RVs as possible and taking advantage of the beauty of the area. Austin guessed they were in the lower west corner of Wyoming now, but he couldn't be sure. And had they been tracked? It was hard to tell, but he suspected that they had— whether that suspicion was made up more of paranoia or intelligence, he couldn't be sure.

Austin thought back to the months prior to the EMP, when he'd been living in the fifth-wheel with Savannah, traveling the country. They'd stayed in various campgrounds and parks of nearly all sorts, but this specimen of resting spot was the kind he'd avoided at all costs. There was no real privacy, and in the tenuous situation they were in now, there was no real cover. He and Amanda couldn't help being exposed as they walked along the narrow paved road that led into the park.

Scanning the grounds, Austin noted that there were only a handful of RVs remaining, and even so, the place looked junky and cramped. The EMP would have hit right at the beginning of the RV season, but occupants had disappeared fast. He imagined it had been an older crowd—people who full-time RV'd after retirement. They wouldn't have stood much of a chance against the soldiers or the hordes of people fleeing the cities.

"Let's start with the motorhome there," he said, pointing to the newer Class A with a slide-out and big sun shields placed in its front window. "I'll stand guard while you go in, and then we'll trade off on the next."

"Got it," Amanda replied, pulling open the flimsy door as Austin stepped to the side.

Almost as soon as she disappeared, he thought he saw movement near the picnic table parked under a single, lonely tree. He swung his gun up to point in the general direction, but whatever had moved was gone.

"Drop your weapon!"

Austin glanced over his shoulder, finding a man in his sixties standing on the one-way road behind him—bearded and thin, and pointing a hunting rifle at him.

"Sorry, mister. Apologies," Austin said, trying to keep his voice calm as he lowered his gun. He didn't drop it, but he pointed it at the ground as he faced the man. "I didn't know there was anyone around. Is this your place?"

The man smirked, closer now. "You already know who lives here. We've told you before: Stay out of our camp, and we'll stay out of yours!"

Austin shook his head, willing the man to believe him as he answered. "I've never met you before. I don't know who you think I am, but this is the first time I've ever been here. I didn't know it was occupied."

He'd made a point of using 'I' instead of 'we,' hoping Amanda would stay out of sight. If this was the man's place, they could figure out how to get her out once this guy lowered his hunting rifle.

The gun wavered, but remained aimed at him as the man scowled.

"We want to be left alone," he said after a minute had passed. "We're not causing you any trouble. There's plenty of hunting and water for us all to live here in peace. If you keep coming over here, we'll be forced to kill every one of you," he added, sounding almost saddened by the idea.

"Okay," Austin said. "I'm sorry. I'll go," he agreed, no longer wanting to argue about who he was or wasn't. The man seemed decent, and he clearly wasn't NWO. If he wasn't going to shoot his rifle, then Austin had no intention of killing him over what amounted, more than likely, to nothing more than a scrapyard of RVs that was all this man and his group had left.

"Your lady friend needs to go with you," the man said, jerking his head towards the RV.

Austin nodded, and he kept the surprise out of his voice when he called for her to come out.

She emerged with her hands up, still carrying the bag of things they'd picked up at the convenience store. The old man aimed the rifle at her now, silently telling her to leave what she'd found.

"Sorry," she said sheepishly. "I didn't realize anyone was still living here; I was just on the other side of the door. I didn't take anything. This is stuff I've been carrying around for a while," she told him. "Take a look and you'll see it came in with me."

"Drop it. Now. Or I'll drop it for you," the man said, no sympathy in his voice.

Austin widened his eyes at her, trying to tell her to let it go.

Amanda put the bag on the step outside the motorhome as she stepped down. "Sorry. We looked around and didn't see anybody. We didn't realize you were living here."

"Well, we are!" a woman's loud voice snapped from the other side of the park—near the RV by the tree where Austin had spotted movement earlier.

"We'll go. We're sorry," Amanda called out, her voice aimed toward the woman's.

"Go," the man ordered them, using his head to gesture them out of the park.

The man sidled out of their path to the road, and Austin slid his gun into his holster, not wanting to appear threatening in any way. It was nothing short of a miracle that they'd let him keep the gun, but he guessed this man didn't want a fight any more than they did. Reaching the road, he reached for Amanda's arm and kept his ears and eyes open as they headed away from the park, walking in silence until they passed the store and got headed back towards the two-lane highway they'd come in by.

"That was close," Amanda finally said.

"Yes, it was. They don't seem like bad people," he added after a minute had passed. Now that there was no danger to be felt from the man's rifle, sympathy was creeping in.

"Who do you think they thought we were?" she asked.

"Maybe part of the group that has the town we passed locked down, or people from that other campground we passed on the other side of the highway. There are clearly some very marked territories around here, and we stumbled right into the middle of them," he said.

She stopped in her tracks and he turned to face her, meeting her intelligent brown eyes with his—they were one of the few sights he'd enjoyed lately. "Why do you suppose none of them took over the hunting lodge?" she asked.

"Luck?" he joked, but then he shook his head as she turned to keep walking and he fell into step beside her. "I don't know. Maybe there was someone in there and they were run off by one of the other groups. Might not have been empty when they checked it out."

"So, do we keep looking or head back?"

He sighed disgustedly. "We're empty-handed."

"That tends to happen," she replied with a small laugh.

"You remember when needing milk or craving a candy bar meant running to the nearest store? I never realized how easy we had it before all this. I'll never take overpriced convenience store food for granted again—assuming it ever returns," he muttered.

She gripped his shoulder in quick understanding. "Let's head back. Maybe the others had better luck."

He nodded, knowing there was little else they could do. Hot and hungry, he felt more than ready to take off the boots that were making his feet feel like lead. They headed towards the lodge, the road making for a steady climb upwards. A trickling creek ran alongside it, almost nonexistent with the July heat drying everything out. Austin looked longingly at it as they walked, wishing he could dip his feet in for just a few minutes. Amanda drifted away from him, inspecting a car stopped dead in the middle of the left lane of the highway. He moved towards the creek instead, drawn to the crystal-clear water flowing downhill.

And then the silence around them, filled with the gurgling sounds of the creek and the few birds braving the heat over-head, was interrupted by gunfire.

The crack of a rifle, followed by what sounded like a semi-automatic and more rifle shots.

Austin dropped and rolled toward the tree line not a second too soon; as he came up, he noticed where the tree bark had exploded just beyond the highway. His knee slammed into a rock as he backed behind a large boulder. This wasn't anything new. They'd been chased out of towns and little makeshift settlements before.

He waited until the shooting had stopped for several seconds before he popped his head up slightly, eyeing the area. "Amanda?" he whispered.

"I'm good. Sounds like they cleared out." Her soft voice had come from maybe twenty feet away, back behind the vehicle that hadn't moved in several months.

He got to his feet and looked up into the trees before motioning Amanda away from the car. She hurried his way, though there were no further gunshots—whoever had shot at them must have figured they'd gotten their message across.

"They're gone or they killed each other," he muttered as Amanda reached him and they crossed the creek, stepping into the trees together.

"This is getting old. We can't stay here," she said with a sigh. "We've risked our lives one too many times coming down here. It isn't worth it."

"I know. I was hoping to find something, though—anything. And it's not like we have a destination in mind at this point."

She dusted off her pants, taking in a deep breath. "Everything's a risk at this point," she reminded him.

"We need food, supplies, everything," he said, glancing back at the highway. What else were they supposed to do *but* scavenge?

"Maybe the others will have had better luck on their raid to the outskirts of town," she offered.

"I hope so," he replied as they started moving back up the mountain towards the hunting lodge they'd commandeered.

"They're going to figure out where we're living," Amanda said as they walked.

"I know, but I wouldn't call it living," he retorted.

"The lodge is perfect for us, Austin. It's got eight rooms, two huge living rooms, the commercial kitchen, and the trees for cover.... I mean, really, it doesn't get any better than that," she said, her tone wistful.

"We just need supplies," he answered simply, and she didn't argue.

He wiped sweat from his brow, but didn't suggest stopping. The hunting lodge was tucked into the trees a couple miles up the mountain. They'd moved to the lodge after heading west from the small cabin where they'd finally rested for a few days after leaving the prepper house. After the cabin and days spent in the woods, the lodge had seemed like paradise, and it had made sense to stop. The first week had been great, too, but as they'd begun to make scavenging runs into the small town and the outlying campgrounds, they'd realized there was some kind of a civil war brewing between the campgrounds.

But there were benefits to the location. They had enough water with the number of streams in the area, and there were plenty of greens to forage, especially without any so-called weed control in the parks and yards of the homes dotting the area. And while Austin worried that the NWO had tracked them, on some level he knew that they hadn't been covering easy ground. Heading west had made sense, but it had made for rough travel. That in itself offered some measure of safety— or, at least, he thought it did.

Unfortunately, they were in sore need of a steady source of protein. Hunting had fallen off, and while they were surviving, by no means were they thriving. Ennis had managed to harvest a couple of wild turkeys from the forest, but there just wasn't much else to hunt where they were—not with so many people trying to survive off of what they could catch and scavenge from the forests.

Austin breathed easier as they got further from the highway, traveling up the deserted two-lane road that was overgrown on both sides with tall, dry grass that made a rustling sound in the breeze. The lodge they'd taken over was down a gravel road with a gate blocking vehicle entrance. There was even a small barn for the horses. It really was an ideal home for their large group… but the location was wrong.

"He's still out there," Austin said, cutting through the silence. With Amanda, he knew he didn't have to explain who he was talking about.

She was his other half. She knew what he was thinking most of the time, and vice versa. They were so much more than housemates, though he hadn't quite figured out how to deal with what that meant. For now, he was content to keep his relationship with her in a neat little box to be dealt with later. Survival came before romance.

"I know," she replied.

"We don't know if or when Zander is going to show up. I don't believe for a second he's going to give up, Amanda. And as much as I'd like to think we lost him, I can't. With our large group, there's no way we hid our tracks all that well. They're probably not all that far behind us even now," he stated. "If not Zander, his people, ready to report back to him."

It was the same thing they'd been saying every day for the last several weeks, ever since they'd lost Nash and the house—everything had changed that day. They'd been on the move, crossing the land toward the upper part of Utah and the lower part of Wyoming, heading loosely toward Oregon on what Tonya had joked was their own version of the Oregon Trail. They'd done their best to stick to the mountain areas, preferring to stay out of the small towns that had dotted their way west.

"Are we supposed to keep running?" Amanda asked.

"I think we have to," he said, knowing it wasn't a permanent solution.

It took a moment for her to speak, and he almost didn't hear her when she did.

"I can't," she whispered.

He swallowed down arguments, knowing just how badly she wanted to remain at the lodge—and how badly he felt the need to keep going. "Sarah is working on those files," he reminded her. "That's what we're working toward. There's a chance we can end all this; we just have to be patient and stay alive long enough to make it happen." Beside him, she'd come to a stop and leaned on a tree, all but demanding he stop and listen. He did.

She leaned back, and glanced up toward the lodge before she spoke. "Austin, look what we have here. At some point, we have to stop, and there's no guarantee Sarah's going to come up with anything. We have to be realistic. I can't imagine the entire NWO operation can be taken down with a single USB stick. I mean, look what they've managed to accomplish thus far! They aren't going to be easy to beat, and I don't see how our little group is going to save the world. What are we going to do, blackmail them? We have nothing. And I know you think they're following us, but we can't be sure of that."

Her face looked pained, and he knew she was speaking reason, but it just didn't ring true. "We have the key, I just know it," he answered. "You can't give up on that yet."

She let out a long sigh. "I'm willing to try, but we have to figure something out. I don't want to keep running."

"Amanda, we don't have any other options!"

He stared at her for full seconds, willing himself not to give in. She was tired, yeah; they all were. But his gut told him that the NWO were following. And he couldn't do this without her. Finally, she pushed off the tree and gave him a quick nod—of acquiescence if not agreement—and they began walking again.

They made it up to the lodge and found that everyone else was already back. As Austin stepped into the main living area with the huge brick fireplace as its focal point, he automatically looked around for Savannah. He didn't see her, though. Lately, she'd been doing a very good job of keeping herself separated from the rest of the group.

"Did you get anything?" Wendell demanded, leaning forward from a chair pushed up against the wall dividing the kitchen and living space.

Austin just looked at him, still not all that pleased to have him along. Even though the guy's alcohol withdrawal was long gone, there was no denying that Wendell was generally unpleasant to be around. He was separated from the others, moody as always, and doing what he did best—nothing but watching and eavesdropping.

"I guess not," the man muttered, as if he would have done better.

"What happened?" Ennis asked casually.

Austin shrugged, but let out a sigh and sat beside his brother to take his boots off. "Same thing that always happens. What about you guys?" he asked Malachi and Jordan, who were sitting at the table with a chess set.

"We got chased out almost immediately," Malachi replied, grimacing.

Jordan nodded. "Got confronted about half a mile from the campground on the east side of town. Guys were convinced we were from the other campground. We decided it was best to walk away."

"You walked away? No fighting?" Tonya Loveridge asked, entering the room as she wiped her hands on a dish towel, kissing her son on his head before she moved to sit down.

Malachi looked down at the chess board. "Basically," he replied after she'd turned away.

Tonya shook her head, but didn't look surprised. Malachi had managed to convince her to let him go on the run with the agreement that it wouldn't be dangerous. There was no way any of them could have guaranteed that demand, though, and she knew it.

"Did you have to use the gun?" she asked.

Malachi put the chess piece he'd been holding down and finally met her eyes. "Nope. We talked our way out of it." After a moment, his mother nodded, but Austin didn't miss the fact that her eyes were more concerned than they'd been earlier. Doubtful, even.

"Same with us," Amanda broke in. "I don't think any of them are all that violent, Tonya. They're all just trying to survive. Honestly, I say we leave them alone," she added, earning a nod from Gretchen, who was sitting on one of the overstuffed sofas knitting with some yarn she'd found in one of the rooms. Drew echoed the sentiment as he continued using a knife to whittle a frog gig.

Tonya finally smiled and reached out to pat Amanda's arm as if in thanks for the reassurance. Austin knew how she felt, though. As Malachi's mother, she wouldn't stop worrying about her son any more than he could stop worrying about his daughter. It didn't matter whether or not these kids wanted to be treated as adults—they weren't there yet. He knew where his daughter was, too—she'd be in her room upstairs or out on the back porch, one or the other. The doctor, on the other hand...

"Where's Sarah?" he asked.

Ennis pointed up, meaning that she was upstairs again, locked away in the bedroom she'd claimed for herself. It had been a point of contention at first, but Austin had argued in favor of her having her own room. She was spending long nights awake, going through the files on the laptop after letting it charge on its solar charger during the day.

"I'm going to have dinner ready in about an hour," Tonya announced before anyone could bring up the subject of the single room again.

There were a few grimaces around the room, everyone knowing the only food available would be the greens Gretchen had harvested from the wild and the squirrels Ennis had managed to snare early that morning. The wild turkey had run out days ago, so they'd been eating squirrel and dandelions for days. It was getting old.

"Sounds great!" Harlen offered enthusiastically.

Austin suspected he was only trying to be nice, but at least someone was. Unlike Wendell, the man was a genuinely nice guy, and his counseling background had set him up as the natural mediator in the group.

"Where's Savannah?" Austin finally asked, though he could guess well enough.

"She was on the upstairs balcony," Malachi answered.

She'd been spending a lot of time up there or out back, alone and staring at the trees. Austin knew Nash's death had hit her hard. Trying to give her space hadn't seemed to do any good, and she seemed less and less inclined to make herself part of the group anymore. She was carrying a lot of guilt, still. No matter how much he, Amanda, and Ennis tried to assure her that there was nothing she could have done to stop Nash from going to the mine, she wasn't buying it.

But, he had some time before dinner—he'd go up and keep trying to convince her.

2

Wendell had been watching the group for weeks, listening to the way they talked and interacted with one another, always excluding him. He knew they didn't like him. He'd done nothing really wrong, but they looked at him like he was a pile of useless garbage. That's the way he felt, at least. Everything was worse since they'd lost the prepper house, too. He hated being sober, and hated having to deal with everything and everyone.

And, for his part, Austin hated him. He could feel it every time the man looked his way. That's what burned the most. Wendell had always thought Austin was some kind of God. He was the guy who'd had everything Wendell wanted. He'd been good-looking, popular, athletic and smart when they'd all known each other in school. The girls had flocked to him. Everyone had wanted to be around him—just like now.

Anything and everything Austin did was perfect. All the Bible thumpers treated him like he was the Messiah. They couldn't see that Austin's obsession with the stupid USB was going to get them all killed. Zander wouldn't even be after them if Austin weren't with them, but no one could see that. No, they were all mindless followers, and nothing Wendell said would make a difference.

Wendell had given up on telling them the truth—that if it weren't for Austin and his sweet little princess, Zander would leave them alone to live out their lives. All they had to do was leave the two of them behind.

But instead they were all on some crusade to save the world.

It was ridiculous. To think one man with no military training could stop the NWO, and with just their little rag-tag group to help. But Austin was leading them on, pushing them to believe it. The man had an inflated ego, and always had in Wendell's opinion.

Wendell let his hatred for Austin settle in his gut as he looked over to the one man he'd previously been able to count on. Even Ennis had been cold towards him lately, ever since they'd nearly died inside the house and he'd opted to get drunk rather than suffer a slow death. They acted as if he'd committed some horrible crime because he'd had a few drinks.

It wasn't like they could have done anything else. They'd been pinned down inside a burning house. And he wasn't the one who'd killed Nash, Audrey, or Bonnie. He'd been doing his part and protecting Savannah. Of course, Austin hadn't even bothered to say thank you for saving his daughter. He never would. So, yeah, there was mutual hatred between them at this point, and Wendell didn't expect it to go away any time soon.

His eyes drifted to where Malachi sat with his best buddy Jordan. The two of them had become very friendly. In fact, everyone seemed to like Malachi, too. Wendell couldn't understand why, though. It was Malachi who'd been a jerk towards Nash. It was because of Malachi and Austin's precious princess that Nash had been driven away from the house, alone and unprotected.

Wendell actively chose not to acknowledge his own role in encouraging Nash to leave. If anything, he'd pushed the inevitable—really, he'd only been looking out for the guy's best interest. He couldn't have known the idiot would go and get himself killed.

Yet, he did know he needed to do something, and fast, if he wanted to stick with the Merryman brothers and the God Squad. As much as he disliked them, they did prove useful. They were keeping him alive, albeit on squirrel, and that was a big deal. Unfortunately, his freeloading had gotten more and more noticeable since they'd left the house. Now that he'd even lost Ennis's friendship, he'd begun worrying they were going to make him walk the plank, so to speak. He had to find a way to contribute now that the withdrawal was behind him, no matter how lousy he still felt.

He was ready to get involved and take down a deer or do something to redeem himself. He had to. He'd work on Ennis first, he decided. Down deep, Ennis was a good guy who'd welcome him back into his warm embrace now that he'd had some time to cool off. Wendell just had to prove himself, and he could do that. Then, he'd apologize, blame the alcoholism they were all so sure he suffered from, and vow to stay sober —it wasn't like he had a choice.

"Ennis," Wendell started, "I was wondering if I could go with you tomorrow?" He hoped he sounded cheerful about the idea.

Ennis glanced over at him with a puzzled frown. "Where?"

He forced a smile onto his face. "I overheard you say you're going hunting in the morning."

On the other side of the room Malachi and Jordan looked up from their chess game. "We were," Malachi said in an unfriendly tone.

"I'd like to go," Wendell said again. "I can help drag back the deer if you get one."

Ennis hesitated briefly before nodding. "Fine. It'll do you good to get some exercise and fresh air."

Amanda, bossy as always, raised her eyebrows. "Are you up to that, Wendell? Sure you've regained your strength?" she asked, slightly sarcastic.

Yeah, he'd played up his weakness. He could admit he might have overplayed his hand just a touch, but so what? They'd get over it.

He gritted his teeth to keep from snarking back at her. He couldn't tell her to mind her own business. He had to play nice.

Smiling again, he cleared his throat. "I'm feeling a lot better. I appreciate everyone's understanding as I went through a very difficult time," he added, looking around to meet everyone's eyes—except for Austin and Savannah, who were upstairs, which he didn't mind a bit. "I know I've not been a huge help, but I'm feeling good, my mind is clear, and I'm ready to be a part of all this. I appreciate the prayers," he said, smiling at Tonya.

Harlen, the man who'd decently helped in his detoxing, smiled and nodded before anyone. "You've made the first big step, beating the disease and admitting you have a problem. The hardest part is behind you. Your journey to sobriety is going to be a little easier than it would be if we were in the old world, too! You won't have alcohol on every corner, tempting you, but you are going to have cravings. I think we all need to be there for Wendell as he gets through the next stage of his recovery," the former drug and alcohol counselor said, looking around as he finished up another over-the-top pronouncement in that deep baritone voice of his. He had been helpful, even if he'd become a bit insufferable since the worst of the with-drawal had actually ended.

Wendell wished he could slap him, but it wasn't like that would go over well.

"Thank you, Harlen. I appreciate the support," Wendell forced out. "All of you have been amazing and I hope to repay your kindness." He wrapped up with his best, charming smile.

The others didn't look quite as accepting of his supposedly new outlook, but he knew the revivalists wouldn't openly discourage him. After all, they were all peace, love, and joy, and talked nonstop about saving the sinners of the world. Forgiveness was their shtick. He had a few sins that were pretty dark—too dark for them to stomach, for sure—but he'd play along. He'd use his problem to his advantage if it gained him sympathy and kept him in the group.

"I'd like to go along, as well, if that's okay," Harlen said. "It's about time I learned how to hunt."

"Works for me," Ennis said. "The more of us that know how to track and hunt, the better it'll be. We need to be doing weekly hunts to keep our bellies full; dividing to conquer will make it easier."

Wendell smiled, pretending he believed that statement. He wasn't for one second looking forward to going out at the crack of dawn to look for a deer, which seemed to be everywhere until there were rifles around.

"Great. I'm looking forward to the time outdoors and clearing my head," Wendell said.

"It's going to be an early morning. We'll all need to be plenty rested," Ennis reminded him.

"I'm going to go fetch some water from the stream," Harlen announced, getting to his feet.

"I'll help," Ezra said, putting down the months-old magazine he'd been reading in the corner of the room.

Wendell knew they were waiting for him to volunteer to carry one of the jugs of water. He inwardly grimaced while pasting on a big, fake smile. "I'll go along," he volunteered, taking the first steps back into the good graces of the household.

Ennis's look of surprise didn't go unnoticed, but Wendell ignored it and followed the other men outside as if this was truly going to be his new norm.

"You're doing well," Harlen said as they walked towards the running stream.

"I'm trying. I know I have a lot to make up for," Wendell said, doing his best to sound contrite.

"I think we've all made mistakes. Don't get too hung up on that part of your recovery. You have to focus on yourself," Harlen said. "Just keep going forward, being positive, and you'll be a-okay."

Wendell hid a smirk. He was absolutely going to focus on himself, and that meant staying alive long enough to get away from these people. There was always something better. He only needed to bide his time until that something better came along.

3

Austin stepped out of the bedroom he shared with his brother with a bit more optimism than he'd felt in days past—one thing about this new world: he was tired enough to sleep well most nights, if not every night, and that did something for his morning outlook. Plus, talking with his brother the night before had put his mind more at rest. Austin felt grateful to have his brother by his side as they navigated this new world. Ennis made him crazy, sure, but Austin knew the man was very capable, especially in this new survival situation they'd found themselves in. Weirdly, things had been good between them since the house had burned down. Good as things could be, anyway, when they were on the run from a madman intent on killing them slowly and painfully.

But, as brothers, they were doing good. They'd had their fight and it was in the past. It had been a way of relieving the pressure and stress that had been building for years, all intensified by the situation of the world in chaos. Now, it was just a matter of surviving.

Ennis already stood in the living room, preparing for the hunting trip.

The sun was barely rising in the sky, providing little light into the lodge through the tall windows that faced west. The building was one of those fancy ones that rich guys would have paid thousands of dollars to stay in for a single night. No doubt, the place would have served delicious meals and top-shelf liquor as guests relaxed by the fire each night, regaling each other with stories about the big one that got away. The lodge had been quite luxurious at one point.

Working with his brother, he checked over the few hunting rifles they'd managed to retrieve from secret caches around Ennis's house back in Colorado. The whole of the arsenal they'd built up had been lost in the fire, but they still had a few guns and minimal ammunition to get by—most of what they'd had prior to what they'd gotten from the NWO soldiers, really. They'd certainly never be able to win a war with what they had, and they all knew it. They were constantly searching for more weapons and ammunition as a result.

Austin hoped his brother managed to get a deer today. He could really go for some venison steaks. Meanwhile, Austin, Amanda, and Drew were going to make another attempt to scavenge in an area they hadn't previously tried. They'd gone down the mountain and into town, but they hadn't tried to go south because the terrain looked rougher. Austin believed there had to be housing, though—and possibly more camp-grounds or another town they could reach. He wasn't ready to give up on finding candles, clothing, and more supplies in general.

Tonya, Savannah, and Sarah would stay at the house with Gretchen and Mike. They'd be safe enough. Austin was confident in Gretchen's ability to shoot to kill if need be. He'd seen it once before. Savannah was capable, as well, if she really needed to be.

"You'll be back by late afternoon?" he asked Ennis.

"That's the plan. Probably earlier, unless we actually manage to get something. I'll field dress it out there. I don't want to bring in the cougars and coyotes I know are around."

"Cougars?" Austin echoed. He hadn't even thought about dealing with those.

Ennis nodded, closing up a backpack with supplies as he did. "I saw some tracks the other day when I was out scouting. We'll be fine as long as we keep our heads up."

Austin grimaced. "Great. I'll keep that in mind."

The entire household was awake now, and Austin walked over to Savannah where she stood in the kitchen, staring out the window.

"It's pretty out there," she commented.

"It is. You going to help Tonya around here today?"

She didn't look at him, only continuing to pull her hair up in a ponytail. "We're supposed to go look for huckleberries. Gretchen says they're in season. We just have to find them."

"Huckleberries sound delicious. Remember when we stopped at that little roadside stand last year? That lady's huckleberry jam was amazing," he reminisced, practically tasting the stuff.

His daughter shrugged. "It was okay."

But there was a small smile on her face, he noticed. "I bet Tonya's got a recipe to rival it," he said. When she didn't seem inclined to say more, he gave her a quick hug and then caught her eyes before letting her go. "Keep that thirty-eight on you, and use it if you have to." He hated that he even had to tell her that at all.

"I know. I will," she muttered, already pulling away.

"I'll see you tonight. Good luck."

Ennis and his hunting party were walking out the door when he returned to the living room. After a quick conversation with Gretchen and Mike about firing two shots into the air if they needed help, he headed out with Amanda and Drew.

"How's Savannah?" Amanda asked.

"She's still in a funk," he answered. "They're going to look for berries today. Maybe Gretchen will get her to open up. She certainly isn't talking to me."

"Don't take it personally, Austin. She's got a lot to deal with. She's taking Nash's death harder than any of us," Amanda said.

"I know, and I understand why, but I can't let her shut down. Have you seen how much weight she's lost?" he asked.

"I can try talking to her," Drew suggested. "I worked as a youth pastor back in my twenties. Sometimes it helps to talk to someone you don't know very well. Couldn't hurt, anyway."

"I'd appreciate that," Austin said after a moment. "She has to work through this or it's going to eat her alive."

Drew smiled. "I'll try and pull her aside tonight."

With that, they seemed to come to a silent agreement to focus on moving forward, and Amanda took the lead in heading south. But they'd only been gone around twenty minutes and walked less than a mile when Austin heard a single gunshot.

"Ennis?" Amanda asked, all of them going stalk still as they exchanged glances.

Austin held up a finger, his head cocked to the side as he listened for a second shot. It was a few seconds later when it rang out, echoing around them. It sounded like the shot had come from a different caliber of gun, but he couldn't be sure.

That might have been the second shot to signal trouble, connected to the first.

"Something's wrong," Austin said, his sweat going cold.

"Was that two shots or is that the guys hunting?" Drew asked.

Austin was already moving back the way they'd come, and he answered over his shoulder. "I don't want to take any chances. We head back."

They'd only gone a quarter mile back toward the lodge when more shots sounded. Austin began running through the trees, his heart pounding as he thought about Savannah being hurt. He knew it was risky to run over the rough terrain, and that he was taking a chance on spraining an ankle or worse, but he couldn't stop. Adrenaline and fear pushed him to keep going.

"Wait!" Amanda shouted. "We have to see what's going on. Don't run into a gun battle without surveying the situation!"

After seconds more of running, her reason got through to him and he slowed, his breathing ragged with stress and exertion. She caught up quickly, Drew right behind her. This was Amanda's area of expertise. She was battle-trained, and he had to follow her lead. He forced himself to breathe slower and fall into step alongside her as she continued moving towards the lodge, but at a much slower pace.

"It's not the lodge," he said when more shots rang out, realizing the noise was coming from lower down the mountain.

"No, it isn't, but those shots are way too close for comfort," Amanda said.

Austin moved faster, hoping Savannah and the others hadn't left the house yet. The idea that the gunshots could have been directed at his little girl made him sick to his stomach. He didn't want to think of them being somewhere in the middle of the shooting just because they'd gone looking for berries.

A sharp whistle pierced the air. He looked to the right and immediately saw Mike gesturing to them. Austin pivoted to head his way, up a small, rocky outcropping.

"Where's Savannah?" he asked when he reached the other man.

"I'm here," Savannah said, standing up from where she'd been crouched low behind some green bushes. Gretchen stood beside her, waving a distracted greeting as Tonya stepped into view from behind another tree. They'd only been hiding.

Austin breathed a sigh of relief.

"Where's the shooting coming from?" Amanda asked.

Mike shook his head. "We'd been out maybe five minutes when we heard the first shot. It came from down the hillside a bit. I couldn't tell you exactly how far, but the other shots, those are moving in this direction."

"Sarah's still in the lodge," Savannah said quietly.

Austin's relief disappeared. They couldn't risk losing Sarah. She held the key to everything—at least, he hoped she did.

"We need to find Ennis and the others," Amanda said.

"Who's shooting, though?" Drew asked.

"I think it's those other groups fighting each other," Austin answered. "Has to be. Let's move. Mike, take them higher. We'll go after Ennis and the others."

Mike nodded, leading the way up the steep hill, away from the action happening further down the mountain. Austin followed Amanda's lead, taking a wide berth around the lodge and staying high above whatever was happening below.

"Austin," he heard, immediately recognizing his brother's voice.

"Ennis?"

"Here," Ennis replied, emerging from the trees about twenty feet away.

"Is everyone okay?" Austin asked, watching as the others came out of the trees.

"We're good. We didn't get far."

"Neither did we," Amanda muttered.

The sound of gunfire seemed to be getting closer.

"We need to see what's happening. It could be a hunting party," Austin suggested, though the words didn't ring true to any of them.

Ennis just looked at him. "You know what it is."

"No, I don't. Not until I see it with my own two eyes. But we need to get Sarah out of there if she's still inside the lodge, too," Austin said, not willing to back down. "And the laptop," he added as an afterthought.

"Let's split up. We'll fan out, moving towards the lodge and trying to see what's happening. We can't up and leave if there's no real danger," Amanda said, looking from one brother to the other.

"Then we make it fast. I don't want to risk getting caught or getting hit by bullets meant for someone else," Austin replied.

"Let's go," Amanda said, taking the middle position.

The rest of the group fanned out, forming a flat V as they moved downhill towards the lodge. As they moved closer, the gunshots grew louder. Austin could see the lodge through the trees. It was Malachi who raised his hand, giving a short whistle and drawing the attention of the others. He pointed to the small parking lot in front of the lodge. There was a man lying on the gravel.

"They're coming," Dr. Bastani's deadpan voice commented from behind them.

Austin spun around and saw her standing next to a tree, the laptop and its charger cradled in her arms. "What?" he asked.

"One of them came into the lodge. He didn't know I was there. I heard someone rustling around in the kitchen and went to investigate. He didn't seem like a bad person," she said flatly, her eyes wild.

Shock, he realized.

"What happened, Sarah?" Amanda asked, her voice offering a calm that Austin didn't remotely feel.

"He said it was theirs. He said he was taking the lodge," Sarah replied, devoid of emotion.

"Who said that?" Austin asked.

Sarah pointed through the trees to the man lying in the gravel. "Him, the man I shot. He said we had to move, that his wife wanted a real house and not a camper. He followed someone here. He wasn't a bad man," she repeated, shaking her head.

"Then what happened?" Amanda asked.

Sarah looked at the man and then back at Amanda. "I killed him," she said. "I stabbed him in the jugular vein. I told him he would die in a matter of minutes. He tried to run, and that's where he landed," she added, looking to the man's body once again.

Wendell cursed nearby, as shocked as the rest of them. For once, Austin didn't blame the man for his reaction. No one said anything for a few moments more. Austin was stunned. The woman barely spoke, barely showed any kind of emotion besides irritation, and now she'd just explained how she had stabbed a man.

"Are you hurt?" Amanda asked.

Sarah shook her head. "No. But they're coming. We have to go."

"Who's coming?" Austin asked, wanting to shake the woman out of her stupor.

"His family. He said they were moving into the lodge. They're going to be very upset when they find him dead," she added casually.

Austin looked to his brother, then Amanda, the two people he relied on the most. "Who's doing the shooting?"

"I'd guess that guy was planning on moving his family to the lodge and someone in the other camp got wind of it. Either way, they know about the lodge," Ennis said with a sigh. "Now... I'd bet you ten to one they're fighting over it."

"We can defend it," Wendell argued.

"At what cost?" Amanda replied.

"She's right," Ennis said, though disappointment sounded in his voice. "We need to leave for now. We can't get into a gunfight. We risk someone being hurt or killed. We hide out and maybe they'll kill each other off."

Austin agreed. A gun battle was too risky. "Okay."

"Leave the lodge?" Wendell asked, his voice high.

"We move now," Amanda said, taking charge. "Grab every-thing you can. Roll silverware, food, supplies, everything into the blankets. We'll all carry a bundle. Take two blankets if you can," she finished, already moving back towards the lodge.

They burst into the lodge as one, half of them rushing upstairs to strip the blankets from the beds while the others raced into the kitchen, grabbing the knives and rope they'd found along with the box of foil and sandwich bags. The rushed packing was hectic, but the gunfire was getting closer—they could all hear it. They only had minutes to get what they could and run before they'd be sucked into the war happening in the woods.

"The horses!" Amanda called out suddenly, whirling to see Austin coming down the stairs.

"Right. Get out now—head up the mountain to Mike and the others," Austin ordered the rest of their group as he and Amanda headed outside.

The bar wasn't far, and he heard the others already moving uphill as they reached it.

"We can't ride them out of here. The terrain is too rough," Amanda said, bridling Raven hurriedly.

Austin took charge of Charlie, all but throwing on the saddle and reins before following Amanda out of the small structure. He breathed once they got into the trees. The others, with their bundles in their hands and the backpacks they'd been traveling with on their backs, were already on the move.

"You! Stop! We'll shoot!" someone shouted from behind them, but a quick look backwards told him that the order hadn't been directed at them. At least for now, they hadn't been seen.

"Hurry!" Austin pressed Amanda. Thankfully, the horses were sensing their urgency—they were all but pulling him and Amanda along now.

Several shots rang out behind them, and Austin guessed they came from the lodge's front porch. "This is ours!" someone shouted.

"Left! Go left!" Amanda called out. They'd caught up to the rest of their group, who were moving uphill just ahead of them now, packs in hand.

With Amanda directing them, they moved fast and quiet. The sounds of gunfire faded behind them and eventually stopped. The groups had either killed each other or one had taken possession of the lodge. Either way, Austin knew they weren't going back.

It wasn't long before they met up with Mike and the others, and Austin didn't hide his relief when he finally got to hug his daughter close again, the latest brush with guns behind them.

"What do we do now?" Dr. Bastani asked, holding the laptop against her chest.

Austin looked to Amanda before glancing over to Ennis. He was open to suggestions.

"We have to move," Ennis grumbled. "Just when we were settling in, we have to move."

"At least it isn't the NWO we're running from right now," Ezra commented.

"This area is too populated," Amanda said quietly, sounding as if she was being forced to admit it to herself as much as anyone.

"Too populated? There's nothing but trees for neighbors," Wendell scoffed.

Austin glared at him, wondering why the guy bothered talking when he could never seem to be helpful. He added no value to the group.

"We need to move," Amanda reiterated.

"Where?" Austin asked.

The group fell silent, none of them having an answer.

"We could follow the mountain range north," Ennis suggested. "Maybe Canada is in better shape?" he offered.

"Back to the Oregon Trail," Tonya offered half-heartedly.

There were a lot of groans, no one interested in the idea of another grueling trek over rough terrain, and with no protection from the elements or any place to rest their weary bodies. The miles on their feet were taking their toll.

"We need shelter. We need access to food and water," Amanda said, eyeing her horses.

Austin nodded, knowing her well enough to know she was going to suggest something. "What? What are you proposing?" he asked.

"We split up," she said simply, and then she kept going before he could argue. "Two groups. Half of us will go north and the other half south. We'll meet at that huge Douglas Fir with the clearing on one side," she said. "Where we made camp the night before we found the lodge. Most of us have gone back to forage often enough that we know where it is in our sleep and won't have trouble meeting up there."

"Amanda," he started.

She shook her head. "It makes sense. There's enough of us to split up. There's no point in all of us going one way only to turn around and go the other. We save time and energy by dividing into two groups. The sooner we find a safe place, Austin, the sooner we get on the path to steady food."

"We don't know that the lodge is lost," Wendell argued.

"It's too dangerous. We already know there are warring factions near the lodge. Even if the lodge isn't taken over this time, it will be. Do we really want a repeat of what happened at the house? I wanted to stay in the lodge as much as anyone," Amanda admitted, looking around, "but it's no longer safe."

The group went quiet.

"She's right," Ennis said, breaking the silence. "Better to abandon the lodge than lose more friends. We need to move, and meeting in the clearing makes sense."

Austin hated the idea of splitting up. No matter how much sense it made. And what if it backfired on them?

But he couldn't think of anything better, and a quick glance around told him that too many of the group were waiting on him to decide the vote. So be it. "Okay," he said on a sigh.

"I'll lead one group, and you take the other," Amanda suggested.

"No," he answered immediately.

"Austin, it's better that way," she said, her eyes meeting his in that silent way she had of telling him to be reasonable. When it came to her and Savannah, that was hard. Harder every day, in fact.

He tried to think of a good reason to keep her with him, but he couldn't. She was right. She was a natural leader, and had the skills to lead a team back safely should there be any fighting. She'd already proven herself, and everyone, not counting Wendell, trusted her and her ability to lead.

"I'll go with her," Ennis said.

Austin nodded, feeling a little better knowing that his brother would have her back. "Good. Sarah, you're with me," he said, looking at the doctor.

"It isn't safe out there," she mumbled.

"It isn't safe right here," he retorted. "Savannah, you're with me, as well," he said, leaving no room for argument. He wasn't letting her out of his sight.

The rest of the group was divided as equally as possible, along with the weapons. Wendell was the only one who hadn't declared what group he wanted to be a part of, but Austin assumed he'd go where Ennis went.

"I'll go with Austin's group," Wendell announced, as if reading his mind.

Austin looked at Ennis, pleading with him to take his friend with him. Ennis just gave a slight shrug, earning him a glare from Austin.

"Fine," he muttered. "What about the horses?" Austin asked Amanda.

Amanda grimaced. "I don't think they'll be helpful in this situation. But I'm not abandoning them!" she added quickly, as if anyone would have suggested it.

"How about leaving them in the clearing?" he suggested. "My group will be headed just past it. We can take them up there and leave them overnight till we get back to them and the clearing tomorrow. We'll meet then, no later."

Amanda chewed her bottom lip. "I guess that's safer than taking them with either group. Make sure you tie their lead ropes loosely enough that they can get to that stream. They should be okay just for the night."

"Okay, then it's settled," Austin said. "We'll leave them by the stream near the clearing."

"Keep your heads up and we'll meet at the clearing tomorrow," Amanda said. "If not before. If you find something promising for the group, just head back to the clearing. Or if something stops you," she added pointedly, all of them knowing that was more likely.

Guns could stop any of their journeys early, to where they might as well head to the clearing and brainstorm what would come next. Splitting up for now made sense, and Austin knew it, but that was assuming they'd find anything of promise. It was far more likely, he thought, that they'd end up back at square one. He knew what Amanda and Ennis would say if he brought that up, though. And they were right. They had to try.

Austin looked at Amanda, meeting her eyes and saying all that he could without speaking. She offered a small smile in return before walking away. He watched her for a few seconds before collecting himself and turning to face his group. Wendell was looking at him in a way that sent a shiver of apprehension down his spine, but he didn't let it show in his voice when he spoke.

"Let's go. And, pay attention. There could be more people with guns out there just waiting to shoot," he warned them.

Ezra nodded. Austin was going to be counting on him to be his back-up. He didn't have much hope of Drew or Wendell being quick enough to eliminate a threat and keep his daughter safe.

4

Amanda knew she was pushing them hard, but she had to. They'd managed to stumble into a mid-sized town that seemed more industrial and factory-based than anything, but with plenty of trailer parks that had been burned to the ground, leaving only the skeletons of the trailer homes standing. It was a grim sight that held no real promise for them, but they had to keep moving through before they could set up camp for the night.

"What's that building?" Malachi asked from her left. Ahead of them, the huge square of a factory loomed above smaller businesses and houses that had been left to rot. It looked sturdy enough in comparison, if foreboding.

"Looks like some kind of factory; notice the huge stacks?" she asked, studying the building.

"We should ignore it," Harlen said. "I don't like it here. It's dark, dirty… and I can smell death."

"That could be a good thing. Empty is good. Safer," Ennis commented, "and we need a place to set up camp for the night, right?"

"It would be nice not to sleep outside," Tonya pointed out.

With that, the group spread out, staying far enough apart that, if they were ambushed, they wouldn't all be taken out in one sweep. Amanda remained a little surprised to have found the town deserted. It was an eerie sensation to walk down a street devoid of all signs of life, as if something had swooped in and snatched up the people who'd once lived and worked in the town. As they moved, she couldn't help but feel like they were being watched; from where, she couldn't immediately identify. They passed small stores that had been burnt out along with what had once been a clinic. There was no point in going in to scavenge—it was clear to all of them that anything left behind had been burned to a crisp.

"Why?" Malachi whispered.

"The burning?" Amanda asked.

"Yes, why would someone burn everything? What's the point?" he asked.

She shrugged, not bothering to stop walking. "I don't know. Control? Maybe it was the people who lived here… if they were being run out of town, they weren't going to leave anything behind. It's hard to say."

"It's so sad," Gretchen said as they passed another building that had been reduced to a pile of rubble.

Coming up on the building Malachi had originally pointed out, Amanda had to agree it looked pretty intact—more so than anything else they'd found anyway. "Okay, listen; Harlen, Tonya, and Gretchen, you three stand watch while the rest of us make sure the factory is empty. Since it's one of the few buildings standing, it might be occupied." Amanda directed them to the side, and then headed to the main entrance, holding her gun at the side of her leg. So far, it seemed as deserted as everything else in the town.

Malachi, Jordan, and Ennis followed her inside, where she silently directed Ennis and Malachi to go left while she and Jordan went right. The windows high in the room gave them some light to see by as they made their way around the bottom floor, seeing nothing but a catwalk high above and a row of offices on the back wall. The building appeared deserted and mostly empty.

"I'll get the others," Ennis said once they'd cleared the place.

"Everyone, spread out and see what you can find. Check for stashes of snacks in the desks and cabinets in those offices and bring whatever you find to the middle of the space. You never know what we might be able to use," Amanda said.

The sounds of their movements echoed as they separated off to search. Judging from the boxes of plastic cutlery strewn about, she surmised this place had been some kind of plastics factory that had manufactured disposable utensils. Too bad they didn't have more room to carry utensils—they could pack up some, but not enough for a lasting supply.

Aside from bags of utensils, the grand total of their scavenging resulted in a single bag of potato chips that had been stored in a cabinet and a half-roll of mints from a desk. The factory had been pillaged; no stone left unturned.

It was a meager dinner with everyone sharing a single bottle of water, knowing they had to ration what they had. They still had a long walk back up the mountain tomorrow.

"Does this mean we failed?" Malachi asked.

"Failed?" Ennis repeated, one eyebrow raised.

"We didn't find a house, we didn't find supplies, and we can't stay here," Malachi answered. "This place is creepy. I don't like it."

Amanda shrugged. "It isn't a failure. We were supposed to be scouting, and we scouted. Hopefully, Austin and the others had better luck."

The mood remained subdued as they unwrapped their blankets, which were filled with nothing truly useful in their current situation. The cement floor wasn't going to be conducive to a good night's sleep, but the roof over their heads was a bonus. They piled up cardboard to create beds, making for a slightly softer night, but kept close together.

"I'll keep watch," Ennis volunteered once their temporary camp was as good as it would get.

"Wake me in a couple hours," Amanda told him with a nod of thanks. "Everyone, we need to get up early, before the sun preferably. I want to move in the early hours and get back up the mountain before we run into any unfriendly folks who might be roaming about."

Amanda rolled onto her side, away from the others. She couldn't help thinking about the group. Maybe they'd had better luck. Every time she tried to sleep, she longed for a home—somewhere she could go to bed at night and feel safe, with a full fridge and running water to make it last. The prepper house hadn't been perfect, but it had been the closest thing to normal that she'd had in a long time. Thinking of it, she closed her eyes, hoping to be able to sleep for a couple of hours.

She awoke what felt like five minutes later to the sound of Ennis shouting, followed by several gunshots. Her gun was on the floor in front of her. She reached for it on instinct, already looking around for the threat.

"Amanda!" Ennis shouted.

"Where?"

"Outside, across the parking lot!" he shouted.

Amanda rolled to her feet, running to the door where Ennis's voice was coming from. She could hear the others scrambling around behind her, gathering up their few belongings.

"How many?" she asked.

"I don't know. I heard something and opened the door and saw a few shadows. One of the shadows aimed a gun at me and I shot back."

She grimaced, knowing a lecture wasn't appropriate in the exact moment, but he'd probably given them away. They might have been able to hide out. Now, whoever was outside knew there was someone armed here.

"Someone's trying to come in," Tonya whisper-shouted from nearby. "In back! I can hear them," she added more loudly, panic in her voice.

"What do we do?" Gretchen asked, looking back to where Tonya had been pointing.

"They're pushing us out the front," Amanda whispered, realizing they'd been surrounded in their sleep. Ennis must not have given them away after all—they'd probably been watched this whole time.

"What?" Ennis asked, shock in his voice.

Amanda briefly closed her eyes, willing herself to calm down and think straight. "We fight."

"Amanda, we don't know how many are out there," Ennis said under his breath, pulling her closer in an effort to keep the conversation between them.

"No, but staying in here leaves us just as exposed," she said, hating the options they were left with. Her eyes were moving around the dark room already. There were several trashcans along one wall, and bins filled with bits of plastic placed around the space.

"Grab those trash bins and get them over here. Ennis, get those desks pushed in front of that back door," she ordered, command back in her voice.

Ennis and Malachi jumped into action, racing across the factory floor to the desks. Gretchen and Tonya ran for the bins, dragging them across the floor. Amanda pressed herself against the side of the door, watching for activity outside. From what she could gather, the folks outside were lining up one side of the parking lot, creating a wall of sorts that would block their way back into town—the only option was the land across the parking lot, which didn't offer a lot of cover beyond occasional abandoned cars. And she was positive they were planning to open fire as soon as she and the others were forced to flee by those trying to gain entrance from the back. It's what she would have done if she'd wanted to keep an enemy out of her territory. A firing squad chasing the enemy in the opposite direction was a pretty effective You-Are-Not-Welcome sign.

"Done," Ennis said out of breath as he and Malachi got back to her side, helping Tonya and Gretchen with the last of the bins. "Those desks will hold them out for a little while, but not long; they're just not that sturdy."

"Guys, this isn't a guarantee, but it's the best I can offer. We're going to do our best to toss these cans as far as we can, and in different directions. The cans will draw the fire and add some chaos, giving us time to run," she explained.

"That sounds risky," Tonya whispered.

"It is. I have no other ideas. Run as fast as you can. Don't run in a straight line. Zig-zag. If you fall, keep rolling until you can find cover. There are a few cars around the lot and weeds on the side of the road as we get closer to trees. Then we run, but not back through town—we have to cut through the trees along that side road we saw off-shooting from the highway. Get there and stay flat."

She looked at the grim faces in the dark. The pounding in the back of the factory grew louder, more intense. They didn't have long. She didn't have any other ideas, though, and they didn't have the luxury of time to come up with another option.

"Let's do this. Amanda, let me and Malachi up front to throw the first cans," Ennis said. "You throw one as you start running, and shoot as soon as you get some distance; Tonya and Gretchen will go out after you while we throw the rest before following."

She nodded, knowing they'd be able to launch them further than she could. She knew the idea was horrible, and guessed it would probably end up with at least one of them dead, but there was no way she was going down without a fight. She'd shoot as many of their attackers as she could and hope that most of their small group survived the escape.

5

Austin led the crew down the trail running into the back of what looked like an elementary school—or what had once been a school, anyway. There was a playground on one side, along with an area that had once been a lawn. A single school bus was parked on the side of the beige building, which itself had a collapsed roof and a huge chunk missing out of the side. He could see desks and chairs inside. Books were laying in various stages of ruin around the area.

"A school could be useful if there's anything left," Wendell offered. "Cafeteria and all that."

As if that isn't obvious. "Everyone, stay low. We don't know what we're going into," Austin said, his voice just above a whisper.

He glanced Savannah's way, making sure she was close. The town looked like it had been bombed, and this school itself wasn't much better. Their vantage point above gave them a view of the flattened town. There was a water tower that had been toppled, the massive cistern lying across what had once been a road. Bricks and debris littered the area where buildings and homes had once stood.

"Dad, why bother? Look," Savannah said, gesturing to the ruins.

"She's right, probably, but we have to try." Austin sighed, not a few seconds later. "Ezra, you're with me. The rest of you, stay up here. Watch us. If we signal it's clear, come in; if not, get out of here and we'll catch up."

"Shouldn't I go with you?" Wendell asked.

"No, stay with the group. Don't let your guard down," he said simply.

With that, he and Ezra moved down the hill, both of them carrying handguns. It was eerily quiet. Austin expected to hear a stray dog or crickets, anything, but there was nothing.

"This doesn't feel right," Ezra whispered.

"No, it doesn't."

They walked alongside the road leading up to the school, their eyes darting left and right.

"Oh God," Ezra groaned, pointing to what looked like the decaying bodies of several adults.

Austin stopped walking, doing a full three-sixty and seeing more of the same further along the ground, closer to the school itself and over near the road approaching the back of the building. Something about the place felt really off now, dangerous. A flash of red caught his eye, partially hidden under what looked like part of a black tarp near a cluster of trees. He moved towards it, focused on the red plastic.

"Oh crap," he murmured, realizing it was the remnants of a biohazard bag.

"What is that?" Ezra asked.

"Biohazard."

"What?" he asked, taking a step back.

"It's a biohazard tag. I don't know what was here, but I know we don't want any part of it. We need to go. Don't touch anything," he said, already moving back towards the hill where the rest of the group waited, cutting across ground now instead of following the road. The important thing was to get out of this area as fast as possible.

Suddenly he heard a moan followed by some shuffling, and Austin whirled around, gun raised and ready to shoot. A soldier in an NWO uniform stumbled out from some bushes between them and the abandoned playground. He had blood on his uniform and clutched one arm against his chest. Austin froze, searching the area behind him for more soldiers, but it seemed he was alone—and he didn't make it far before falling to his knees and collapsing to the ground. Austin walked towards him slowly, motioning Ezra to keep his eyes on the move, looking for trouble.

The soldier himself had stopped moving, and Austin prodded him with his boot, pulling another moan from him. He'd been badly burned all up and down one arm, and his leg was bleeding.

Reaching down, Austin disarmed the soldier without any fight, handing his sidearm and knife back to Ezra. "What happened here?" Ezra asked, speaking up before Austin could. The man just groaned into the ground, and Austin prodded him with his boot again, repeating Ezra's question.

"Infection," the soldier muttered. "Burned it out."

"Bad enough to burn a whole town?" Austin couldn't believe that an infection could have hit that quickly, but a part of him wondered if maybe it had been manufactured. It wouldn't have surprised him, all things considered.

The soldier nodded before asking for water, but they'd left their packs with the others. Austin gestured to the small pack on the soldier's back and the man nodded as if he'd forgotten it. Austin used a knife to cut the straps off and then placed the pack on the ground in front of him. Opening it, Austin pulled out a small canteen, popped the drinking spout, and handed it to the soldier, who managed to drink some of it before dropping it to the ground.

"Shouldn't we keep that for ourselves?" Ezra asked quietly, but Austin shook his head. He did pick up the pack, though.

"Let him have it," Austin said. If there'd been infection around, they didn't want that water, and there hadn't been much in the canteen anyway. Rooting through the pack, Austin pulled out a couple of 2-way satellite messengers. Turning one on, he saw that the batteries were dead. If the solar charger for the laptop would recharge them, though, these could be handy if he and Amanda had to separate the group into teams again. On a whim, he tried to turn on the other one and was surprised to see that it still had some juice. A message popped up, and he looked at what appeared to be a date, accompanied by a countdown.

Grabbing the soldier's shoulder, he gave him a shake. "What's this date?" The soldier flinched at the contact and Austin jerked his hand away as the soldier began to gasp. Not ready to let him go just yet, he got over his surprise and grabbed him again. "Don't you dare die yet. What. Is. This?"

"Countdown," the soldier finally answered before laughing out loud suddenly and rolling onto his back.

"Countdown? Countdown to what?" Austin grabbed the soldier again, gripping his bad arm and making him cry out. "Answer me!"

"Doomsday," was all the soldier said before passing out. Austin looked at the countdown and then tried to wake the soldier. He got no response, and the man's pulse was slow. Too slow. He'd be dead soon.

Realizing the soldier wasn't going to say anything more, Austin stood up and showed the message to Ezra. "We have to get back to the others."

"What do you think happened here?" Ezra asked as they cut toward the group.

Austin took a deep breath. "I have no idea. It could have been a hoax meant to scare people and it got out of hand, or it could have been something as serious as Ebola. For all we know, the NWO could have introduced some sort of biological warfare as a test on this town."

"Why would they leave their own behind?"

"He's a grunt; probably expendable once he got hurt. There's no point in trying to guess, Ezra. We need to get out of here. We can't take the risk of it being the real deal and contracting some horrible virus. I don't want to touch anything in the town. I'm going to wash my hands in that creek we passed just from touching that soldier, but I think he's dying from injury anyway, not illness. Even if there were supplies to be had here, it's too risky."

"I guess that means we struck out. I hope Amanda and the others fared better," Ezra replied.

"Well, we have the messengers, and a date, but what that date means, I don't know. 'Doomsday' sure as hell doesn't sound good, though, does it?"

"And just under a month away, from the looks of it," Ezra commented.

Austin paused for a moment; something about the other man's speaking the timeline aloud brought it home to him in a way that the countdown message hadn't. But there was nothing else to say. After a moment, he kept walking and caught up to Ezra at the stream.

After washing as best they could, they met up with the group and gave them a quick rundown before deciding to head back to the meeting point. Going any further would delay their return since they'd have to bypass this town, and Austin didn't want to be walking at night.

By the time they reached their camp for the night, they were all exhausted. Austin sat down under the lean-to they'd built from branches they'd hacked down; one of the few things they still had from the prepper house was a hatchet, which had come in handy over and over again. The weather looked to be holding, which meant they wouldn't get rained on. Keeping the laptop dry had been a priority—at least for him. It was probably the only working laptop in the civilian world.

By light of the laptop, Sarah examined the messengers; she also hooked the dead one up to the charger to see if they could get it working. Then, with nothing more to do but wait to see if it charged, she went back to work on the laptop, where it created a soft glow in the lean-to.

Savannah was lying on her side, facing into the lean-to but not really looking at anyone. The others were cleaning up at the stream near the clearing, where the horses were settled. With his reluctance to search the town, they hadn't found any food or supplies they could use, and the messengers might well turn into paperweights if they couldn't get them to charge. That meant the day had very nearly been wasted. But, at the same time, he worried about what the soldier had said about the countdown. Doomsday? Sarah hadn't said anything much when he'd mentioned it, though her face had gotten even grimmer, if that were possible.

"Have you gotten anywhere on that?" Austin asked Sarah suddenly.

"Of course, I've gotten somewhere," she snapped, not looking away from the screen.

"What does that mean?" Austin asked, settling onto the ground beside her.

"It means I'm still working on it," she said, clearly irritated.

Savannah half-turned her eyes to him as she interrupted, lost in her own thoughts. "Tell me again what he said," Savannah said, bringing up the topic of Nash yet again.

It was something she'd been doing almost nightly, and it wasn't healthy. She was dwelling on Nash's death instead of letting herself move past it.

Austin could only sigh in response. He wished there was some way he could help her move on. Grief was a fickle beast, and everyone handled it differently, but he wondered if it was the amount of grief she'd endured in a relatively short amount of time that was making it especially hard for his daughter to move on.

"He didn't say much, sweetie. Just that same word. Amanda said it was all she got out of him, as well," he said gently.

"I told you I knew what he was talking about, or at least a good idea of what he was trying to tell you," Sarah said.

Austin looked at her. "What? Who? Nash?"

"Yes," she said, still tapping on keys and not looking up.

Austin reached out and stopped her hand, unable to understand how she could be so blasé. "Sarah, stop! You've told us almost nothing about Blackdown. Nothing useful, anyway. I'm tired of it. You tell me everything you can. Now."

She quit tapping and looked up at him. "I only knew what I suspected. I never had concrete proof until now, until this countdown you found. It was a lot of theory and speculation, Austin. Callum wasn't the only one who realized something was going on. He was just more brazen about his digging."

"But now you know more about Blackdown? Without a doubt?" he questioned. "And you know what to make of this countdown?"

She nodded. "Yes, but I *still* don't have all the information on their plan; that's why I haven't said anything tonight. I didn't want to present the information until I could give you all of it. Saying their plan is called Blackdown only does so much good if we don't understand their intentions."

He rubbed a hand over his face, searching for patience. "Tell me whatever it is you know now. I don't care what you don't know. Tell me what you *do* know."

Intrigued, even Savannah sat up. They both stared at Sarah, waiting for her to speak.

"Blackdown is nothing more than their term for a series of codes for the US missile defense system," she said. "The question is why they matter."

Austin glared at her. "I don't understand."

"The missiles could be used to shoot down the satellites that are hovering above the earth, ready to detonate another EMP —or worse."

"Worse?" he asked.

She nodded, her eyes going to Savannah and then back to him. "Worse, as in total annihilation. Those satellites are holding nuclear warheads."

His mouth went dry as he stared at her. "They would drop nuclear bombs on us? Doomsday?"

She shrugged. "They could, but I don't believe that's their end game. The nuclear warheads detonated high in the atmosphere would create another EMP. The satellites are strategically positioned to disable the entire country—possibly the world, should our government make headway in restoring the power grid. However, the NWO is clearly a group of narcissistic individuals, who'd very likely drop nuclear bombs and destroy everything if things didn't go their way. 'My way or the highway' and all that nonsense. I'm sure they have a bunker they could live in until it would be safe enough, in their minds, to emerge and start the world anew with them at the helm," she said, her lip curled with disgust. "Those codes could keep that from happening."

Austin swallowed. Why were they only hearing this now? "You have the codes and can stop them from dropping bombs on us?" he asked. "Or triggering another EMP?"

"Yes, but much more than that," she said.

He looked at her, waiting for her to tell him more. "Sarah, explain it to me as if I were a five-year-old," he said through gritted teeth.

She took a deep breath. "The codes could prevent them from initiating a nuclear attack or more EMPs, but won't fix the damage that's already been done. Those satellites are the NWO's plan B. In case the government gets back up and running against them."

Austin nodded, thinking. "We have to assume someone, somewhere, is already working to restore our electrical grid. There's no way our government wouldn't have some kind of countermeasures to this type of thing. We know they've trained and prepared for an EMP strike for decades. It's probably already in the works!"

Sarah rubbed her face. "Yes, they have, and they are, I'm sure. Right this minute, there are people at work trying to right this. Those satellites are positioned to knock out the grid again if it should come up. The NWO is watching and waiting for the right time to strike, and these codes can keep that from happening. But the NWO knows the government is already working against them. They have to. So, their plan has to be setting off another EMP just when it will do maximum damage to the grid and what supplies the government had stockpiled separately. Killing the government's back-up plan, so to speak."

"The date that was on the messenger we got from NWO soldier. Could that be it? When they plan to set off another EMP?"

Sarah nodded, grimacing at the laptop in front of her. "No doubt coordinated to do maximum damage based on whatever they know of what the government is doing."

"So, we shoot them down with the missiles you were talking about," he reasoned. "We don't let them set it off."

Sarah looked up from the laptop with a frown. "It isn't that easy. You have to get to the silos to launch the missiles, and I haven't been able to unencrypt the file. I know the codes are there, but I don't actually know what they are. And while I'm getting close to the codes, we also don't know everything we need to. That's why I haven't said anything."

"We just head to the silos, right? Where are they?"

She shrugged. "There are silos all over the country. I have to believe those silos are going to be heavily guarded, though. The NWO will know if you manage to get in."

"So, we'll be prepared!"

"There are more files I need to get through, Austin. I think Callum knew where the back-up computer centers would be. If I can find them, we can cut off the head of the snake," she said. "Shut down their control so that, when we fire those missiles, the NWO won't be able to counteract anything we do —it'll be too late for them and their back-up plan will be in the wind."

"You mean we can take down the NWO?"

"Yes, that's what I'm saying. They'll have some kind of technology center where they can man the satellites. They're likely communicating with one another here and across the world with that same technology. We find where the center is, use the codes, and we remedy the threat of any forward progress being destroyed. Otherwise, finding the missiles could just be delaying whatever they do next, if even that, and there's the potential that they could interfere with our directing the missiles at all. Countermeasures against our strike, essentially. Our first strike option is taking out their control of the satellites with those codes before firing any missiles at all, which means finding the computer centers and shutting the NWO out for good."

"Can we track them with the messengers?" Austin asked.

"Those aren't like cell phones or tablets. You can send limited texts, like if you're lost or in an accident, but you can't send files," she said.

"So, we can see what they're sending?"

"In theory, if they send out a message and we're on the right frequency. Assuming we can get them charged."

Austin refused to be deflated. They were further along than they'd been yesterday, and that was something. "We have a date, which is more than we had before."

"You mean we can end this? We can win?" Savannah asked. "Is that what you're saying?"

Austin smiled. "I think that's exactly what she's saying."

Sarah held up a hand. "No, I'm saying there's a chance, a very slim chance. I have to work on these files. I have to find the computer center where the NWO is manning those satellites. That date and the codes mean nothing if we can't get to the missiles. There are a lot of moving parts, and everything has to fit together perfectly. We can't have one piece of the puzzle and get anywhere."

"I understand. There's hard work to be done yet," Austin said.

She scoffed. "It isn't necessarily hard work. I would have arranged these files differently. Callum's method is messy. He should have known better," she said tightly.

"I think Callum was under some pressure," Austin retorted, feeling the need to defend the dead man who'd given his life to pass them the information.

"If he really wanted to help, he could have simply said what all this was," she argued.

"Can you prioritize getting a bead on locations? We only have so much time. If you figure out where we need to go, we can head in that direction while you keep working on the codes."

Sarah seemed to consider it for a moment, looking between him and the computer. "There are limited options..." she began, and then cut herself off. "Let me work on it tonight and think about it. If we're moving anyway..."

"Right," Austin said. "And we are. Try, alright?"

After a moment, she nodded, and Austin grinned when the woman went right back to typing.

The snapping of a twig outside the shelter drew Austin's attention. He looked up to see Wendell slinking away.

The man had obviously been eavesdropping. Austin didn't trust the guy, not at all, but he thought it best to keep his enemies close. He could keep an eye on him better that way. He didn't trust him to watch Amanda's back. It was better to have Ennis looking out for her.

It wasn't long before the others came back to set up makeshift beds around the lean-to. The warm night meant they didn't really need a fire. They wanted to avoid drawing any attention to themselves anyway, and had opted to skip dinner for the night, saving their few provisions for when the full group of them would be reunited. Austin volunteered to take the first watch, knowing he wasn't going to be able to sleep.

Sarah's revelation about Blackdown changed everything. There was a way out. He could see an end in sight, and felt willing to do just about anything to take out the NWO and make a better world for his daughter.

He looked up at the moon where it hung high in the sky, the night crystal clear with what looked like a million stars. He thought about the satellites mingling with the stars. The satellites that were threatening to keep the world under the thumb of some very bad men. He wished he could personally shoot down the darn things while the people behind the NWO watched. He wanted to see their faces when he destroyed their little experiment to run the world. He wanted to make them pay for all the lives they had cost and the destruction their propaganda campaign had caused. There was no punishment that would ever feel like it was enough.

6

Amanda's heart beat so fast it hurt. There was a sharp pain in her side, too, making it difficult to draw breath. They had to keep running, though. She'd been doing her best to keep track of everyone, but the dodging and weaving and diving behind dead cars made it extremely difficult. All she knew was that they had to keep running for the hills—literally.

"Amanda!" Ennis's voice rang through the night.

It was only then that she realized there was no more gunfire. She slowed her pace, dropping behind a semi stranded on the two-lane road they were taking out of town. She guessed she'd run at least a half-mile since they'd burst out of the factory. It had been chaos. She closed her eyes, reliving those terrifying moments when they'd fled, the gunmen shooting at the garbage cans rolling towards them and through the parking lot. It hadn't been long before the gunfire had turned in their direction, making their escape extremely dicey.

Ennis joined her behind the truck she'd crouched beside. The two of them stood bent over at the waist as they tried to catch their breath.

"Where's everyone else?" she gasped.

"I don't know. I saw shadows running out of town. I got pinned down not too far from the factory. Everyone was gone by the time I was able to make a break for it."

"We need to find them," she breathed out.

"Are you okay?" he asked.

"I think so. You?"

He chuckled. "Other than feeling like my lungs are going to explode, I'm good. I didn't get hit. I didn't see anyone drop when we headed out the door, either. I think we all made it out of there."

"Thank God. Maybe they were just trying to scare us out of the factory and not actually hit us," she said as they began a slow jog down the side of the highway, sticking to the shadows.

He made a coughing noise. "Those guns were real. You don't shoot at someone if you're not actually trying to kill them."

"They must have watched us go in and then waited," she said.

"You think?" Ennis asked.

"I'm thinking either they saw us come into town and were lying low, waiting to see what we'd do, or else they were watching the factory."

"Maybe there was something in that factory to be had and we didn't find it," Ennis agreed.

"I should have been more alert. I should have known it was too easy," she said, chastising herself.

"Amanda, is that you?" Gretchen's voice cut through the night.

"It is. Who's with you?" Amanda asked, looking blindly into the field of dry grass where Gretchen's voice had floated from.

"All but Ennis," she replied, her voice grim.

Amanda breathed a sigh of relief. "I'm with Ennis. Is everyone okay?" she asked, heading toward the voice.

"Harlen took a hard fall, but none of us are shot. Your garbage can trick worked," she said, emerging from the shadows.

"Thank God. We need to keep moving now that we're together again. There's nothing here for us," Amanda replied, giving Gretchen a quick hug when they met up on the side of the road. It didn't sound like they were being followed, but she didn't dare stop.

Still, she could feel the defeat hanging on them like a heavy cloak as they moved up the road. They'd walk through the night, the mountains providing their only real safety. It was clear the towns were no-go zones. Even the ones that looked abandoned were too dangerous.

"What do we tell Austin?" Malachi asked.

"The truth. He isn't going to be upset that we didn't find anything. We knew this was a possibility," Amanda said.

"Where do we go from here?" Tonya asked.

"I don't know. Civilization is breaking down. I don't see anyone welcoming new community members. I think we're stuck with each other," Amanda said, attempting a joke.

"We can't seem to find anywhere to settle down," Tonya said, exhaustion evident in her voice.

Ennis let out a long sigh. "That's our goal. We find somewhere we can live and protect, just like all these towns we've encountered. All these little groups have found their little corner of the world. We'll find ours, Tonya. We just have to be diligent."

"We can't settle down with that man wanting to kill Austin, and the rest of us by extension. We stop moving with him, we die," Harlen stated.

Ennis chuckled. "There is that."

Of course, it wasn't that simple, and they all knew it. None of them would ditch Austin, but that didn't matter. By now, Zander had a good idea who most of them were, or at least their faces. Even if they asked Austin to leave the group, Zander would still kill them. He was a ruthless, evil man who wouldn't hesitate to take some kind of revenge on any one of them for their part in the battle at the prepper house. An image of Nash's face popped into her mind. None of the people walking alongside her could make it through that kind of torture and not give up their secrets. She wasn't even sure of her own ability.

"How are we supposed to see once we're away from the road?" Gretchen grumbled. "Shouldn't we stop for the night?"

"We'll figure it out. I'd rather go into the woods blind than stay back here and wait for angry people with guns to kill us," Ennis replied.

Amanda's legs burned as they made the second steep climb of their journey back. "I don't remember it being so steep when we went into town," she complained.

"Funny how it never feels like that until it's time to make the return trip," Ennis said with a strained laugh.

The faded yellow lines on the road were highlighted by the moonlight, their only real guide. Amanda wasn't fond of traveling in the middle of the night, knowing there were more than human predators lurking, but it was what it was. "I think we need to turn off up here somewhere," she said, straining to see the mile sign they were coming up on.

"Another mile," Ennis replied confidently.

The group was subdued and quiet as they followed Ennis. He had an excellent sense of direction—far better than Amanda's. She'd gladly follow him.

Ennis stopped in front of one of the milepost signs, and the rest of them followed suit.

"Here?" Amanda asked.

"Here. We need to go about three miles east, up the mountain. With the dark and the terrain, I'd say we'll be there right around sunrise," he commented.

There was a collective moan from the group at the idea of walking all night long, but Amanda cut it off. "Let's keep moving. We'll have a chance to sleep a few hours before the others return."

"If they return," Jordan grumbled.

Amanda ignored him. She knew Austin wouldn't fail. He refused to fail. She only hoped they had found something. The group needed a win. Morale was low, and without a place to call home with plenty of resources, it was only going to get worse. Low morale would cause more problems. She thought back to SERE training. That had been one of the first things they'd been warned about. Low morale would disrupt their very strained relationships within the group. The breakdown would be the equivalent of what they were already seeing in the towns.

It would be every man for himself if that happened.

7

Austin woke to the sound of hushed voices. He immediately rolled to the side, reaching for his gun as he checked on Savannah. She was sound asleep, curled in a small ball in a corner of the lean-to. Ezra, who had been on watch, must have heard the noise, as well; he was already on his feet with the Glock pulled out when Austin emerged from the shelter.

The voices were louder, but it was one voice in particular that stuck out. Smiling, he lowered his gun, slipping it into his waistband at the small of his back.

"What are you doing?" Ezra hissed.

"It's Amanda," Austin said, unable to stop smiling with relief. He was already walking towards the sounds of grumbling people, never having been so happy to see the disgruntled faces of the people he now considered family.

"You're back," he said with a grin when Amanda's tired face appeared in the faint light of the morning.

Exhaustion evident in her sagging shoulders, she only muttered in return.

"Let's get you some water," he said, stepping in next to her.

"Good, we all need it," she replied.

He looked at the faces of disappointment and defeat. "Didn't go well?" he asked as the others followed Ezra back toward the clearing.

Amanda stopped walking, pushing hair out of her face. "No, it didn't. It's a very long story. What about you? Did you find anything?"

"Not exactly. We struck out, and instead of risking missing our reunion, we came back last night," he said, holding back the news. She needed water and maybe rest first.

She groaned. "Great."

"Have you been walking all night?" he asked.

"Yes, we had to. We kind of got chased out of the town we'd stumbled into. Not kind of—we did. We were shot at and had to run for our lives."

Austin froze in his tracks, and then gripped her hand, all but pulling her back to the clearing. He wanted her with him. "I'm sorry. We didn't hear anything all night. I think we're safe enough here to give you guys time to rest. We've got some water. While you guys rest, we'll go hunting," he said.

"I want to say we don't need to sleep, but I'd be lying. I need to close my eyes for a while and then we can come up with a plan. Everyone's feeling anxious about a lack of roots. They're scared," she said.

"I know. I get it, but I think we might have a way out of all this," he said, suddenly anxious to tell her everything.

"You do?"

"I'll tell you all about it after you've gotten some water and rest," he promised.

In their makeshift camp, everyone was up, greeting one another and talking about what they'd seen. Austin and Amanda hung back on the fringes, each of them quietly listening to the conversations. Austin grabbed one of the half-empty bottles of water and handed it to Amanda.

"I'll go hunting," Wendell announced. "We all need some breakfast."

Austin looked at him, his brows raised. "You'll go hunting?"

He nodded. "Sure, I can."

Ennis, standing a few feet behind Wendell, met Austin's eyes and very subtly shook his head. Austin understood.

"I'll go with you," Austin muttered.

"Really?" Wendell asked, clearly surprised.

"Yes, really."

"I'll go, as well," Mike volunteered.

"Good. The rest of you, keep your eyes open. Let the others rest. I want a full perimeter around the camp," Austin said loudly.

"Camp?" Wendell asked with a sneer.

Austin shot him a glare. "It's our camp for now. Build a fire ring and then we'll get going. We'll need to purify more water from that stream."

"I can do it," Savannah said. "You guys go hunt. Find us some hamburgers," she joked half-heartedly.

After a moment, Austin looked over at Drew. "Can you help her out and keep an eye on her?"

"Will do," he said.

With that, Austin grabbed a rifle, handing it to Mike. He wasn't keen on letting Wendell carry a gun, and suggested he wear the long hunting knife they had brought with them from the house instead. The man seemed to understand that the suggestion was more order than anything, and he took the knife.

They headed into the deeper forest, northeast, hoping to find some food for the group. Austin didn't talk. His ears were open, listening for anything they might use as breakfast. Hungry as he was, he'd eat just about any meat he could get his hands on.

"What exactly should we be looking for?" Wendell asked.

"Anything that moves," Austin replied dryly.

"Think we'll find a deer?" the man asked.

"Doubtful. Very doubtful if you don't be quiet."

Wendell groaned rather taking the hint. "More squirrel?" he complained.

"We take what we can find," Mike shot back. "Now, quiet, man!"

Austin's eyes were on the rocky terrain, littered with leaves from the many bushes growing in between the tall Ponderosa pines. He hoped to find some tracks or notice a game trail. It all looked the same, though—wild and untamed.

"Berries!" Wendell shouted.

Austin looked in the direction where Wendell was pointing, towards a sunny, south-facing slope. The pale green mingled with dark green leafy bushes growing wild with plenty of red berries.

"Raspberries," he said with a grin.

"Really?" Wendell asked. "Not poisonous?"

"Not poisonous, which is great. We'll pick a lot, but watch for black bears. This is their food source," he warned the others.

"You got that right. Scat," Mike said, pointing to the ground.

Wendell flinched. "Bear poop?" he asked.

"Yes, bear poop. So, let's hurry. I have one of those grocery bags in my pack," Austin said, shrugging it off his shoulder and quickly unzipping it as they moved towards the berries.

The three men began picking rapidly, dropping berries in the bag while scanning the area.

"I see some wild strawberries over there," Mike commented.

"That'll make an excellent breakfast! Let's get those. I think there's another bag in my pack," Wendell said, clumsily removing his own backpack and noisily fishing around for the bag as he and Mike headed for the next bush.

Austin nodded toward the remaining raspberries. "I'll keep picking these while you guys go for the strawberries. This might be it for food."

Some of the overripe berries squished between his fingers, leaving them stained red and sticky as he picked faster. He kept telling himself to be happy with what they'd found, but he couldn't quite ignore the hunger in his belly for something more substantial. His mind started to wander as he thought about the pantry back at Ennis's now destroyed home. They'd had it good there. He hated that it had all been taken away.

"Austin!" he heard Mike shout, and looked up to see what was wrong.

Wendell had gone pale, the bag of strawberries hanging limp in his hand as he stared toward Austin. With that prompt, and Mike's wide eyes to back it up, Austin slowly turned around until he saw a black bear lumbering towards him as if he didn't have a care in the world.

His mind raced. Did he scare the bear or keep his mouth shut and hope the bear left him alone? He slowly backed away from the berry bushes, hoping the bear wouldn't see him as a threat. The bear stopped about thirty feet away and stared at him.

"Get big," Mike said in a quiet voice.

"That's cats!" Austin retorted.

"I think it'll work for anything," the man shot back.

"What do we do?" Wendell whined.

"We wait. It's a black bear. I doubt he'll attack as long as he doesn't feel threatened," Austin said, hoping he was right.

"Shoot it!" Wendell exclaimed suddenly.

"I have a twenty-two. That isn't going to do anything but make it mad," Austin hissed back.

The bear was staring at Austin. He could practically feel it sizing him up. In the back of his mind, he scolded himself. He knew it was better to stay loud and chatty in bear country, to keep the bears away, but he'd been hoping to find some meat for food and had let that take priority over safety. This bear didn't want to be around him anymore than he wanted to be around it, and this encounter was their fault. They'd been quiet, none of them talking as they picked their breakfast.

Suddenly, a rock the size of a baseball flew past Austin's head, landing a few feet in front of him and skittering over the terrain, sending more small rocks moving.

"What are you doing?" Mike growled behind him.

Austin shook his head, not even needing to turn around to know that it was Wendell who'd thrown the rock, antagonizing the bear. "Wendell, stop. You're going to scare it and it might charge us."

"Stop!" Mike shouted just as another rock flew past him.

"Wendell, knock it off!" Austin shouted, not turning around in case the bear did decide to charge.

The bear stood up on its hind legs, his head swinging back and forth as if the creature was trying to get a better view of the situation. It was an intimidating sight.

"Get out of here! Go! Rawr!" Wendell screamed, throwing more rocks.

"Stop!" Austin shouted as the bear dropped to all fours and did a swaying thing, its big fluffy body moving back and forth.

There was an oomph sound then, and some cursing behind him. Austin half-turned to see Mike tackling Wendell to the ground. When he turned back around, the bear was making a full turn and heading back into the trees.

Austin waited, watching to make sure the bear was going to stay gone before heading towards Mike and Wendell, who were now dusting themselves off and getting to their feet.

"What'd you do that for?" Wendell spat.

"Because we told you to stop and you didn't!" Austin answered.

"I got him out of here, didn't I?" he asked defiantly.

Austin glared at him. "You could have gotten me killed."

Wendell stared back at him, the look on his face actually sending a shiver down Austin's spine. Wendell looked almost satisfied, his eyes beady and boring into Austin's, so that he suddenly wondered if that had been the man's plan.

The thought was disconcerting, and put him on high alert. Mike looked at Austin, then Wendell, taking a step back.

"Let's get out of here. I'm done," Austin said, not trusting Wendell not to try and get him killed again.

They trudged back towards the camp in silence. Austin wasn't sure what had happened; if Wendell's actions had been stupid or intentional. Either way, he didn't like it.

By the time they got back, most of the group was back up and moving. Sarah was under the lean-to, sitting with the laptop and tapping away on the keyboard, a look of pure determination on her face.

Savannah sat next to the firepit, a small fire burning with the single pot they had sitting over the flames. She was staring into the pot, clearly lost in her own little world. Tonya was still under the shelter, lying on her side and sound asleep. The mood was subdued as the others talked in low voices.

"You're back," Malachi said, looking up from the pine cone he'd been carefully tearing apart.

"Any luck?" Gretchen asked from beside him, doing the same thing.

Austin noticed they each had a pile of pine cones beside them. "What are you doing?" he asked.

Gretchen smiled. "Pine nuts. I now understand why they're so expensive in the grocery stores. Or were, I suppose."

He raised an eyebrow. "Pine nuts?"

She reached for the bottom half of a two-liter bottle they had picked up and cut to use as a bowl. He looked inside and saw some tiny pale seeds.

"I know it isn't a lot, but they do have some protein. Ideally, I would want Pinyon Pine or something like that with bigger nuts, but we had nothing else to do and I hate to do nothing. A little is better than nothing," Gretchen said.

"Is that what the chipmunks and squirrels go after?" Mike asked.

Gretchen smiled. "It is. See this one?" She held up a cone that was still green and unopened. "We can collect more of these and set them near the fire. The heat will open them up and we can get to the seeds before the squirrels and chipmunks have a chance. The ones that are already open are what the animals are going after. It's tedious, but we're pulling these apart to get at the remaining seeds."

"Whatever works. It's a good use of time, and we got some bags of berries. Not a bad breakfast, really. Where's Ennis?" he asked, looking around for his brother.

"He took Harlen to try and do some fishing," Malachi replied.

"Amanda?" he asked, doing his usual roll call.

"She went with Harlen and Ennis to collect some water," Gretchen said.

"Did any of you sleep?" Mike asked.

"We tried, and we did get a little rest, but I hate doing nothing," Gretchen reiterated. "Plus, the sun's up—not easy to sleep in bright daylight. You said you found some berries?"

"Raspberries and strawberries," Wendell replied eagerly.

Gretchen and Malachi both grinned, and Mike sat down beside them to have a go at a pine cone with them.

Austin took off his pack and carefully propped the rifle against a tree. "I'm going to the stream to check on the others," he said, wanting to get away from Wendell.

He glanced over at Savannah, but decided she was safe enough with the others around. He headed into the trees that led to the crystal-clear stream, which was only about four feet wide and a foot deep. Great for water, but he couldn't imagine Ennis was going to find any fish in it. No matter. He needed to talk to his brother about his friend.

Once at the stream, he followed it down about half a mile, following the sound of Ennis's voice. When he ran into Ennis and Harlen, they were sitting on a couple of small rocks, staring at the water that was lacking any kind of fishing apparatus.

"What are you doing?" Austin asked.

Ennis looked up and smiled as Austin approached. "If I said we were fishing, would you believe me?"

"No," Austin said dryly.

"Our intent was to fish, but there's no fish to find. We were just taking a breather," he replied.

Austin could see the dark circles under his eyes; he knew he was beat. He could understand the feeling, and didn't blame him a bit for taking some time to do nothing at all.

"I see. We managed to get some berries, but that was it," Austin reported.

"Have a seat and take a load off," Ennis said, patting a rock beside him.

Austin did as suggested. "What happened last night?" he asked.

"We found a small town; looked to be nothing more than a few trailer parks burned to the ground. There were a few buildings, old factories and warehouses. We didn't see anyone when we walked through and decided to hunker down in a factory overnight," he explained, and then went on to tell him about the night in detail.

"Wow. I guess that's a dead-end there."

"What about you? Any luck?"

Austin thought for a moment, processing everything. "Yes and no. We ran into the same problem at the town we found. There was an NWO soldier there, though. Still alive, but he'd been burned and was injured; I'm sure he's dead by now. We found a couple satellite messengers on him, and we're hoping we can charge them with the solar charger. Sarah's working on that. One of the messengers had a bit of juice left in the battery, and there was a message with a date. The soldier called it 'Dooms-day' before he passed out, and it came with a countdown. Less than a month out. We're thinking… what if there's a correlation between that date and the files Sarah's finding on the laptop?"

"What's the date?"

"Twenty-seven days from now," Austin said, his voice somber. "But I've no idea if that's a doomsday countdown or something else, truth be told. We're just trying to put together the facts we have with what we've found."

"I think it's safe to say it isn't someone's birthday," Ennis replied. "So, what's the plan?"

Austin shook his head, still trying to piece it all together. "Sarah has some ideas for how to take down the NWO if we can untangle the information on the laptop and figure out where to go. I'm thinking we might just hunker down here and give her a few days to see what she comes up with and if there's something we can do."

"Can we use the messengers?" Ennis asked. "Maybe contact others who can help?"

Austin shrugged. "Sarah seemed to think so, but there's concern that anyone else with the same units could see our messages if they're on the same frequency, so we'd have to be careful. Who knows if they'll be on our side or the NWO's? But we won't know until we try."

"How did Wendell do?" Harlen asked, changing the subject.

Austin let out a long sigh. "Yesterday, fine. I mean, he didn't do anything great, but he didn't cause any problems."

"But today?" Ennis prodded.

"Today, he nearly got me killed," Austin muttered.

"What? How?" Ennis asked with surprise.

Austin ran his hand over his dark beard, replaying the scene. "We ran into a bear while we were picking berries, or rather, the bear ran into us. I was closest. Wendell started throwing rocks at the thing," he said, exasperation in his voice. "And we're not talking a small bear, guys."

"Maybe he didn't know what else to do and thought he was helping," Ennis offered.

"We told him to stop, several times. Mike had to tackle him to the ground," Austin said.

"What happened with the bear?" Harlen asked after a moment.

"It walked away."

Ennis threw his head back and laughed. "Sounds like ol' Wendy saved your bacon. He wasn't trying to get you killed."

"If you say so."

"Look, he's doing a lot better than he was a few weeks ago. Give him some time. He needs to prove he's part of the group. You know he's always been socially awkward. I don't think he's trying to be mean or get anyone hurt. Seriously, we're all he has. He won't survive out here on his own. He can't afford to hurt or kill any of us," Ennis reasoned.

Harlen looked thoughtful. "I agree. The guy has some issues, but I don't think he's necessarily bad. He needs to learn how to work with others and how to contribute. It's going to take some time."

Austin knew there was no point in arguing. For now, he'd keep his guard up and do his best to keep a close eye on the man. As much as he disliked Wendell, he wanted him close.

Plus, they had other problems.

8

Amanda felt like she could fall asleep standing up. She was so tired after the grueling journey the night before and the lack of sleep, her bones actually hurt. She didn't care that she was sitting on the hard ground with no shelter over her head. Her body demanded sleep. It also wanted something more substantial than berries and greens and nuts, but that was another matter. After breakfast, she'd moved the horses to a flat, open area with lots of green grass after leading them to the water to drink their fill. The simple task had sapped her energy.

She looked up from her spot outside the circle of people sitting around the campfire in the fading sunlight and saw Austin and Sarah in the lean-to, talking in hushed voices. Austin was gesturing and had a look of frustration on his face. The information wasn't coming fast enough for him. She hadn't had a chance to catch up with him yet about what his grand plan for saving the world was, but assumed it was something to do with the USB. It always was. She appreciated his hopefulness and his willingness to do something good, too, but she couldn't help but think they were just a lone group of survivors. They had no chance against something like the NWO. It was an opinion she hadn't shared with him, knowing he wouldn't want to hear it.

She mustered the energy to get up and walk into the lean-to. Austin looked up and held out a hand to help her sit down next to him.

"Why don't you try and sleep?" Austin suggested, his tone gentle. "You took care of the horses, but you need to take care of you too."

She shook her head. "Not yet. You told me you had some news. Can you tell me now?"

He half-smiled. "Well, the good news…. Basically, in a nutshell, this laptop has the codes to missiles that will shoot down satellites hovering above the earth's atmosphere that are holding nuclear warheads. And we think we know a timeline of how long we have to use them."

Amanda blinked, rubbing her face as she tried to focus. She couldn't possibly have heard him correctly. "Austin, do you plan on blowing up the earth?" she asked.

Sarah looked up from the laptop and frowned at her before returning to her work.

He grinned. "No, but it is an option. The satellites would blow up, and the nuclear bombs would explode high in the atmosphere and not touch us here on the surface."

"You're sure about that?" she asked.

He opened his mouth, closed it, and then opened it again to finally answer. "Not entirely, but yes, I think so."

"Why do the satellites matter? How does that help us?"

"We believe our government is already working on a solution to this problem. They have enough underground bunkers to have some technology functioning that would allow them to restore the power grid or to at least get started in that direction. If this thing is worldwide, other countries are going to have the same technology and will be working hard to fight back against the NWO. Those satellites are the NWO's safety net, their back-up plan. At the first sign of progress, they're going to launch another EMP and set us back to square one," Austin explained.

She took a minute to process what he was saying. "Okay. So, what's our role?"

"We get to the missiles and kill the satellites," he said, as if it was as simple as running down to the grocery store.

"You want to shoot down nuclear warheads?" Ennis asked, squatting down outside the lean-to. "Am I hearing that right?"

"Yes," Austin replied without hesitation.

"That seems dangerous," Tonya said, her arm going around Malachi's shoulders where they sat around the fire.

Amanda looked around—they'd been talking louder than she'd realized, and most everyone was present and listening now.

"Living like we are is dangerous," Mike chimed in.

The group erupted, everyone talking at once about the pros and cons of the situation before the arguing transformed into a litany of complaints.

"Stop!" Austin said, holding up a hand and climbing out of the shelter to stand beside it.

Amanda could see his legs and nothing else, but noticed that everyone outside the shelter was looking up at him. They were waiting for him to tell them what to do; for better or worse, they'd accepted him as their leader, and it was his idea they wanted to hear most.

"Let him talk," Ennis said to the crowd when the murmurs started again.

"I know we're lost in every way, but this could be our only chance at fixing things," Austin started.

"Why us? Where's the government?" Ezra asked.

Austin shrugged. "I don't know. I hope they're underground somewhere, maybe Cheyenne, working on a fix to this. I do know that the files that were passed to me were not seen by anyone else. My friend did a lot of digging to get those files. He tried to tell the bigwigs at the Pentagon and no one would listen. He entrusted me with finding someone willing to pay attention. Unfortunately, things happened fast, maybe because they knew Callum was onto their operation and was about to shut it down. I don't know. I do know I'm tired of living like this. I'm tired of worrying how I'll keep my daughter safe and worrying about her future. I have to do something. We have the knowledge, and I think we owe it to ourselves and our country to do something about it."

"How are we supposed to shoot missiles? Isn't that a little more technical than pushing a big red button?" Gretchen said.

Sarah cleared her throat. "It is. It requires specific codes—which I have."

Amanda whipped her head around to stare at the woman. Austin dropped down low, staring into the lean-to. "You do?" he asked with excitement. "You got them?"

Sarah offered a rare, tired smile. "I do."

Amanda turned back to look at Austin, who was grinning like a fool. "Austin, I have one little question."

"What?" he asked, still grinning.

"Where are we supposed to find missiles?" she asked.

Austin's grin faded as he looked to Dr. Bastani. The woman grimaced. "I'm working on it."

"What about Cheyenne?" Harlen asked. "Isn't that a huge underground bunker with missiles and all that?"

Amanda nodded. "It is."

"We also have to disable the systems controlling the satellites," Sarah said, looking at Austin pointedly as if he should have remembered this part.

"How are we supposed to do that?" Wendell asked.

"We find the control center and disable it. Then, and only then, do we launch the missiles to destroy the satellites," Sarah explained. "It has to happen in order—that's our one shot at ending all this."

Amanda looked to Austin. His simplistic plan had just gotten a lot more complicated. The look on his face was one of disappointment, but he moved to sit back down next to her. "And you're still looking for the locations? So, how? How do we do that?" he asked, clearly not giving up on his goal of winning the war against the NWO.

Sarah looked up from the computer, seeming to notice for the first time that all eyes were on her. Everyone was waiting for her to give them the secret.

"There are three likely places the NWO would be commandeering to guide the satellites," she started. "I don't know where for sure. Once the guidance system is disabled, the missiles could be launched. Unfortunately, the computer center and the missile silos are not going to be in the same place."

The group fell quiet again, all of them struggling to understand the information.

"We find the computer center, disable it, and then find the missiles," Amanda said, breaking it down.

"Yes," Sarah said firmly, "but the problem is time."

"What if they move to another one of those three places you're talking about while we're trying to find missiles?" Drew asked.

"That's another problem," Sarah muttered.

"It has to be a coordinated attack. We have to take out the guidance system and launch the missiles shortly after," Austin said, summing it up.

Wendell scoffed. "Oh, so simple."

Amanda shot the man another glare. She was cranky, in need of sleep, and had zero patience left to deal with his snide comments. "Anything is possible."

"You don't know where these potential sites for computer centers might be?" Ennis asked.

Sarah shook her head. "Not yet. I'm digging. These files are buried deep. I just need more time."

"Do we sit here and wait?" Ennis asked, looking to Austin.

Austin looked at Amanda. She really had no answers, and gave a little shrug.

"How long do you think it will take you to unlock those files?" Austin asked.

Sarah looked up. "It could be in five minutes or five years, I don't know. The fact that I found the codes already is promising... but there are no guarantees."

Amanda scowled. The woman's response wasn't exactly encouraging. She turned to look back at Austin, waiting to see what he would say.

"Well, we only have so much time," he said, and with that he filled the group in on the countdown and messengers they'd found on the NWO soldier. "The fact is," he finished, "if we move now, we could be moving away from where we need to be to make a move against the NWO. And there's only so much time. This isn't an ideal location, but we're doing okay. I say we give Sarah a few days to work on this rather than moving needlessly. We'll do what we can to rest up and get ready to move when we can. If she hasn't found it in a week or so, we can re-evaluate."

Tonya nodded, though she didn't look excited. "Meanwhile, we can think about what to do if Sarah doesn't find those locations—if we can't do anything against the NWO," she said gently, her eyes on Austin. "Where do we go if that date passes and nothing has changed?"

Amanda met Austin's eyes and saw the worry there, but he didn't argue.

Everyone looked at one another. "We need to get somewhere with a mild climate," Gretchen offered. "A place where we can grow food all year, or at least a good portion of the year."

Amanda smiled, liking the way the woman thought. She was thinking long term. It was smart, and meant she had accepted what was happening. This plan against the NWO was a long-shot, whether Austin wanted to admit it or not.

"I agree," Amanda chimed in.

"I like that idea, but don't you think everyone else is going to have the same idea?" Harlen asked.

"We can't live in the mountains through winter with no shelter," Mike added.

"I agree, but the mountains offer resources that we aren't going to find in the lower elevations," Amanda said. "Plus, we are somewhat sheltered in the mountains."

"I say we head west if it comes to it," Austin said. "Stick to the mountains as much as we can. Without a map, I can't say exactly where we are, but I think if we head towards southern Oregon, we can have the best of both worlds. The weather's fairly mild, and there's plenty of farmland and mountains."

"Works for me," Harlen said, putting his hands in the air.

Amanda nodded. "It's decided then. We give Sarah some time to find those locations, keeping camp here. If she does, we re-evaluate and figure out what makes sense and what we can do. If that doesn't happen, though, we have a plan." While she loved the idea of saving the world, she was more inclined to believe it was a fool's errand. She wanted a back-up plan, a place they could call home and learn to start living once again.

There were more murmurs among the group before it was officially decided they were headed west; all but Austin seemed to assume that the information on the laptop wouldn't bear any fruit, and that this plan would be their next play. Amanda couldn't help feeling the same, but wondered if they'd ever really make it... or, rather, how many of them would survive such a trip, the way the world was now.

She looked at Austin and could see the stress on his face in the way his jaw was set. She reached over and put a hand on his knee. "Take a walk with me?" she whispered, not wanting to attract the attention of the others.

He stood up without more prodding, helping her up and out of the shelter. They walked into the trees, passing by the horses.

"What's up?" he asked.

"You okay with all of this?"

"I don't think I have a choice."

"Something's bothering you," she prodded. "But having a back-up plan is a good thing. We're not giving up, Austin."

He let out a long sigh. "Part of me thinks I should just go to ground with Savannah. Find a place, build a cabin if I need to, and give her somewhere to live. I've dragged that girl all over the place for more than a year. She's been on the move since long before the EMP. That's no life for a kid. She needs stability. I can see her pulling away, Amanda, and it isn't just from me. She hardly talks to anyone. She's scared. I need to give her security and help her find her way back to the living."

Amanda nodded, appreciating his need to take care of his daughter. "You're right. She does need something solid in her life, but, Austin, how much security can you really offer her with the NWO in control? It's always going to be dangerous. None of us will ever going to be safe and comfortable."

"But staying put somewhere and giving her a chance to recover from all she's been through would help," he argued.

"Yes, it would, but you and I both know it isn't that easy. I'll admit, I initially thought your plan to save the world was a fool's errand and, in a way, I still do, but I know you well enough to know you will not be able to let this go. You will not be able to sit back and accept the world for what it is unless you know you did everything you could to change it. I feel the same way. I want to relax. I want to kick up my feet and have a drink after a long night of working in the fields or hunting for game. We all want that. It's human nature."

"How do we get that again?" he muttered.

She chuckled. "We do our best. We try our best to do our part. If we fail, we know we tried. We move on—find our little corner of Oregon and settle down. It will be like the pioneers all those years ago. We plant, we grow food, and we get back to living instead of surviving," she said, not fully believing what she was saying, but doing her best to sell the dream.

He pulled her to him, giving her a quick hug before stepping back. "You're right. Thank you. Now, let's get back there so you can get some sleep. You're about to fall over."

She laughed softly. "You are so right."

They walked back to the camp, finding that the others were either settling in to rest or making plans for hunting and fishing. Mike was planning to lead another group up to those berries that evening. Amanda made her makeshift bed, lying down and ignoring the bumpy, hard ground. Austin sat down a few feet away to work on some sort of rabbit snare Ennis was building. She stared at his profile for several long minutes, comforted by the idea of him watching over her while she slept.

9

E nnis settled down by the side of the firepit and glanced around the mostly empty clearing

"Where is everyone?" he asked Wendell, who was dozing a few feet away, lazily watching the clouds.

"Wandering around. Fishing for fish that aren't there or picking those berry bushes clean, maybe," he said, not looking over.

"I think you mean they're out looking for something to eat," Ennis replied.

Wendell looked over finally, but didn't take the jibe. "Yes, that, and Amanda said she had to do something with the horses. Those horses seem to be more of a pain than a help. We can't ride them. There's only two of them. They take water away from us, and they're loud and they stink."

Ennis chuckled, not letting Wendell's attitude bother him. "They're helpful. Once we start collecting some supplies or need to send folks out on scouting missions, those horses will come in handy."

"I suppose," he said, sitting up and moving in to sit closer by. "Ennis, can we talk for a minute, just you and me?"

Ennis looked around the empty clearing; even Sarah was taking a break from the laptop while it charged on its solar battery—he guessed she was washing up by the stream, which was about the only place outside the clearing she ventured to. "It's just you and me."

"I mean, I want to talk to you, but only you. I don't want it going any further" he said in a hushed voice.

"What's on your mind, Wendy?" he asked with a smile, wishing the guy would relax.

Wendell bristled a bit at the use of the nickname, but seemed to shake it off. "What are we doing?" he asked.

"We're sitting here talking," Ennis replied dryly.

"I mean, what are we doing trying to chase down the NWO? Shouldn't we be trying to get away from them?"

Ennis stared off into the trees, wishing he could just have one day without thinking about the NWO. It wasn't to be, obviously. "Have you ever heard the phrase, 'the best way out is through?'" he asked.

Wendell rolled his eyes. "Probably, but what does that have to do with anything?"

"It means that the only way we get to have our lives back is to get through this tough part. If we can take down the NWO, even a little, it's going to get us that much closer to living a normal life again," he explained.

"Do you really think all the other survivors are following that very poor advice?" he muttered.

Ennis shrugged. "They don't know there's a way out. We do. That's the difference."

"No, we don't know that. It could be a wild goose chase. We could be sacrificing our lives to do the impossible. What good is it going to do us, specifically?" he questioned.

"It's going to help us return to normal before we're old and die," Ennis replied. "It's going to give us a chance to actually live a life instead of fighting to survive every single day."

Wendell studied his face. "You don't want to do it," he said, his eyes lighting up.

"That is not what I said."

"You didn't have to. I can see it in your eyes. You don't want to chase down missile silos. You're ready for normal!"

Ennis sighed. "We're *all* ready for normal, Wendell."

Wendell climbed to his feet, staring at Ennis. "You're ready for it now. So am I. So are a lot of them. We don't have to do this. Let's get out of here; we'll head for Oregon like we talked about. Forget the NWO. People will follow you. You know how to fish, hunt, live off the land and all that. They'll follow you!" he said excitedly.

"Follow me to what, Wendell? Don't you see that's the problem? There's nowhere to go. Oregon doesn't solve the problem. We can't have 'normal' with the NWO still out there!"

"Okay, so we go to Oregon and we don't stop. We head to the west coast and we get a boat. We sail away to an island. There are islands everywhere! We can set up far away from everyone else. We can grow and plant and do all that stuff we've been talking about," he gushed, grinning like a fool.

Ennis found himself listening, though, letting himself believe it was an option. However temporarily. Then… "I can't," he muttered.

"You can't or you won't because you don't want to upset your brother?" Wendell shot back.

"It isn't that. We've come a long way together. He's my brother."

"Your brother is going to get us all killed for nothing! You're the older brother. You should be the one making the decisions," he insisted, crouching down beside the firepit as if to convince him.

"Yeah, Ennis, you're the older one, you should be the boss," Austin said, stomping towards them with Amanda right on his heels.

"Stop, it isn't like that," Ennis said, holding up his hand to stave off another confrontation between himself and his brother.

"Sounds to me like Wendell here wants to separate you from the rest of the group," Austin said, glaring at the much shorter man.

"No, I want to save the group from your reckless decision making," Wendell spat.

Ennis saw his brother's clenched jaw and knew he was on the verge of knocking Wendell into the next state. "Stop, Austin. He's just worried, and he has a right to his opinion."

"Ennis, I thought we all agreed this was the right thing to do," Amanda said. "We wait to see if we can do something, and we have a back-up if not."

"But we have to do something if we can," Austin pressed. "That's the right thing to do for all of us. For everyone."

Ennis felt himself shrugging, looking off into the trees. "I don't know if it *is* right. What chance do we have, really, even if Sarah finds the information we need? And if she doesn't, we've only lost time. Wendell brings up a good idea. We could get to the west coast, find a boat, and sail to an island."

Austin rolled his eyes. "Oh, shoot, that sounds like a much more solid plan."

"Austin, we all deserve to decide our own fate. We've been in this position before," Ennis said, meeting his brother's eyes finally. "Everyone needs to make their own choice for their future. They need to hear the options, and not be pressed into a course that's going to decide their lives."

"Ennis, have you seen a lot of islands in your lifetime?" Austin asked.

"No, but that doesn't matter."

"It does matter. What are you going to hunt?" he shot back.

"Fish. You can fish all day," Wendell chimed in.

Austin shook his head again, but kept his eyes on his brother. "Really? What about water? Do you two have a desalinator handy?"

The plan did have some hiccups, Ennis knew, but so did any plan for going after the NWO. "It's worth a conversation," he said quietly.

"You're dividing the group again, just after we finally all came together," Amanda insisted.

"I'm giving the people a chance to make a choice. They aren't warriors, Austin," Ennis said. "You can't drag them into another fight that's absolutely going to end up with people dying. You're talking about going into a war zone with no real guns, no gear, no nothing. You've seen the NWO fight, more than once, and they aren't going to leave a computer center unguarded. Think about that!"

Because it was true, and they all knew it. What Austin wanted to do wasn't just dangerous—it was reckless, maybe suicidal. So what if they were the only ones who could do it? What did that matter if it was impossible? Wendell might be a fool, but at least he wanted to live.

Austin had gone silent, but Ennis faced him head-on, willing himself to stay calm. "You're family. We're all family now." He couldn't bring himself to say that he was terrified of losing his brother, his niece, or his own life. Austin would just have to understand that, and it seemed he did—his eyes softened, and he took a step back.

Austin sat on the ground, and waited for the others to do the same before he spoke, though Wendell remained off to the side, pacing. "I know it's a huge risk," Austin began. "I know it and I'm struggling to do the right thing. I want to run away and put my head in the sand, but I have to think about the future, Savannah's future."

"But Ennis has a point," Amanda said, siding with him suddenly.

"What's that?" Austin asked, looking at her with irritation.

"We can't force these people into a battle they don't want to be a part of," she offered, her voice quiet. "If they go in there half-hearted, everyone dies. Assuming we do this, whoever wants to fight back has to be all in."

"You want everyone to hear Wendell's island idea?" Austin asked bitterly.

Amanda looked to Ennis, then Wendell. "I do. I think it's better we find out who's on board now rather than later when we really need them."

Austin sighed. "Fine. No one's really doing anything. Let's get this hashed out now. I want to know who's with me and who's not."

"It isn't personal, Austin," Ennis said.

"Feels like it."

Ennis swallowed down a retort and forced himself to speak calmly. "You're making this about you. It isn't only you that has to decide what they are willing to die for."

Austin looked at his brother before turning and walking out of the clearing. Amanda followed, leaving Ennis and Wendell alone once again.

"Sheesh, he acted like we tried to impeach him or something," Wendell said.

"It's a big deal, Wendy. Your idea sounds great in theory, but it amounts to avoiding the fight, and Austin brought up some good points. I suggest you think about how you're going to answer those questions when they're brought up by the others," Ennis said before stalking away into the trees for some shade and some space.

It was hot and miserable—an ugly dry heat that made his throat feel dry.

Ennis watched as Austin and Amanda walked toward the stream together, heading off through the trees. There was a strange symbiosis to the way they moved, as if they were of one mind. Amanda was the only one Austin seemed to listen to. She was the only one who could tell him no without his brother blowing up at her.

It wasn't long before everyone had been rounded up and brought back to the clearing to discuss Wendell's plan. Ennis stood off to the side, torn between his sense of patriotism and his desire to survive and live in a peaceful world, separated from the horrors gripping the country.

"What's going on?" Drew asked.

Ennis quickly told them about the idea of moving west immediately, and finding an island retreat, forgetting about the NWO entirely. The discussion got lively quickly, and Ennis only watched, no longer sure what he wanted. Off to the side, Sarah was the only other person who stayed out of it, intent on her own personal mission.

"We could fight the NWO with the information on that USB," Austin interjected. "We could fight back and possibly have a real chance at a real future and not a temporary solution to a problem that's only going to get worse."

"We're tired of fighting," Gretchen said, her voice carrying over the group.

Ennis looked around, seeing the others slowly nodding in agreement.

"We want to live a peaceful life," Tonya acknowledged.

"How peaceful will your life be when the NWO finds your island and kills all of you?" Austin snapped. "Or when you're dehydrated and out of supplies because you've trapped yourself on an island?"

"We deal with that when that day comes. The constant fighting isn't getting us anywhere," Gretchen said.

"It's keeping you alive. You can't give up. You give up, you die," Austin stated simply, staring at her until she looked down to the ground.

"Who's to say we can fight the NWO?" Jordan asked. "We can't beat them. The plan you and Sarah are talking about, that's pipe dream stuff, it sounds like. We're just biding time here, waiting to know that for sure. All we can do is keep running from the NWO and hope they don't send out their full army to kill us. It makes sense to stop running sooner than later and find somewhere to live."

Austin was shaking his head. "You're giving up. How can you give up? The island dream isn't a long-term solution."

"The only thing long-term in this world is death," Wendell shot back. "You'll surely lead us all to our deaths if we keep following you!"

Amanda held up her hands, effectively stopping the comeback from Austin and quieting the group. She had that kind of authority which everyone seemed to respect.

"Look, the point is that everybody needs to decide whether to prioritize fighting back against the NWO or not. If Sarah comes up with the information we need, we have to be ready to move if we want to, and those who don't want to fight don't have to. Let's take a day to think about it. Pray or do whatever it is you do, but no matter what you choose, you have to be fully committed to the idea. This isn't something you can change your mind on. Think about your life in a year, five years, twenty years. What do you want? No one can force you to do anything, except the NWO maybe," she murmured. "But let's decide by tomorrow where all of our priorities lie."

Her calm, authoritative method worked. Everyone quieted down, though Ennis doubted any of them knew for sure what they wanted—except maybe his brother and Wendell.

"We'll reconvene tomorrow and see where everyone's at," Ennis said, feeling like a day or two to mull over their options was definitely the right decision. He also needed some time to think it over. What made sense? Running to the battle, hoping they had a shot—if Sarah could even offer them a chance—or running for the hills and accepting this world for what it was, however dark a place that might be?

10

Malachi rubbed his eyes. The wind had kicked up and he kept getting dirt in his eyes. He'd left the clearing behind earlier, tired of listening to the adults fighting and arguing about what they should do. He didn't really get a choice in the matter anyway. His mom would decide what was best for them, though he'd push for them to stay with Savannah and her dad if he could.

"Savannah!" he called out into the woods.

The sun was setting, blinding him even through the trees when he looked to the west. He squinted, seeing her figure moving down from the area where the horses were; he must have just missed her when he'd left the clearing.

"Savannah! Wait up!" he called out, jogging towards her. He'd been trying to talk to her the past couple of weeks. He felt horrible for treating her so badly. She'd wanted to be friends and he'd pushed her away. He hated watching her suffer in silence, though. She hadn't been the same bubbly Savannah since Nash had died. Malachi felt his own share of the guilt, but Savannah was taking it the hardest of any of them.

"Hey," he said when he finally caught up to her.

"Hi," she returned, not offering anything more as she continued down into the woods. He fell into step beside her.

"What are you doing out here?" he asked.

She shrugged a dainty shoulder. "Taking a walk."

"It isn't safe for you to go out walking alone," he said, noting that she didn't have a thing on her that she could defend herself with.

"There's no one out here," she replied.

"We always think there's no one here until there is."

"It's fine. I'm fine," she said, not bothering to look at him.

"How are you doing?"

"I'm fine," she repeated.

It was the same answer she always gave him.

"What do you think about the options they're talking about up there," he asked.

Her hair got caught in a pine's limb and she angrily pulled away from it. Usually, she used her fingers to comb it and tie it back. He'd noticed she hadn't done much with her hair in days. It was like she was wilting away right in front of their eyes.

"I don't know. I don't care."

"You have to care. I know you have an opinion," he teased.

"Not really," she said flatly. "It doesn't matter if I do. My dad is going to decide for me regardless of what I want to do, and he should. I'm terrible at making decisions. My decisions get people killed."

Malachi bit back a groan. He'd hoped she'd gotten beyond blaming herself so much. "That isn't true. Savannah, you saved all of us. Your decisions kept us alive before we got to your uncle's. I know we wouldn't be here today if not for you," he insisted.

She let out a long sigh, staring out into the overgrown trees. "I hate this. I hate all of it so much."

Fighting the urge to give her a hug, Malachi came to a stop beside her as she leaned on a tree and simply reached out to hold her hand. She let him, which seemed like progress, and he finally answered, "I know. I do, too."

"Is it worth it?" she asked.

"Is what worth it?"

"All of this pain and suffering. We're probably all going to die anyway. I don't want to die like Nash did. I want it to be over and done with fast. He suffered a long time. Did you see his face?" she whispered.

Malachi winced. "You can't keep thinking about that. It isn't healthy."

"How can I not think about it!" she wailed, tearing her hand away from him and crouching down against the tree as if to shrink into the ground. "I did that to him. I was horrible to him. He left because he was mad at you and me. We made him feel like he didn't belong."

Malachi crouched in front of her, pulling her hand away from her face and holding onto it, gripping it as if that could send some of his reason into her. "I'm sorry for what I did. I pray to God every night to please forgive me for my part in him leaving. But we didn't actually hurt him, Savannah. You can't think like that."

"I do think like that! I can't stop thinking like that! I hate myself for what happened to him. Every time I close my eyes, I see his big, bright smile…. He was a nice person, so nice. He saved my life, and look at how I repaid him. It hurts, Malachi. I mean, it really hurts," she said, putting a fist against her chest as tears began flowing down her cheeks.

His heart ached for her suffering. "Savannah, will you pray with me?"

"For what? Forgiveness? No. I don't want forgiveness. I don't deserve it!" she hissed, scrubbing at her tears.

"Yes, you do. You made a mistake. It was Nash's decision to leave the group. No matter what happened at the house, it was his decision to go to that mine by himself. He knew it was dangerous."

She covered her face with her hands, shaking her head. "I can't deal with this. I can't do this anymore."

He acted on instinct then, reaching out and pulling her into his arms, hugging her tight. She tried to get away, but he refused to let go. Instead, he held her until she quit fighting and relaxed into his arms, both of them there on the ground leaning against a giant pine. Her soft sobs tore at his heart. He hated to see her suffering, but the only thing he knew to do for her was be there and pray she found peace.

11

After spending some time with Malachi, Savannah had felt moderately better, but then she'd come back to the clearing. The adults were bickering over what made sense, and it brought all of the stress she'd felt lately pounding back into her head. The tension in the group made it all the more difficult to cope with her own heartache. It felt like there was nowhere safe to turn. Everything was life or death, and there was no safe place to just let her guard down, and simply feel.

Malachi was a good friend, and she was glad to have him around, but he was about the only thing keeping her sane. He'd assured her things weren't as bleak as she'd thought. Yes, they had made mistakes, but they were in the past. Crying had actually helped her calm down, weirdly enough.

Unfortunately, things were never easy. She was convinced she wasn't meant to be happy. It was one horrible mistake after another for her.

Now, Savannah felt like crap as she watched Amanda calm Charlie, whispering nothings to him as if Savannah weren't even there. Amanda stroked his nose, softly whispering as she ran her hand over his neck.

Finally, Amanda turned to face her, gathering his lead in her hand. "You should have been paying more attention—horses aren't dogs that you can just give half your attention to!"

Savannah shrank back from the woman's anger. "I just wanted space from the clearing, and I thought that part of the stream would be a nice change of pace for him. And me. I wanted his company and didn't think you'd mind."

"I wouldn't have, if you'd acted responsibly!"

Amanda turned away from her without another word, leading Charlie back up toward the clearing. The set to her shoulders made her frustration clear, and she had every right to be angry—they were lucky Charlie hadn't gotten hurt. Savannah had looked away for only a moment, but she'd been holding his bridle too loosely, and something had spooked him. Amanda guessed it had been a snake, but one way or another, he'd bolted. Savannah had screamed for help and run to catch him, but these woods were so thick... they were lucky his bridle hadn't gotten caught on something and broken his neck.

Ahead of her, Amanda suddenly pulled Charlie to a halt and swung around to face her. "I know you've been wrestling with a lot on your mind since Nash died, but it's time to get your head out of the sand. We could have lost Charlie today just because you weren't paying enough attention and wanted to be alone. Life and death decisions are being made, and if you persist in walking around ignoring everything, you could get hurt, or worse, cause someone else to get hurt."

Again. While Amanda didn't say it, Savannah heard it loud and clear. She was responsible for Nash's death, and just as Amanda said, they could have lost Charlie today because of her—this sweet horse who didn't hurt anyone. Just like Nash, the sweet guy who'd only wanted to help everyone survive. "I'm sorry. I would never purposely hurt him."

"I know that, Savannah. I do," Amanda said, stroking the horse's side. "But it being an accident doesn't change anything."

Savannah felt tears on her cheeks. "I'm sorry," she whispered again.

"Look, we're all under a lot of stress, and sometimes we want to get away and forget about our responsibilities, but that doesn't make them disappear. Even if he hadn't broken his neck like I said, what if Charlie had stumbled and broken his leg? I'd have had to put him down. Or what if he'd knocked you against a rock or down a slope and broken your leg?"

"Well then, you'd just have to put me down," Savannah bit out. "At least I'd be put out of my misery." Savannah swiped at the angry tears on her cheeks.

Amanda stepped towards her, concern all over her face. "Savannah, that's not what I meant."

Savannah knew that, in her heart, but it didn't matter. Amanda was right—this could all have gone so horribly wrong, and it would have been her fault all over again. Without giving Amanda a chance to say anything more, she turned and ran, going nowhere in particular. She couldn't go back to camp. The horses were more useful than she was. Amanda didn't have to say the words for it to be true. She herself may not have done it, but it was her fault Nash was dead and she'd almost gotten Charlie killed. She ran blindly, down toward the stream and along its bank, finally stopping when she couldn't see through the tears anymore.

She collapsed to the damp ground there, burying her face in her hands. The pain and anguish that had plagued her since Nash had died was erupting in loud sobs that she couldn't hold back anymore. She struggled to draw a breath, pain radiating through her body. Life was not okay. The *world* was not okay.

"Savannah!" she heard Malachi's voice coming through the trees.

She wanted to crawl under the prickly bushes she'd found herself next to. The last thing she wanted was to have Malachi find her. She looked a mess.

"Go away," she croaked out when he came crashing in next to her.

He was beside her anyway, breathing hard. "Are you okay?" he gasped out.

"I'm fine. Just leave me alone. I'm toxic!" she wailed.

He dropped to his knees beside her, putting his hand on her back and gently rubbing. "You're not toxic."

"I am. I got Nash killed and I almost killed Charlie."

Malachi looked at her. "Savannah, I told you, you can't blame yourself for what happened to Nash. He chose to go off on his own, and you certainly didn't do anything to Charlie. We found him and he's fine; all he did was go for a run and give the rest of us some exercise. Probably figured we'd been sitting still in the clearing long enough." He smirked a bit at that, but Savannah couldn't muster a smile. Nothing was okay. Not for her.

"Malachi, I didn't fit in anywhere before the EMP and I don't fit in now. I have nothing to offer the group. Face it—I'm dead weight," she said, her heart twisting and cramping as she struggled to breathe.

"I'll stay here with you while you calm down," he replied simply, settling down beside her on a rock.

"No. Go back."

"I'm not going to leave you out here by yourself," he said.

She wiped her face with her hands. Knowing how stubborn he could be, she took a few deep breaths to try and slow her breathing. And then, as if it were carried on the stream, a sudden sense of calm washed over her. It was like, in that moment, the proverbial clouds parted, and she could see clearly. She knew what to do. It brought her peace and a little fear, but the fear would ease.

Big decisions were always scary; that's what her dad always said. She'd work through the fear and everything would be okay.

"Okay," she said.

"You'll come back with me, or you want me to stay with you?" Malachi asked with confusion.

"I'll go back with you," she said, getting to her feet and wiping the dirt from her pants.

"Oh, okay, great," he said, getting up and quickly falling into step beside her.

She didn't speak as they moved up through the trees. Her mind was already planning. She knew what she had to do.

Her dad was standing off to the edge of their camp when they returned, his arm around Amanda's shoulders. They both had their backs to everyone. The sight was difficult to see. Her dad was more worried about Amanda than he was her. Savannah looked away, glancing around the faces of the others sitting around the campfire. The way they looked at her, with annoyance and irritation... it hurt to see how useless they thought she was.

"Hey, you," Ennis said, coming up to her and giving her a big hug. "Are you okay? You just ran off," he said.

"I'm fine," she snapped, a little too abruptly.

"Why don't you have a seat by the fire?" he suggested softly. "Have something to eat. You've hardly eaten anything these last few days."

"I'm not hungry. Besides, it's better that someone who doesn't make so many mistakes should get the food instead of me."

Savannah felt Malachi trade looks with her uncle and come to some silent agreement—he walked over to his mother, and she cringed. Even Malachi thought she was a useless child.

"Savannah, we all make mistakes." Her uncle reached out to her, but Savannah didn't think she could handle another pity hug.

"I'm tired and I think I want to go to sleep," she said flatly, stepping away from him.

"It's early," Ennis protested.

She shrugged. "I was up early."

After a moment, Ennis nodded and let her go. She walked behind the lean-to—something she'd been prone to doing lately. The space out of sight of the others allowed her to be with the group, but still separate. It was the only place she felt alone.

The others stayed up late into the night, sitting by the fire and talking. She needed to get her rest, and did her best to calm her brain. Despite her best attempt to sleep, though, she couldn't get her mind to stop running. It was nonstop. Thoughts of the past, before the world as she'd known it had been stolen away. Then Nash had died. So many people had died. She had to get away; that was the only way to shed the pain that seemed to be following her.

Darkness fell. Slowly, one by one, everyone crawled into their own little spots and settled in. She didn't know who was on watch, but didn't care. And while Sarah was most certainly awake, she'd still be absorbed in the laptop. They wouldn't see her leave. That was another benefit to crashing behind the lean-to. When she heard no more voices, she sat up, waiting to see if anyone noticed. No one said anything. She grabbed the backpack she had carefully positioned under a bush behind the shelter. No one had noticed, or if they had, they hadn't mentioned it.

She crawled on her hands and knees in a straight line, keeping the lean-to behind her as a shield from sight. The dark night was perfect for her grand escape. Little rocks and sticks poked her palms and her knees, causing her to wince, but she never stopped moving. When she felt confident she was far enough away to be seen, she got to her feet and moved cautiously around to the other side of the clearing, coming to where the horses were tethered and being sure to keep the horses between her and the camp.

Not hearing any noises from the camp, she quickly tacked up Raven. Charlie was Amanda's baby, and while the woman would miss Raven, Savannah thought she'd understand and just be glad that Savannah herself was gone. She wouldn't make another mistake around horses, and Amanda would know that once she thought about it. Plus, Amanda would still have Charlie.

But by the time they found that Raven and her tack were gone, Savannah would be long gone with her.

She took a deep breath, feeling a huge weight lift from her shoulders. She knew being alone was dangerous, but it felt right. She needed some time alone to work things out in her head. She couldn't take any more looks of sympathy, pity, or outright anger.

She needed to be free.

12

Austin's eyes popped open when the sun was barely breaking over the trees. He felt like something was wrong. He couldn't put his finger on it, but it was there. He rolled his head to the left and saw Amanda's sleeping face. Then he scanned the area. He could see the others all still sleeping, some of them under the trees, others partially under the shelter. Sarah was passed out, as well, just inside the lean-to with the laptop hugged against her chest.

He sat up, rubbed his eyes, and saw Ennis sitting up, leaning against the trunk of a tall pine. His brother looked over at him and gave him a small wave.

"Anyone else up?" Austin asked as he approached.

"Nope. Probably not even five yet."

He got to his feet, doing a quick roll call in his mind as he looked around. He moved to check behind the lean-to where

Savannah had gone to bed last night. He could see the pile of pine needles where she'd slept, but she wasn't there. He assumed she must have already gotten up and moved into the trees for some private time.

He went back around and sat next to Ennis. "So, an island?" he started.

Ennis chuckled. "It's an option. Look, I don't want to fight over this. I know you don't like Wendell, but he did bring up a valid point."

"Ennis, we could do something to end this whole thing. Don't you want to have a normal life again? Don't you want to have a house with running water and electricity? Drive a car, surf the internet, go to a restaurant?" he asked.

Ennis let out a long sigh. "I do, but, Austin, you have to be realistic. Do you honestly believe we have a chance of ever getting into the computer center or into a missile silo?"

"I do," Gretchen said, sitting up.

Austin's mouth dropped open. The previous night had been nothing but arguing about what to do; their group had broken up in the afternoon, saying they'd all think about it, but squabbles had broken up from then on until late into the night. Gretchen especially had been staunchly against the idea. She'd been one of the loudest voices pushing for a peaceful existence far away from society.

"You do? What changed your mind?" Austin asked.

"I did. God did," Tonya answered, propping herself up on a shoulder. "If we have the opportunity, we'll try to help you make your plan work."

"We prayed on it, Austin, and after giving it to God, we listened to our hearts. We are against violence, but we are all for helping our fellow man. We have the tools—most of them, anyway. We have to try and help our brothers and sisters. If we can save lives, even if it costs us our own, we're ready for it," Gretchen said.

Austin looked over to Amanda, who was still lying down but had her eyes open. With Gretchen and Tonya on board, Austin was convinced that the rest would follow suit. They did all share the same God. Maybe Wendell would disagree, but so what if he did?

Austin blew out a loud breath. "Great! Sarah thought she was getting somewhere last night—let's see if she did."

He'd been thinking about what the soldier had said continuously since they'd gotten back, and he couldn't shake the idea that if they didn't stop this madness before that date, it would be too late for them, for the U.S.—possibly the world.

The doctor sat up, and he could see her taking a minute to shake herself awake. Then, she looked around. "What's the verdict?" she asked. "Are you all cutting and running for Oregon?"

Austin grinned despite himself, trading a look with Amanda before he looked back to the doctor. "No. You have to find those locations for us so we can move against the NWO. Any chance—"

He didn't get a chance to finish.

"I narrowed it down to three locations. That's as good as we're going to get if we want to have time to make it work."

Austin's heart stopped for a moment. "You mean it? You found what we need?"

She didn't even bother responding—apparently, his pushing her had put a fire under her that had resolved into an all new resolve. "We need to move now, before they figure out that we've figured out the codes; I don't think they'll be able to tell that I've been searching through data on this laptop or that I know what I do, but I don't want to wait and find out."

Austin nodded, moving over to stand closer even as the rest of the group gathered up, only Wendell hanging back. "Okay, what do we do? Where do we go?" he asked.

Sarah's lips pursed, and then she began explaining. "There are three locations where the computer centers might be located. There could be others, but after reading a lot of the information Callum included, I believe they're in southern Idaho and that these are our best bets. All of them are within a few hundred miles of where we are."

"So, we leave today, and start with the closest location first," Austin said, no further thought needed. "One by one, and then on to Cheyenne." Because, very simply, it was time to move. Waiting only gave the NWO more time to dig in. Every day they waited was a day the U.S. government could be working to restore the power. If they turned on the lights, so to speak, the NWO would fire their missiles and undo everything that had been done. If that happened, it would likely be the last attempt to restore order for a long time. The country would be bound in darkness until the NWO decided when it was time to turn on the lights, and then, if it happened, the country would most certainly be at their mercy.

He looked over at Ennis, and could see his brother still wasn't totally on board. His eyes drifted over to Wendell next, who looked downright murderous—clearly not happy to see his plan to separate Ennis from the others failing. That alone gave Austin a great deal of satisfaction and renewed energy.

"That alone won't work," Sarah replied, bringing his focus straight back to her. "Not one by one."

"Excuse me?" Amanda asked from behind him.

"We need to get to these locations fast. Are you listening to yourself? Thinking of distance? We can't get to all three fast enough, assuming we won't get lucky to strike gold on our first try, and then get all the way back to Cheyenne to launch the missiles. It makes more sense to divide and conquer," she announced.

"What? But we have to stay together!" Malachi spoke up.

Austin wasn't exactly fond of the idea, either, but he understood the woman's reasoning now that he thought about. They needed to move fast with this countdown in play, and with that distance.... It would take days, possibly a week, to reach the location of the first potential center, and then another week or possibly longer to backtrack and head in the opposite direction, even assuming they got lucky on the first center having what they needed.

"I think we need to consider the idea of splitting up," Austin said, his heart already sinking at the thought. Because he knew what made sense, again—him and Amanda leading separate groups.

"How are we going to divide?" Ennis asked.

Sarah cleared her throat. "We'll need three groups. One heading to each computer center."

Austin grimaced. Two groups stretched them, but three groups seemed extremely risky. In his mind, though, he was already putting Savannah with him. That was what mattered most. As much as he wanted Amanda to be with him, as well, it didn't make sense. She was a strong leader and would be able to help keep a group alive. They'd find each other again after everything was through.

"Two groups," Amanda said. "Three groups is setting us up to fail, and by *fail*, I mean be killed."

Austin looked at her. "What?"

"I understand the urgency to find the center, but three groups is too risky. Are four people expected to go up against an army of soldiers?" she asked.

Austin looked to Sarah. She didn't look happy to have her idea argued against, but couldn't seem to bring herself to disagree.

"I'm with Amanda on this," Ennis said.

That was a rarity. Ennis and Wendell were always on the other side of anything when it came to Amanda. Amanda's eyes met his. She was waiting for him to back her up.

"She's right," Austin conceded quietly.

Malachi was sitting on the ground next to his mom, his eyes roaming the group. "Where's Savannah?" he asked.

Austin glanced around, only now realizing she hadn't come back from her bathroom break. He got to his feet and moved through the circle the group had created for the conversation. "Savannah!" he called out, looking behind the lean-to. "Savannah!" he shouted again, cupping his hands around his mouth as he stared into the trees.

Malachi was beside him a moment later. "Was she here earlier?" he asked, his voice full of dread.

Austin looked down at the teen, remembering he'd assumed his daughter must have gone just into the trees to be by herself —just as she'd done so often lately. He hadn't even considered... "I haven't seen her."

Malachi groaned. "She took off."

Austin froze, staring at the boy beside him. "What do you mean she took off?" he asked, dread washing over him.

Malachi was shaking his head, his hands fisted by his sides. "I should have known something was wrong. She came back too easy last night. I should have known she would do this!"

Austin took a deep breath. "Do what? What do you mean she came back too easy?"

"Last night, the horse thing with Charlie really upset her. I found her, yeah, but she wouldn't come back with me at first. I told her I was going to stay with her. Then, she suddenly changed her mind and said she'd come back. Like she'd never walked off."

Austin knew his daughter; he knew the turmoil she'd been in after Nash's death. He should have been keeping a better eye on her. His eyes kept looking towards the tree line, and suddenly he realized... there was only one horse. "Where's Raven?"

Amanda came up beside them, and the look in her eyes was enough to tell him what had happened. "She took off on Raven," he whispered. "Sometime during the night."

"I'll go look for her," Malachi said. "I can catch up with her if I take Charlie, and I'm the best of us at tracking. It'll be okay."

Austin turned and looked behind him, seeing the group talking amongst themselves. "This changes everything." He looked back to Malachi and nodded. "Pack up some supplies. You'll go out in one direction on Charlie and I'll go in the other. We'll find her."

He moved back, staying just outside the circle of people, and caught his brother's eyes, using his head to gesture for Ennis to join him. Ennis got up and walked over immediately. "What's going on?"

"Savannah's gone," Austin said, the words feeling like daggers in his gut. "Possibly on Raven."

Ennis's mouth dropped open. "Gone? Gone where?"

Austin shook his head. "I don't know. I think she might have run away in the middle of the night."

Ennis's eyes widened, and then he reached out and gripped his brother's shoulder. "We'll split up and start looking for her," Ennis said immediately.

"What about the mission?" Wendell asked, joining them.

Austin glared at him. "My daughter is missing. I don't care about the mission."

Wendell scoffed. "I thought our whole lives depended on the mission. Aren't we supposed to be saving the world?"

"Not when my daughter is missing!" he shouted, and silence descended around them, even the birds stopped chirping.

"Missing!" Tonya repeated belatedly.

Austin realized everyone was looking at them. There was no point in trying to keep it a secret. "She's not here. I suspect she ran off at some point last night. Possibly on horseback."

"Who was on watch?" Amanda asked.

Austin shook his head, not wanting to point fingers and cause tension. "It doesn't matter—she was sleeping behind the lean-to and easily could have snuck off." His daughter was head-strong. And she was smart enough to have used the lean-to to hide her escape, as well as quiet enough to do it without anyone noticing.

"It doesn't matter. I have to find her," Austin announced.

"The mission. You can't abandon the mission!" Sarah said, practically panicking. "You said we'd stop the NWO and I've worked nonstop to make it possible. Don't you dare give up because of a teenager's temper tantrum!"

Austin glared at her. "I can't abandon my daughter. She comes first!"

"I'll find her and bring her back. We'll catch up with you," Malachi said, stepping in front of him. "I can do it. I know how to think like her, Austin. I'm the only one she's going to talk to, too, and you know it. She feels horrible about Nash, still, and the thing with Charlie yesterday was just the icing on the cake," Malachi said. "You need to let me do this while you focus on taking down the NWO—that can't wait," the boy pressed, holding his gaze.

He stepped back, away from the group, fighting the urge to either sob or scream. When he spoke, it was as much to himself as anyone. "I've tried talking to her. I've tried giving her space and time to grieve," Austin said, knowing it was no defense for his ignorance of how hard she'd been taking everything. He'd known she was upset, but to run away...

"I'll go. I can find her. I can track her," Malachi insisted.

"Austin. Let Malachi go, and we stick with the plan," Ennis said.

Austin stared at him with horror. "You can't be serious! I'm not leaving her behind!"

"I can do it, Austin. I promise you I can do this. I'll find her and bring her back," Malachi said again, putting up a hand to stop his mother from cutting in.

"We need you to lead one of the teams," Ennis said.

Austin glared at him, wondering what he could be thinking. "You can lead the team. You're the one who was just making a big play to be the leader—so, lead. I'll catch up to you once I find my daughter," Austin argued.

Amanda stepped in beside Malachi, catching his eye. "I think Ennis makes a good point. Austin, you are the one who pushed for this. Malachi is a capable young man. He can take Charlie. He's better on horseback than you are and can make better time," she said. "Plus, he's been the only one of us to have any real luck with tracking, and his eyesight will allow him to do it from horseback. He's the smart choice here."

"Okay, but so what if he is?" Austin answered. "That doesn't mean I can just walk away from this clearing. I should be here looking for her. Malachi can help me."

"Austin, think about this," Amanda begged, stepping in closer and lowering her voice. "If she sees you, she might not even want to come back. What'll you do, drag her back to the group? Malachi is right; he's the better choice to get her to return. She'll listen to him." Amanda's voice had gotten softer as she spoke, as if she knew she were telling him hard truths.

In front of her, Austin cringed. It killed him that she was right. The idea of leaving Savannah tore him up; torn between saving his daughter or saving the world *for* his daughter. He looked at Malachi again, and then thought back to the journey to get Sarah, and the way Malachi had helped his daughter cross the country to get to Ennis's house. It had been Savannah who'd directed them, but Malachi who'd made sure that his whole group didn't abandon her. He'd not once stopped looking after her, and the trip to get Sarah had more than proven the teen was strong and capable. He'd shown how capable he was several times since then, in fact.

"Malachi, are you sure you can do this?" Austin asked quietly. "And I mean absolutely, one-hundred percent positive?"

Malachi held his gaze, and then looked over to his mom before facing Austin again. "I can do this. I can find her." Tonya let out a sob, and Malachi looked over to her. "Mom, I'll be fine. You know it. I need to go now, though," he said, meeting Austin's eyes. "Every minute we stand here arguing, it's another minute she's getting farther away."

Austin gulped down the lump in his throat. "Tonya, I understand if you don't want him to go. If the roles were reversed, I wouldn't want my kid leaving alone, either. Don't feel pressured to do something you're not comfortable with. If you say he doesn't go, he doesn't go."

Tonya looked like she was in pain, but she only threw her arms around her son and squeezed him tight. "Don't you dare do anything that will get you hurt or worse! You better come right back to me, got it?" she asked, tears in her eyes.

Malachi nodded, giving her a quick kiss on the cheek. "I got it, Mom. I don't want to get hurt, either. I'll be back with you in no time."

Amanda stepped in then, putting her hand on Austin's shoulder. "It's settled then. Let's get Charlie ready to go. We need to give Malachi all the extra food and water we've collected so he can focus on finding Savannah and not have to scavenge. With any luck, he'll bring most of it back to us," Amanda said. "Meanwhile, let's figure out where he needs to meet up with us."

Austin nodded, sick to his stomach as he thought about leaving. He felt like the worst father in the world. He knew he should be putting his daughter first, but he also knew that the mission was ultimately putting her first. He was doing it all for her. He was doing it because he wanted her to have a bright future.

Sarah stood by anxiously, and he knew this was her cue. He could see she was just waiting for permission to set the plan in motion.

"What's the plan, Dr. Bastani?" he asked, forcing himself to switch gears and focus on the end game. He had to focus on something while Malachi got ready.

"We need one group to head to Blackfoot, Idaho. That's the first possible location of the computer center," she explained.

"We're probably somewhere close to the southwest corner of Wyoming," he guesstimated. "How far are we from Blackfoot?"

"I'd guess it's approximately two hundred miles, or just under. That's why we need to move."

Austin winced. "We can move at twenty to thirty miles a day if we push hard. It's going to take us at least a week to get there. Do we have that kind of time?"

"Assuming the date on the messenger is correct, we have about twenty-five days to do this. So, we don't stop for anything. We push ourselves until our feet are blistered," she said vehemently.

Austin grimaced, not looking forward to that or to walking two hundred miles. He hoped his leg was up for it. "The other group? Where do we send them?" he asked.

Sarah had her answer ready, at least. "I think we have the first group search Blackfoot, then move on to Twin Falls, Idaho, and if there's no luck there, on to Boise. These are somewhat close together, so one group can go for all three and deal with whichever one works out, wherever they find the computer center. The missile silos are much farther away. As much as I want to find the computer center first and put our focus there, it makes more sense to have someone at the missile silo, ready to activate the codes. There should be military personnel there to help with the activation itself as long as everything else is in place. Someone with military background might make things go more smoothly," Sarah added, looking pointedly at Amanda.

Austin nodded. "Where are the missiles?"

At this, Sarah looked down at her feet. "Warren Air Force base."

"Where's that?" Tonya asked.

Amanda's face twisted. "About four hundred miles east, near Cheyenne."

Austin exchanged a look with the vet. It had been their original plan to try and get to the base. If only they could have known then what they knew now.

"Okay, so we're up for a long walk," Amanda muttered. "But it should be me headed that way. I'm former Air Force and have a little more working knowledge on how things work on the base, and maybe my background will hold sway with whoever's there if there's still U.S. military installed. We thought there would be then, and I haven't changed my mind. And even if there aren't… well, I can't say I've ever launched a real missile, but I do know my way around computers."

Austin agreed with the logic in play here, but hated the idea of sending her out on such a long journey, especially when he'd be heading in the opposite direction. He turned to Malachi, seeing that the kid was fidgeting, shifting from one foot to the other as he waited to get going.

"Malachi, you'll come to me when you get Savannah," he said simply, and then he set about giving him a general set of directions to follow. "Head for Blackfoot—that's where we'll go first. If you get delayed…" he choked off at the thought, and then forced himself to keep going. "If you get delayed, assume we're far enough ahead that you should bypass us. In that case, go to Boise. Use your best judgement. I hope to see you by tonight, but that'll be the plan if not. We'll stick to the highway. If it's close to dark, I'll leave some kind of signal to let you know where to look for our camp, alright? And we'll keep our eyes open. I'm trusting you to do this. Be safe, Malachi, and please bring her back to me."

"I will." Malachi nodded once, and then just to be safe, Austin went over the plan with Malachi again, outlining the course of their journey for the next few weeks. They'd plan on doing this in three weeks. It was hard to imagine they could have everything resolved in twenty-one days, but that was the plan. Twenty-one days for Amanda to get to Cheyenne, with a couple extra days for padding. And, on his side, they had three weeks to find the computer center and disable the satellite controls before she got there. With the messengers both charged from the laptop's solar charger, Austin could let her know once the satellite controls had been disabled from the computer center, and then she'd be free to figure out the missile launch. Sarah even thought they could send a message to the base from the computer center, but one way or another, they'd find a way to get her word that things were good on his end if they got that far.

That was a big *if*, he knew, but worse came to worst, she knew the countdown as well as he did, and could launch the missiles just before they hit it if need be. At that point... well, at that point, there'd be nothing to lose.

Malachi loaded onto Charlie and rode off, giving one final promise to stick to the directions Austin had given him—with the understanding that, worst case scenario, he'd head to Boise if they got delayed. Austin watched as he rode away. His heart felt like it was being ripped out, but he reminded himself he'd probably see Savannah that evening. She wouldn't be far—she couldn't be—and with them on horseback, they'd catch up to Austin and the others in no time.

He hoped.

A part of him also realized that it might be awhile before he saw his daughter again. He made a silent prayer to any deity listening that Malachi found her and they both returned safely.

"Let's get a fire going and get the bottles filled," Ennis said, taking charge while Austin grappled with his decision. "Mike, you and Gretchen go gather up the last of those berries. We leave this afternoon."

"We need to talk about groups," Amanda said.

Austin nodded, taking her to the side as the others began prepping to leave. "I'll take Wendell with me. I want him where I can see him," he said, still not trusting the guy.

"Ennis?"

"I'm sure Wendell will insist he goes where Ennis goes at this point, so I'd say they both come with me. Are you okay with that?" he asked.

"Of course."

"Sarah?" he asked.

Amanda cringed. "She seems to trust you, and she'll be better with the computers. It's probably best she goes with you."

He nodded. "The rest can go with you. I want you to have plenty of backup."

"No, I'll feel better if one more guy stays with you since we don't know if Wendell will take off or not—I wouldn't put it past him. Ezra?" she suggested.

Austin agreed now that he considered the point, but wanted Ezra with Amanda. "You take him. I trust him. He can handle himself pretty well."

"Jordan?"

Austin thought about it. He wanted to set Amanda up for success. "Take him, as well. I'll take Harlen; he's better with Wendell than Jordan. And Gretchen can shoot, remember. She goes with you, as well."

With the groups established, things were soon prepared and there was nothing left to deal with but the goodbyes. There were some tears as everyone wished each other well. Finally packing up the charger and electronics, Sarah came over and handed Amanda one of the messengers.

"Amanda, leave it off till you need to. Then, when you make it to the base, turn it on and wait for the signal from Austin. If you fire the missiles before I can enter the coordinates, it will all be for nothing," she said. "Unless we hit the countdown date... if you haven't heard from us then, you might as well try."

"Will do."

Tucking away the other messenger, Sarah added, "It took me a while to get them both charged and I've no idea how long the charges will hold, as I think there's a problem with them. So, seriously, don't turn it on until the last possible minute."

The last chore done, Austin pulled Amanda away from the group. They didn't usually need to say much to communicate, but he wanted at least a moment with her. "I *will* see you in a few weeks," he told her. "You wait for me at that base."

She smiled. "I bet I see you first."

He forced a smile. "Watch your back, Amanda. Don't let those guys push you into something you don't think is right. You have excellent instincts."

"Thank you. And you watch your back. You have Wendell with you. I still don't trust him," she whispered.

"I know. I will."

They stared at each other for several seconds.

"Take care of yourself," he said finally.

With that, he leaned in and gave her a quick hug. He refused to let himself think it would be the last time he saw her. He had to believe Malachi would bring Savannah to him within a couple of hours, and by next month, the world would be back on track, and he'd once again be with his daughter as well as Amanda.

13

Zander stomped into the old-school military-style tent they'd set up about five miles north of the burnt-out house Austin and his cohorts had been living in. He was still stewing over the fact that Austin had escaped again. The guy was proving to be a real pain, and Zander swore he'd be putting a bullet in Austin's head the next time he saw him. He wouldn't give him the chance to escape. Not again. Austin's continued freedom made Zander look bad in front of his bosses, and that wasn't acceptable.

He'd been forced to report back to them about the man, admitting he'd screwed up again. And a gun had been put to his head. He'd thought he was going to be killed in that instant. It was nothing short of a miracle that he still breathed. He wanted to believe it was because they trusted him, but he knew otherwise; it was only because they knew he was ruthless. There were few men on the planet that were as ruthless as he was.

This was his last chance, however. They would not hesitate to kill him if he failed again—that had been made clear. He had a feeling the death they would wield on him would be slow and painful, too, so he'd take care of the matter himself if Austin escaped again.

He'd been so hopeful that he would one day be at the top in the organization. Cream always rose to the top, and he knew he was smarter, better, and more efficient than most of the people he worked with. He deserved a seat at the big table... and he was going to get it one way or another. Austin and his little brat weren't going to get in the way again.

"Sir, we've got a report," one of his sergeants said from behind him.

"Come inside," Zander ordered, gesturing to one of the folding chairs set up inside the tent.

"Sir, we've found them! I'm sure this time."

"Are you positive?" Zander asked, tired of the false leads they had been chasing.

His man grimaced. "A group with a young girl and a man who match the Merrymans' descriptions, and a few of the others, were spotted northwest of here. It's about two-days' ride, maybe three at most. They had taken over a hunting lodge, but according to some of the locals in the area, they were forced out."

"Forced out? Are they dead? Please, tell me they're dead," Zander answered.

"No, sir. But there was a note found at the lodge, proving that it was them there. Our men found it stuck in a window," the sergeant said.

"And?" he prompted, gesturing with his arm and encouraging the man to keep talking.

"It's addressed to you," the soldier said, producing a plain white envelope from his uniform's pocket.

He handed it to Zander, who snatched it from his hands. The word 'Crane' was scrawled across the front. Zander stared at the envelope, growing angrier by the second. Merryman was taunting him. He thought he was so funny because he'd escaped, though it hadn't been clean. His men had found three graves when they'd returned to the house. Zander had hoped one of those graves had been Austin's, and he'd ordered his men to dig up the bodies for identification. Unfortunately, they hadn't held Austin or his brat daughter.

Since then, they'd been scouring the area for weeks, trying to find some clue as to where Austin had gone. Zander had even feared—or, at times, hoped—that he'd take his little army into Denver once again and try to take out the headquarters. His men had been on high alert, prepared for an attack that, so far, had never come.

"Are you going to open it?" the sergeant asked eagerly.

Zander looked up and shot him a dirty look before running his finger under the seal and pulling out a small piece of paper. "I want to help you. Go west," he read out the simple, cryptic message aloud.

He flipped the paper over, next checking the envelope to try and find a clue about who had written the note, but he found nothing. It couldn't be from Austin.

"Is that from our guy? Why would he want us to catch him?" the sergeant asked.

Zander shook his head, grinning suddenly. "No. I would say our guy has a traitor in his midst. Get the horses ready. We're going to that lodge."

"Sir, the lodge has been searched. It's empty. They cleared out several days ago."

Zander glared at him. "They're on foot. We'll find them. Get my horse and get the rest of the men ready. We leave now!" he ordered.

His sergeant scrambled out of the tent and started barking orders. Zander looked at the note again. He couldn't stop smiling. Austin was arrogant. He acted like he was above everyone else. It was satisfying to see he wasn't so saintly that he inspired full loyalty. He'd made at least one member of his little band of misfits angry, and all it took was one. Zander had found his weakness, and he was going to capitalize on it until he put Austin six feet under.

14

Austin and Ennis led the group down the hillside, following a two-lane highway headed west. It was risky to walk along the road, but also the fastest method of travel and the easiest way for Malachi to find him when he brought Savannah back. And the open space would make it easier to leave trail markers if they changed paths or made camp somewhere off the main road.

"He'll get her," Ennis said from beside him.

"He better," Austin grumbled.

"If it takes him all day to find her, they'll take shelter for the night and start moving first thing in the morning. It's what you'd tell them to do," Ennis pointed out.

Austin grimaced, knowing his brother was right and at the same time hating the idea of his daughter being out in the forest alone all night. Or alone with Malachi all night, for that matter. He looked up at the sky and determined it to be late afternoon. There was no way to know how far they'd walked, but he already felt tired—in large part due to stress, no doubt.

"Do you think we'll be able to keep up this pace?" Austin asked in a low voice.

Ennis shrugged. "Today, yes. Tomorrow, probably. The following day... doubtful."

"Then we push hard today and cover as much ground as possible."

"We'll need to find water and real food tonight," Ennis said. "We're burning through calories walking at this pace. It's a mild day today, too, but if it warms up tomorrow, it's going to be brutal. I'm vaguely familiar with this area, but if I remember correctly, southern Idaho is mostly dry farmland with lots of sagebrush, and very hot."

"I agree. We'll stay on the highway for now. There's a few seasonal streams for water right now, at least, although I don't like what I'm seeing ahead of us," Austin added, looking at the bland landscape.

Ennis laughed. "You're too used to the trees and mountains."

"It's so barren. What are we going to hunt out here?" Austin asked, looking at the flat terrain stretching on forever. The highway was lined with power lines, sage brush, and tall, dry grass.

"Antelope is a possibility. I'm more focused on the plants at the moment. I never realized how much sagebrush stunk until this moment," Ennis complained.

Austin chuckled. "We're practically walking in a sagebrush farm. There has to be animals hiding out in those bushes."

"None that I'm going to try and catch right now," Ennis retorted.

Austin wiped his brow. With no shade to be had, it was hot and uncomfortable. He turned to look behind him. Harlen and Wendell were walking side by side, Sarah right behind them. She wore one of the few backpacks they had with the laptop tucked inside. They'd used some duct tape to tape the solar charger to the outside of the pack in order to charge the laptop while they moved. With the direct sunlight, Austin guessed the thing would be fully charged in no time.

"Hey, we're back in Utah," Ennis said with a laugh.

"Why do I feel like we're not getting anywhere?" Austin said.

"At least we're going downhill. Look over there." He pointed to an area up ahead and to the west, which had signs of life in the way of trees.

"Water?" Austin asked.

"Or a pond. We could eat frogs for dinner. It wouldn't be hard to fashion a few gigs," Ennis said.

"We'll make camp over there. We should be able to keep an eye on the highway," Austin said, still thinking about Malachi finding them.

"This is all cattle land, so where are all the cows?" Ennis asked.

Austin laughed. "I'm sure they've taken off, died, or already been butchered." For a moment, he thought about the idea of butchering a cow and having a fresh steak or a juicy hamburger. A cow would be a great find, but not while they were on the road. No, they were stuck with small critters that were easy to get and more plentiful.

"What about that farmhouse?" Sarah called out from behind them.

Austin looked in the direction she pointed. He could barely make out the roof of a house in the middle of a vast pasture. He glanced at his brother, silently asking his opinion. Ennis shrugged in response.

"It's early, and we probably have two more hours of daylight," Austin said aloud, reasoning with himself. He wanted to stop. His leg was throbbing, and he could see the exhaustion on the faces of the others. Just moments ago, he'd planned on them getting as far as they could... but they'd traveled close to twenty miles. He figured that was a good enough start on their journey. Part of him didn't want to go much further, either, in order to give Malachi and Savannah a better chance at catching up to them.

"How about we check it out," Ennis suggested. "If it's empty, it would be nice to have a roof over our heads and hopefully no bugs to sleep with. Maybe, we'll get really lucky and find food."

"Alright, let's cut across the pasture. There's nowhere to hide out here. If that house is occupied, they may very well shoot first and ask questions later. Pay attention," Austin reminded everyone.

Once they'd left a red flag of fabric by the highway to signal Malachi, should it come to it, they spread out, forming a V shape with Austin at the point to lead the way. He knew he'd be the first person shot if there was someone in the house, but he refused to put that on anyone else in the group.

The pasture that would normally have been mowed down by grazing cows had some green patches, but the rest of it appeared to be nothing more than dry grass. Far in the distance, he could see a tractor in a field. He imagined the EMP would have hit at a time when fields were being prepped for alfalfa growing to feed the cattle during the winter. He saw no signs of life, though, human or bovine.

"Anything?" Harlen whispered.

"Nothing. I don't think anyone's here," Austin replied, keeping his voice low.

"There's an old truck in the driveway," Ennis said.

"Hello!" Austin called out in a loud voice as they got closer.

"What are you doing?" Wendell hissed.

"If someone is here, I want to know now before they think we mean harm and decide to shoot," Austin shot back.

"You're announcing our approach! Seems stupid to me!"

Austin ignored him and kept walking forward. The house was of an average size and looked to be at least a hundred years old, worn down and lacking updates. Whoever had lived in the house certainly hadn't put any money into fixing up the place. There were run-down outbuildings scattered around the property, highlighting the fact.

"We'll clear the house first, and then we need to check every building," Austin said before shouting out again to announce their presence.

"Oh God, what is that smell," Harlen moaned as they came up the drive.

Austin's lip curled and his stomach turned. He pulled his t-shirt up to cover his nose and mouth. The others quickly did the same.

"That is the smell of death," he grumbled, dreading what they'd find as he led them around the corner of the house.

"There." Ennis pointed to an area that would probably have been considered the home's backyard. A rotting cow carcass lay on the ground with a swarm of flies hovering around it.

"That is disgusting," Wendell snarled.

"I think that's a good sign this place is empty. No one would purposely butcher a cow that close to the house," Ennis said.

"I'd bet that was an animal kill," Austin said.

"Animal?" Wendell asked, his voice high. "What kind of animal would take down a cow?"

"Wolves, cougars… really hard to say. If this place is empty, those predators would be at the top of the food chain," Ennis explained.

"Let's go in," Austin said—not hopeful they'd find much in the way of food, but obligated to check anyway. Plus, getting inside would get them away from this smell, for what that was worth.

15

Amanda surveyed the freeway ahead of them, littered with cars and huge semi-trucks that had all been rendered useless at the moment the EMP hit. They'd been walking all day and encountered nothing but barren land. There weren't any towns along I80. Not yet. That meant their group's only option was to check as many vehicles as they could for food and other supplies, though they couldn't afford to spend a lot of time doing it. It was a catch-22. They needed food and they also needed to keep moving. She'd made the executive decision not to check any more vehicles until it was closer to nightfall. That's when they would make camp for the night, only to get started first thing in the morning.

Her group was subdued, or maybe it was her own quiet attitude influencing the others. It felt strange to be apart from the rest of the group—from Austin, especially. They'd been through hell and back together the past couple months, spending almost every night together along with every meal. They'd seen death, they'd triumphed, and they had dealt with more setbacks in three months than the average person dealt with in a lifetime. She felt like she was missing her right arm.

She told herself she was way too caught up in the man. She'd been lecturing Savannah about the appropriate time to think about romance, and yet she herself kept going there. Austin was her friend, probably her best friend in the whole world, and this was not the right time or the right place to think about anything more than a friendship. She didn't want to get caught up in a love affair only to lose him or have him lose her. She knew what he'd lost already, and didn't want to think about him having to grieve the loss of another woman he loved. The thought made her scoff even as it came to her. She was really getting ahead of herself. There had never yet been talk of love or anything else in that realm.

"You okay?" Gretchen asked from beside her.

Amanda offered her a smile. "Fine. I was thinking about our journey."

"It's a lot of pressure, but I'm confident we'll get there in time," Gretchen replied in her usual serene way.

"If we move an average of twenty miles a day, we'll be there within twenty-two days. It's day twenty-five when we try to put a stop to all this," she said, still not sure it was a task they could complete. "I feel like I'm carrying the entire future in my pocket," she commented more quietly, patting the zippered pocket of her cargo pants where the paper with the launch codes was sealed inside three Ziploc bags. They couldn't risk it getting wet and blurring the ink they'd used to jot the codes down.

"You're like the President of the United States in this moment," Gretchen said.

"I don't think I enjoy that. These codes feel like I'm actually carrying the missiles themselves," she said with a grimace.

"It's going to be okay. I have faith," Gretchen said.

"So, do I," Tonya added. "We all do. God wouldn't have put this path in us if he didn't think we were up for the task."

Amanda smirked. She wasn't quite as sure about that as they seemed to be, but she'd go along with it.

The fluffy clouds overhead did little to cast any real shade over them as they walked along the hard surface of the black-top. She knew walking along the grassy edges of the highway would be cooler, but it would also slow them down, and they'd risk tripping over rocks or little bumps in the path. The smooth blacktop was easier. Not to mention that she was pretty sure they were in rattlesnake country. They couldn't risk getting bit by an angry snake.

"Listen," Mike said, stopping and holding out his arm to halt the others beside him.

Amanda stopped and cocked her head to the side. "What is that?" she whispered.

"An engine?" Jordan replied with confusion. "Do I hear a car engine?"

"That's a diesel!" Mike exclaimed as the sound grew closer.

Amanda looked up and down both sides of the divided highway. She couldn't see anything, but the sound was definitely coming closer. "It has to be the NWO. They're the only ones that would have an operational vehicle."

"It could be our military," Gretchen suggested.

"Either way, we need to get out of sight until we know what it is we're dealing with," Amanda said, already looking for somewhere to hide.

There was nothing but flat land around them. There were hills far off in the distance, but they'd never make it there in time. Up ahead, though, she saw a semi with a trailer. The roll-up door was about halfway up. It would have to do; she just hoped there was nothing dead or hiding in the trailer.

"I see something coming—they're on our side," Mike called out.

"The trailer! Go!" Amanda shouted, already on the move.

One by one, they scrambled into the back of the trailer. There were boxes strewn about, just waiting to be searched. She waited for her eyes to adjust before she tried to identify what it was the truck had been hauling. She broke into a smile when she recognized the big red target signs on the outside of the boxes.

"No way," Jordan exclaimed when he picked up one of the boxes.

"Yes, way," Amanda said with a smile. "But before we start digging through these Target boxes, we identify the risk," she said, turning back to the truck's back opening.

Amanda flattened herself against the inside wall of the trailer, hoping she wasn't visible to the coming vehicle.

"Humvee," Ezra said from the other side of the trailer.

The large vehicle was traveling slowly—around thirty-miles per hour, Amanda guessed. They could see it weaving around the other vehicles on the road, driving in and out of the median as it moved closer. She couldn't tell if it was military or NWO.

"A vehicle would sure make our journey easier," she whispered.

"Rifle?" Jordan asked.

She cringed. She hated the idea of shooting a true military person, even though the likelihood of the Humvee being military seemed nil. They'd traveled the country and not seen a single military vehicle.

"We shoot," she said, her decision made.

"What are you going to do?" Tonya hissed from the back of the trailer.

"I'm going to shoot the driver," she said coolly.

She expected arguing and pleading for the driver's life, but it didn't come. She had a feeling they were just as eager as she was to be in a vehicle again. They were only on the first day of their journey, and it was proving to be physically exhausting. Amanda dropped to her stomach, knowing the rifle wasn't the best choice, but it was the only option she had.

She lined up her shot, waiting until the Humvee was a little closer. The reflection of the sun made it difficult for her to actually see the driver, but she could make out the general outline. As soon as the Humvee came back onto the road and was about fifty feet away, she pulled the trigger. Her shot rang true, piercing the windshield.

Only then did she realize her plan's flaw. "Oh no," she whispered when the Humvee started to rapidly accelerate before making a sharp left and slamming right into the back of a semi truck's flatbed trailer. The corner of the trailer nearly sheared off the top of the Humvee. If the driver hadn't been killed by her bullet, he was certainly dead after that collision.

"Is there anyone else in there?" Ezra asked.

Amanda kept her rifle aimed on the destroyed vehicle that now had smoke barreling out from the front of its destroyed engine area, which sat wedged underneath the trailer. If anyone else had been in the front passenger seat, it was more than likely that the impact had killed them, as well.

They all waited, none of them moving. After several long minutes with no one attempting to get out of the back of the Humvee, Amanda decided it was clear.

"Ezra, with me. Jordan, take the rifle and cover us," Amanda instructed.

She took the Glock Jordan held out and handed him the rifle before she jumped out of the trailer, landing on her feet and immediately moving towards the vehicle. Ezra was just behind her. Her heart pounded fast as she moved to get a better view of the driver's seat. The front end of the Humvee was nothing more than a pile of twisted, crunched metal, the vehicle's engine pushed into the front seating.

"On the count of three," she told Ezra, who reached for the handle of the back door.

He nodded his understanding. She aimed her gun, ready to shoot if anyone moved. Ezra yanked open the door only to find it empty, minus the splatters of blood from the driver.

"I don't think we'll be driving this anywhere," Ezra said dryly.

Amanda winced, angry with herself for not thinking the plan through. To be fair, she'd only had a split second to make a plan. It just hadn't been the right one.

"Let's get all the supplies we can from here. He has to have a go-bag in here," she replied, ignoring his comment about driving away.

"Hopefully, it wasn't in the front seat," Ezra said, shuddering at the gruesome scene.

"Check the back," she ordered. "It's clear!" she shouted to the others waiting in the trailer. "Start going through those boxes and see if there's anything useful!"

"On it!" Jordan called back.

Amanda moved to the back of the Humvee and yanked open the hardtop on the slant back military rig. She smiled when she saw the boxes of rations along with a flashlight, a wool blanket, and even an old cot folded into the space.

"I've got food!" she hollered with excitement.

"Good, because I've got nothing but blood and brains up here," Ezra complained.

He came around the back and immediately reached for the Maglite and turned it on. When the light shone bright, he and Amanda couldn't stop staring at it.

"Wow," she said with awe.

"This is going to be a huge help out here," he said with a grin, turning it off to save the battery.

"Grab some of those MREs and let's go see what's in that truck," Amanda said, grabbing a handful of the brown packages.

They walked back to the truck with their hands full, placing their goodies on the edge before jumping inside. Jordan held up a handful of what looked like little girls' summer dresses. "Are they your size?" he teased.

Amanda scoffed. "Finding anything useful?"

"I'm finding a lot of little kids' clothes, shoes, and some toys, but so far nothing for adults," Gretchen called out from the back corner.

"We can use the clothes, even the small shirts and dresses, to cover our heads with. We'll be able to protect our heads and the back of our necks from the sun," Amanda said.

"We could make the hobo-style bundles with some of the dresses as well—the larger ones, that is," Tonya suggested.

"Good thinking. With only three backpacks between us, we need a way to carry as many supplies as we can. We're in some pretty barren territory and need to bring everything we can," Amanda said.

"Any use for all these sandals?" Drew asked, holding up some child-size summer sandals.

Amanda stared at the sandals, trying to think out of the box. Nothing sprang to mind, though she knew everything had a purpose. Everything could be reused in some way to aid survival. Unfortunately, with limited carrying ability, it didn't make sense to carry stuff that may not prove helpful.

"I don't think so, unless someone else has an idea," Amanda muttered.

After searching every single box and determining the load was nothing more than summer clothing for kids, they decided to make camp inside the trailer for the night. The MREs were passed around for everyone to enjoy.

"Should someone keep watch?" Jordan asked.

Amanda thought about it before nodding. "It's probably for the best. We'll pull this door down and just leave a small gap, and use a few of the boxes to keep it from closing all the way.

All those clothes will certainly make for nice bedding," she added with a smile.

"I'll take first watch," Jordan offered.

Amanda agreed before heading to the back of the trailer and fluffing her own bed made from children's clothes. It wasn't a Memory Foam, but it would be awfully nice to have a secure place to sleep with no bugs crawling all over her.

16

Malachi slid from Charlie's back, crouching low to look at what he was convinced was a hoofprint in the dark, soft earth. He dropped to his knees and leaned in, studying the print just like Ennis had taught him. It was definitely a hoofprint, and it was fresh. He got to his feet and stared in the direction the print was pointed. Savannah was headed north.

He'd spent most of the afternoon traveling in a semi-circle out from the camp. Now he knew the general direction she'd gone in, but it wasn't until he saw a few strands of her hair hanging from a low branch that he got his first real clue. He'd been intermittently riding the horse and walking, not wanting to miss anything, but now he got back on Charlie to give more range to his voice.

"Savannah!" he called out. "It's me, Malachi! I'm alone!"

He waited, listening for any sign she was close. He hoped she would answer him and not run farther away. When he heard nothing, he started walking again. He'd gone another mile when he came to the edge of a two-lane road. To the right, he saw a brown sign.

"Ha! I know where you are," he said, feeling sure that a state park would be just the place she'd choose to hide out. It would be filled with resources like water, shelter, and plenty of foraging opportunities in the surrounding area. Savannah was excellent at fishing, and he knew she was capable of setting various traps. She could survive off the land easily enough thanks to Ennis teaching her so much about survival.

Malachi got back on Charlie's back and trotted toward the sign, then turning and following the narrow road that led into the park.

Charlie's hooves clopping against the pavement echoed around him, feeding the eerie silence. He knew how dangerous the other campgrounds had been and hoped this one wouldn't be the same. It was then that he had the horrible realization that Savannah could have been kidnapped if there were people already claiming the campground for their own. Would she have thought of that and been on her guard?

His eyes scanned the area, noticed the small wood building that housed the visitor's center and a lone camper trailer parked in the lot out front. He kept going, heading to the day use area that had access to the small lake. A familiar scent caught his attention. He inhaled deeply and identified it as the smell of a campfire. He wanted to believe it was Savannah, settling in and making camp for the night.

"Shh, boy, shh," he said, stroking Charlie's neck when he neighed softly.

He checked the first day use area and found it empty, minus trash strewn about. Dejected, he moved on and checked a second and a third, wondering if the smell of fire was coming from another direction. Just when he was about to give up hope of finding her, he saw the faintest trail of smoke rising from a firepit in the last day use spot.

He jumped off Charlie and raced to the firepit, where he crouched and felt the heat from the ash. Someone had been there recently. He looked around, hoping to find Savannah asleep somewhere nearby. She wasn't.

"Savannah!" he yelled, frustrated he hadn't found her.

He'd thought he would already be back with Austin's group by now, with Savannah in tow. He'd promised Austin he would find her and bring her back.

A glimpse of something shiny caught his eye. He walked a few feet away from the firepit and saw the wrapper of a chocolate chip granola bar. It was the exact same kind they'd had in their stash back at camp. It wasn't weathered, which told him it had only recently been discarded.

It had to be her. He could feel it in his gut. She'd been there. She'd had a fire, and probably boiled some water and eaten a snack before moving on. He did a slow circle, his eyes glued to the soft ground around the firepit, slowly moving outward and looking for a sign of which way she would have gone.

The fading light made it difficult for him to see clearly. Savannah would probably already be making camp for the night, he realized. Malachi wanted to go in search of her while she wasn't moving, but he was too worried he'd miss clues to guide him in the right direction. After a great deal of thought, he decided to use the ash from her fire to start another one for himself.

"Come on, boy," he called Charlie, leading him to the water's edge to drink.

He pulled off his backpack and removed one of the two full bottles of water he carried, taking a long healthy drink for himself. Austin had given him one of the empty tin cans they had saved from some beans they'd found. That's what he would use to purify more water to refill the empty bottles. He'd get a fresh start in the morning.

"I'm coming, Savannah, I'm coming," he whispered into the night.

17

Savannah hated the night. She hated hearing the rustling in the trees and wondering what it was.

Her grand plan for running away wasn't feeling so grand after a long, cold night sleeping on the ground underneath a fir tree. She'd lain awake for a long time, just waiting for the sun to come up, for the moment when she'd see the first bit of pink haze from beyond the canopy of the tree she lay under.

When she did, she rolled to her feet and ran her hands over her legs and then her arms before bending at the waist and shaking out whatever bugs had decided to crawl into her hair during the night.

One of the perks to being completely alone was not having to worry about trekking too far into the woods to use the bathroom. With personal business taken care of and more light flooding the area, Savannah decided to stick with her original plan and head deeper into the forest. She hoped to find an old hunting cabin to make her own. It wasn't like she had to ask anyone their opinion on the matter. She was alone and free to do what she felt was right, so it was just a matter of finding the right opportunity.

One day away from the pitying looks of the others, and she was already feeling better about things. She decided she'd been born to be alone. She was supposed to be a hermit, like Sarah had been. She could do it, too. She could totally live on her own.

She walked back to her tree, pulled her bottle of water from her pack, and took a drink. She'd wait to eat breakfast, she decided. She wasn't all that hungry anyway. She was too anxious to find her new home. Her mind briefly went to thoughts of her dad. Would he be sad or relieved she'd left? She'd seen him with Amanda and felt real jealousy. She didn't like the way it had felt, but maybe he'd be better off.

Truthfully, she liked Amanda. She admired how strong and independent the woman was. Savannah even wanted to be like her one day, but the only way that would happen was through the same practice Amanda had gone through. Savannah needed to be alone and gain her own strength and wisdom.

With her pack on, she bridled Raven and took up her reins, mounting the horse easily before guiding her back up the small hill they'd climbed down last night to find their resting place. There was a hiking trail she'd been following and wanted to get back to, though she hadn't wanted to risk making camp too close to the trail and having someone stumble upon her.

It was a cool morning filled with the songs of birds and bugs she couldn't identify. The sound reminded her of a channel on TV that had played nothing but nature sounds—supposedly to help a person relax. After living with the sounds day in and day out, and knowing that bugs went along with those noises, the harmony wasn't quite so soothing anymore.

She preferred the mountains to flatland because they were so much cooler. Riding was easier when she wasn't hot and uncomfortable. The downside to the forest was the bees and other flying insects that bit when they landed. She didn't know if they'd come from flies or bugs in general, but she was covered in little bites up and down her exposed arms. She decided to find a stream and dig for some mud to slather over her skin; that would give Raven a break, as well. She'd also keep her eyes down in areas that were exposed to lots of sun and look for plantain. It was a plant Gretchen had shown her several times. When the leaves were crushed and macerated, it could be applied to bee stings and bug bites to limit itching and stinging.

The sound of Raven's steps over the pine needles and leaves littering the trail, which appeared to have been ignored for months, was cathartic. The quiet gave Savannah time to think and mull over everything. She hastily pushed aside any guilty feelings for taking Raven. She knew deep down that she should have left her behind—especially after what had happened with Charlie—but she also knew that her only option had been horseback. Otherwise, her dad and the others would have been sure to follow and catch up with her. This way, they didn't have that option. She only hoped Amanda would understand. It was one more thing to feel guilty over, though.

She couldn't help thinking about Nash's death, too, which then had her thoughts turn to Malachi's father's death and the other losses they had suffered. Wrestling with thoughts of everyone they'd lost, she didn't even have to think about being alone and away from her dad to start feeling saddened by everything.

Lost in thought, she wasn't truly paying attention to her surroundings when she nearly ran right into a little boy. Raven stopped in her tracks, neighing softly. Savannah's first reaction was to go on the defense and look around for his family. She grabbed the stick she had whittled down to a point and been using as a spear, waving it menacingly from atop the horse.

"What are you doing?" she snapped.

The boy stared down the trail, his face dirty and his clothes hanging off him, covered with dried mud. It was like he didn't see her. She guessed him to be maybe eight or nine. He was also very thin, and looked unkempt.

"Hello! I asked, what are you doing out here? Where's your family?" she demanded.

When he turned to look at her, his big brown eyes were so blank that they creeped her out. Savannah tugged on the reins, encouraging Raven to take a step back. He kept staring up at her, his face pale and hollow at the cheekbones. His eyes had big, dark circles under them, so that he reminded her a great deal of something out of a zombie movie. She didn't believe in zombies, or at least she didn't think she did, but it was hard to deny what was right before her eyes.

She decided to use a different approach. Dismounting, she kept the spear at the ready and approached the boy slowly. "Hi," she said, her voice soft. "Are you lost?"

The boy stared at her before slowly shaking his head.

She offered him a smile. "Are your mom and dad around?"

He nodded.

Not a big talker, she mused. "Why don't I take you back to them? I bet they're worried sick about you."

He stared at her, and she thought she sensed pain and fear. Maybe he'd run away from them. Maybe they'd been mistreating him.

He slowly started to walk up the trail, and she followed behind him with Raven, still worried it was a trap. The starving boy thing could be an act meant to trap others into feeling sorry for him, only for them to be jumped and attacked by his family. Savannah kept her eyes and ears open, just in case someone was lying in wait.

Suddenly, there was an assault on her senses. Flies buzzing, the stench of rot, and what smelled like copper nearly made her vomit. Raven didn't want to follow and tugged against her reins, so Savannah looped them around a low-hanging branch and continued without her. They broke through some trees and she immediately noticed a red tent set up in a clearing with a firepit in front of it. There was a makeshift clothes line strung between two trees with a tattered towel hanging from it. It was clearly a camp where the boy's family must have made their home.

Savannah almost smiled despite the smell, imagining making her own comfy home in a place like the one she was looking at. Her eyes moved to the left of the firepit then, and she stepped forward so that she could see just to the side of the tent, where she encountered the most horrific sight she'd ever seen.

"Oh God!" she cried out, slapping her hand over her mouth and turning away.

The little boy stood five feet away from the two bodies of a man and woman lying grotesquely askew, their throats nothing but gaping holes and their bodies lying in a pool of congealed blood. The woman's hair, long and once blonde, was a deep brown, clumpy mass.

Savannah grabbed the boy's arm and pulled him away, running through the forest back to where she'd left Raven. Grabbing the reins, she headed back to the trail. Once they were back on it, she stopped to inhale clean, fresh air, realizing that the boy at her side still hadn't spoken. Her stomach was rolling and she couldn't stop shaking. There were goosebumps covering every inch of her body as her mind kept replaying the horrible vision.

"Was that your mom and dad?" she finally managed to ask.

The little boy looked at her before slowly nodding. Her heart jumped in her chest, imagining what the poor kid had lived through. That was a scene she would never forget for as long as she lived. She wondered if the boy had been there to witness the horror, or if he had simply found them.

"Can you tell me your name?" she asked, bending down to look him in the eye.

He opened his mouth and then closed it before swallowing. "Andy," he whispered.

"Your name is Andy?" she asked, thrilled to have finally gotten something out of him.

She took off her backpack and fished out the bottle of water, handing it to him. "Take a drink, Andy."

He took it and started drinking like he hadn't drunk in days. Water ran down his chin, creating streaks of pale skin under the dirt and grime. She reached for it after he'd had another few swallows, carefully taking the bottle and putting the lid back on. There wasn't much left, but they could go back to that stream she'd passed earlier and resupply.

She took a deep breath, trying to think of what to do next in general. She couldn't take care of a child. She was struggling to take care of herself. She knew there had to be more people hiding in the forest, though, so she'd have to make do till then. She'd take Andy with her until she found one of those camps and could drop him off with adults who could care for him.

She looked down at the little boy with mousy brown hair that hadn't been properly cut in a while. She suspected his selective mutism was the result of something horrible he'd lived through. He was clearly traumatized. Heck, she was traumatized after seeing the aftermath. She shuddered again, the forest suddenly feeling too big and too dangerous. Whoever had done that to those people could still be out there.

But... maybe not. She wasn't an expert in decomposing bodies, but she'd seen her fair share of fresh dead. Those people had been there for at least a few days, she guessed. And Andy had survived this long, hadn't he? But there was no putting off traveling away from here, either.

"We need to go, Andy. We're going to get on Raven and ride out of here. We'll look for a place for you to stay, a new family for you to live with," she said in a gentle voice.

If the boy heard her, he wasn't saying. Leading him over to Raven, Savannah lifted him up, situating him on the horse before mounting behind him. Giving the reins a bit of a snap, she kicked lightly at Raven's sides with her legs and the mare started walking, setting a slow pace. Andy held tight to the pommel, never speaking a word.

18

Malachi plodded along on Charlie, following the narrow hiking trail he was convinced Savannah would be sticking to. The trees were thick in the area, and trying to walk around them and avoiding getting tangled or tripped up wouldn't be her first choice. The trail seemed relatively deserted, though, with no signs of humans going back at least a mile by his estimate.

He walked for a long time, stopping and surveying the area, looking for any signs she'd been there. It was late afternoon when he picked up a scent wafting through the trees—not a pleasant smell. It was something rotting. He assumed there might be an animal carcass left to rot, but decided to check it out. There was a slim chance Savannah had caught an animal and that the heat of the day was speeding up the decomp process.

"You stay here, boy," he whispered to Charlie as he looped his reins around the branch of a tree.

Something felt off. He didn't want the horse revealing his presence. He crouched low, choosing every footstep with great care, setting the heels of his feet down first before carefully shifting his weight to the balls of his feet and taking one slow step at a time. All of his senses were on high alert. He could feel something wrong. He kept telling himself to turn back and walk away, but the chance that Savannah could be ahead, and potentially in trouble, pushed him to move forward.

And then he recognized the smell. He hovered in the trees and surveyed the scene, seeing no sign of Savannah. The bodies of a man and a woman were gruesome. He couldn't bring himself to go any closer, though, and chose to head back for Charlie and get as far from the horror as he could. He wondered if Savannah had come across that scene, hoping she had not.

He climbed on top of Charlie and spurred him on, all the more desperate to catch up to Savannah before nightfall. He did his best to look for tracks or signs of her from atop Charlie, but was finding nothing. He opted to stay on the trail instead of venturing off again, too afraid of what he might find hidden in the trees. He rode for almost an hour, growing more and more worried that he wouldn't find her before nightfall. The sun had already started its downward slide to the west. It got dark fast in the mountains. He had less than two hours to find her before he'd have to make camp for the night.

A scream cut through the air, causing Malachi to pull up on the reins and bring Charlie to a dead stop. His body broke out in goosebumps as he turned his head, trying to better identify where the scream had come from. It wasn't far. After the initial shock, he spurred Charlie into a fast trot, racing towards the screaming. A little boy stood in the middle of the trail. Once again, Malachi pulled Charlie to a stop and jumped off the horse to rush to the little boy.

"What's wrong? Are you hurt?" he asked, looking the boy over for obvious signs of injury.

The boy stopped screaming, his eyes wide as he stared at Malachi.

"Are you hurt?" Malachi asked again, his heart pounding hard and fast against his chest.

The boy pointed it to the trees. Malachi followed his gesture, not seeing anything. He shook his head and looked at the boy again. "What? Why were you screaming?" he demanded, frustrated by the boy's lack of communication.

"Bad men," the boy whispered.

"There are bad men in the trees?" Malachi asked.

The boy nodded, and held up a small piece of cloth that Malachi immediately recognized as Savannah's. They all had small rags they carried for cleaning up with, and this boy had Savannah's. His eyes darted towards the direction the boy had pointed.

"Did they take her?" he asked, his voice revealing his desperation.

The boy nodded again. Malachi only had a second to make a decision. Clearly, Savannah had been with the boy. He couldn't leave him, either, but he couldn't very well drag him along on a rescue mission.

"Do you know how to ride a horse?" he asked.

The boy nodded before pointing off to the side, where Malachi suddenly noticed Raven happily munching away on some grass perhaps twenty feet away. Malachi thought quickly.

"Okay, we're going to play a game of Hide and Seek. Or, in this case, simply Hide. Do you think you can do that?" At the boy's solemn nod, Malachi led the boy and Charlie over to where Raven was. Grabbing both sets of reins, he took the boy's small hand in his and gently pulled him over to a crop of trees that was set off even further into a thick wooded area. Looping the reins around some branches, he made the boy sit down against a tree. "I need you to stay here with the horses and hide, and I'll be right back," he told the boy. He hoped the trees would be enough to hide their presence.

"You stay right here, okay?" Malachi asked.

The kid nodded. Malachi wasn't all that sure he understood him, but it would have to do. He patted Raven's nose before pulling the small gun from the back of his waistband, choosing to carry it at his side like Amanda had taught him. His finger rested along the barrel, staying off the trigger in case he tripped or got spooked. He didn't want to shoot his foot.

With that, he moved fast, light on his feet and heading across the trail in the general direction of the aforementioned bad guys. He had no idea how many there were and hadn't thought it worthwhile to ask the boy—who knew if he'd gotten sight of all of them. Silently, Malachi prayed it was only one or two. In the back of his mind, he remembered the look on Austin's face when the man had agreed to let him go after Savannah. Malachi couldn't let him down.

"Stop! Let me go!" he heard Savannah shout.

His blood ran colder as he picked up the pace, hoping to use the sounds of the struggle to hide his approach. It was another trick Amanda had taught him—moving with the surroundings to better hide his movement. The sound of snapping twigs and rustling leaves could be easily ignored when the subject he was pursuing was making the same sounds. When the noises stopped, he stopped, doing his best to breathe through his nose to keep from panting loudly.

Malachi could hear Savannah's muffled shouts and screams, and knew she'd been gagged. The sound was enough for him to follow. He hoped she kept fighting, and kept leaving him a sound trail to track her with. He could tell they were on the move, and he couldn't let them get away. Through the trees, he finally got a look at who it was that had kidnapped Savannah. He counted three men, scrawny and gross. They had long, greasy hair and looked like they had either spent the last few years in prison or a meth house. Savannah was being held by a tall, skinny man. Malachi saw her thrashing about, kicking back as she fought against him. When she whipped her head to the side, he saw the dark piece of cloth tied around her face, effectively gagging her.

Distracted by the sight of her, he stepped on a stick, making it crack loudly. One of the men turned to look in his direction. That's when he saw what had to be blood staining the yellowed t-shirt. The splatters covered the front of his pants, as well. Malachi shuddered, suspecting part of the clumpy texture he could see was also dried blood.

They were deadly. He sent up a silent prayer, asking God to forgive what he was about to do. Then, using everything Amanda had taught him about shooting, Malachi aimed, using a tree as his shield, and released the breath he'd been holding and pulled the trigger.

The sound of the gunshot combined with the man dropping and the other two spinning around to face him all in the span of a second was stunning. He refused to let himself be distracted again, however. He stepped forward, letting Savannah see him. She knew exactly what to do when she did, and dropped like a sack of potatoes. Malachi could practically hear Austin speaking to him, Amanda guiding his aim as he pulled the trigger again, hitting the next attacker in the chest.

Savannah was crawling towards him as the third man just looked at him, wild-eyed. Malachi hesitated, his natural instinct telling him to let the guy go, but Austin's voice and Amanda's teaching told him never to leave a threat open. He prayed again, pulling the trigger, and his aim rang out true. The young man dropped to the ground in a heap.

Malachi immediately moved to Savannah, who ripped the gag out of her mouth and spat several times. He moved to check the men next, holding the gun on the fallen attackers as he kicked a knife away from the first man. They were all dead.

"Andy?" Savannah asked, seeming rather calm for a person who'd just been kidnapped. Shock, maybe, Malachi guessed.

"Andy? Is that the little boy?" he asked.

"Did you find him? Is he okay?"

"Yes, he's fine. I have him hidden with Raven and Charlie. Are you okay?" he asked, looking at her face and then over her body.

"I'm fine."

They stared at each other for long seconds before Malachi pulled her into his arms. Relief washed over him. He'd been terrified when he'd seen her being dragged, and could feel himself starting to shake with the emotion of it all as the adrenaline of the moment bled out of him.

He stepped back when he thought he could speak without his voice shaking. "We should get back to the kid."

"What are you doing here?" she asked as they started to walk through the trees.

"I came after you," he replied.

"Oh," she said belatedly.

He scoffed. "Did you actually think me or your dad—or your uncle or any of us, for that matter—would let you walk away?"

"I wish you would have," she muttered.

"Never going to happen."

When they made it back to the trail, she looked left and right. "Is it just you?" she asked.

He winced, knowing she was probably going to be a little hurt that her father hadn't come along, but she didn't know all that was happening.

"It's just me. We're supposed to catch up with your dad. He's on his way to Blackfoot, Idaho. I was hoping to have caught up with him yesterday, but you moved fast," he grumbled.

"I've got to get Andy somewhere safe," she said, ignoring the subject of catching up with her dad. "His parents were butchered; I'm guessing by those jerks that nabbed me."

"I figured that. I saw that scene," he muttered. "He's not far."

They found the boy sitting on the ground, his legs crossed in front of him as he stared at nothing. Malachi's heart went out to him. He couldn't imagine what the little guy had gone through. Malachi had watched his own father die and it had gutted him. He couldn't imagine being Andy's age and watching the horrifying acts that had killed his family.

"Andy, it's time to go now," Savannah said in a soft voice, kneeling on the ground in front of the boy.

He shook his head. Savannah smiled and reached for his hand, helping him to his feet as she got up.

"Savannah," Malachi said, stopping her when she turned to continue in the opposite direction from where they needed to go.

She let out a long sigh. "I have to get him to someone who can take care of him. We can't leave him here."

"We'll find a camp or a town on the way to join your dad," he insisted.

"We know what's that way," she whispered.

Andy shook his head and started to tug on Savannah's hand.

"Savannah, they're going to do something to try and stop all this. Amanda is on her way to Cheyenne and your dad is headed to check the first town in Idaho where they think they can shut down the NWO's satellite control," he explained.

"Malachi, I'm not saying I won't go back, but I have to find somewhere safe for him," she said again.

"No!" Andy shouted, pulling at her hand.

"What's wrong?" she asked him.

He was shaking his head. "Don't leave me," he whined.

"Andy, I'm going to take you somewhere safe, somewhere to live with good people," she told him gently.

With that, the kid became hysterical, shaking his head, screaming, and pulling at Savannah's hand as if to draw her to the ground beside him. "No, no, no!"

Savannah looked to Malachi and he took a deep breath. "We might as well take him with us. He trusts you."

"Malachi, what if it's dangerous?" she hissed.

"It's dangerous everywhere. He's attached himself to you, though, and he's not going to leave you easily," he said, looking at the fear in the boy's eyes.

She looked pained, but slowly nodded, letting out a long breath. "Okay." She turned to face Andy. "You can stay with me, Andy. We'll take care of you," she whispered. "But we're going to get going, okay?"

The kid nodded, wiping at tears with the back of his hand.

"Let's put him on Raven while we walk. It doesn't look like he's eaten in a while. We'll move away from... from the scene, and set up camp for the night," Malachi said.

With that, Malachi helped Andy onto Raven and they began to walk back the way he'd come. As they neared the camp where Andy's parents lay slain, Savannah stopped.

"We should check for supplies. I saw a tent," she said in a low voice.

He grimaced, not keen on stepping foot in the camp, but he knew that, regardless of the nasty scene, they were in desperate need of supplies. "Okay. I'll go. You stay with him since he likes you and knows you."

"Be careful," she said as they prepared to separate.

The growing darkness made him uneasy as he crept through the trees towards the area that was undeniably the place of death. He saw the red tent and avoided peering at the bodies as he quickly scoured the area in search of supplies. He came up with a few packs of dried soup buried in a shallow hole. There was a small pot he grabbed along with a tiny first aid kit tucked inside an old butter container. It wasn't much, but it was something. Thankfully, the tent was one of those that went up easy, with a pull string on the top. Shelter would be a very good thing. He didn't see the sleeve to hold the tent, but didn't think they needed it. He'd figure out a way to strap it to one of the horses while they walked.

Feeling a little better about their situation, he headed back to where he'd left Savannah and the boy. "Got a few things, but not much. Let's move. We can go another mile or so before it's too dark to move," he said solemnly.

"Thank you, Malachi," she said.

He wasn't thrilled to be in charge of a little kid, but could take comfort in knowing they were on the right track. And, most importantly, he'd gotten back Savannah. Hopefully, they could make good time and catch up to Austin.

19

Zander walked into the tent that had been set up by the men under his command. It made him feel powerful to be the king, even if he wasn't the king of the world—yet. Five years ago, he couldn't have imagined being a man with men jumping to do his bidding. He'd been a nobody, a petty thief without a penny to his name. He'd been homeless, in jail more often than out.

Now, he was a man on the rise in the organization, and felt confident he'd soon be sitting at the king's table. Assuming he got Austin Merryman taken care of. The guy was elusive, and he couldn't be sure the note was legit, but something told him it was. Austin wasn't like him… he wasn't a leader, and his people didn't fear him. He'd done a horrible job keeping them safe. Now, they were on the run, hungry and scared. That worked in Zander's favor.

Someone didn't trust Austin. That someone was reaching out, clearly understanding who the stronger man was. And there was no doubt in Zander's mind that he was the strongest, most determined man; the people who'd hitched their wagons to Austin's had to be second-guessing their decision.

"We have whiskey, sir," one of his men said, standing outside the tent door.

"Bring it in," he ordered gruffly.

He sat down on the pile of blankets that had been positioned for him. They were on horseback for now, but the goal was to meet up with one of the convoys currently moving towards his location to pick him up. They'd picked up Austin's trail and were going to get him soon—Zander could feel it.

The glass of whiskey he'd ordered was delivered, with the man quickly exiting the tent and leaving him alone. He didn't feel the least bit guilty that some of the men didn't have shelter and that he was occupying a rather large tent all by himself. He'd earned the privacy and the luxury accommodations, even if they weren't quite as nice as the tower back in Denver. Once he turned over Austin and took care of the missing USB drive, he planned to ask for one of the mansions currently being held by the NWO. He was going to get the life he deserved.

He took a sip of the whiskey, letting it roll down the back of his throat. His dinner would be served soon—another perk for being the guy at the top of the totem pole. While he waited, he pulled out the map. He guessed they were about a hundred miles from Blackfoot. The trail Austin's people were leaving certainly suggested they were heading in that general direction. His trackers had gone ahead yesterday and were even now out scouting for clues.

"Sir!" one of the soldiers shouted before rapping on the tent's flap by way of announcing himself.

He rolled his eyes. "Stop shouting. I have a headache," he growled.

The soldier cleared his throat, standing in front of the tent with only his lower half visible through the door.

"Sir, the trackers are back. They have news."

"Send them in. Also, where's my dinner?" he groused.

"I'll check, sir," the man replied before he scurried away.

Shortly after his departure, two more sets of legs appeared in the doorway. The tent wasn't the usual military tent he took along with him. He'd had to settle for a standard eight-man tent with a door that cut off the heads of his visitors. He didn't have to worry it was an enemy. His men were guarding him with their very lives.

"Come in," he said in a stern voice.

The first tracker through presented him with a piece of paper, rife with familiar handwriting that made his heart beat faster. It was another note from his source on the inside.

"Meet me in Twin Falls at the Evel Knievel Jump Monument," he read aloud.

Zander looked up at the men he'd sent ahead, questioning them without words.

"That was folded and placed inside a bag that we found hung from the rearview mirror of a vehicle along the highway to Blackfoot. We're convinced that's their destination," the first man said, not looking Zander directly in the eye.

Zander read the note again before pulling the first note from the bag he'd placed it in. It was the same handwriting.

"How far is Twin Falls from Blackfoot?"

"About five days' walk, sir. With our horses, we can make it in four."

"What's the status of the convoy?" Zander asked.

The two trackers looked at each other. "I don't know, sir. We can find out."

"Do we know if they've reached Blackfoot already?" Zander asked, an idea forming.

The men shook their heads. "No, sir. At least two days out."

Zander nodded. "Good, then we ride to Twin Falls and set up. I want to see them coming. I want to know if this is a trap. Better to get ahead than play catch-up."

"Yes, sir," they said, and quickly rushed out of the tent.

Zander stared at both the notes. He had to consider the possibility that the notes had been placed by Austin himself. He didn't think so, but he wasn't about to get taken by surprise. Austin was a formidable opponent, but Zander was convinced he could outsmart and outmaneuver him. Zander had something Austin didn't—no conscience. He didn't care how many people died or how they died. It was all about him getting to the top. He would stomp on fingers, toes, and heads to get there. His men were expendable, too. Every day, more men and women were pledging their allegiance to the NWO. It was all part of the master plan. Break society down until the only option was to join or die.

His dinner arrived, giving him something else to focus on. He tucked both notes into his bag. If it wasn't Austin setting a trap and there was truly a Judas in the guy's group, Zander decided that he'd be the one to tell him. He wanted Austin to know he wasn't a leader, that he didn't have loyalty. It would be the last thing he got to discover before he died. The only question left was whether Zander would kill him slowly or quickly.

20

Austin felt real excitement at finally reaching their first destination, though it was tempered by the fact that Malachi and Savannah still hadn't rejoined them. He knew Malachi knew the plan, and he knew how capable the young man was, and that what they'd done had made sense... but none of that allayed his worries over whether or not they were okay. So much could have happened since they'd all split up, and he couldn't stop himself from thinking the worst. Several times, he'd been tempted to leave the others and backtrack to try to pick up their trail, but logic had prevailed when he'd realized that his daughter could have gone in any direction by now, making it near impossible to find them since the trail would have gone so cold by now. He just had to remind himself that what he was doing would not only save his daughter, but everyone else, as well, even if it didn't stop the incessant worry.

They had all pushed themselves, putting in extra miles every day in an attempt to reach Blackfoot ahead of schedule. Sarah had been the one driving the group on the most, which was a change in pace. But as much as Sarah pushed, Wendell pulled.

"We're here, so can we please take a break now?" Wendell whined.

Sarah, walking alongside Austin at the head of the group, turned around to glare at him for at least the tenth time. "Does it look like we're *here*? We're not *here*," she snapped. "We're just close, and that doesn't mean we can rest."

Austin could hear Ennis assuring Wendell they'd be stopping early that night. It was infuriating to listen to the two of them, and grated on Austin's nerves. Wendell was acting like a petulant child, and Ennis constantly tried to comfort and assure him they were almost there. A five-year-old would have had more endurance.

"We need to get to the computer center. It's on the outskirts of town," Austin said.

Harlen trudged along, as silent and stalwart as he'd been the entire trip. The guy always seemed lost in deep thought. "I hope we'll be able to scout for some more food. We've about gone through everything we picked up at that little store," the man said.

Austin nodded. "That's the plan. We'll get to the computer center and check it out. If there's nothing, we'll spend the rest of the day scouting for food and supplies. Then we'll make camp and head out early tomorrow."

It was a grueling pace, but they couldn't afford to drop the ball. He only hoped Amanda hadn't been waylaid. She had to get to those missiles, though it wouldn't do any good if he couldn't reach a functioning computer center and shut down the satellite target systems. He'd contemplated turning on the messenger to send her a message and check on the other group's progress, but Sarah had been adamant that they wait, which would mean Amanda wouldn't have hers on to get the message anyway.

"It's off this old highway," Sarah announced.

"I thought we were going into the city," Wendell complained.

"No!" she snapped.

They turned right, heading north along a narrow blacktop road with no lines down the middle or either side. It wasn't a road that would have been used often. Power lines ran alongside it, just outside a long line of white fencing. Austin surveyed the flat terrain that would have once been a place for cattle to graze. Farmhouses were scattered about, some burned out; others they had investigated in days past had been the scenes of horrible crimes that had likely left the inhabitants dead.

"How much farther? This is a dead-end," Wendell whined.

Austin had a feeling Sarah was about ready to hit the guy over the head with the laptop secured in her backpack. And if she didn't, he might. They walked for another forty-five minutes before Sarah came to an abrupt stop at a crossroads. The dirt road on the left looked like it headed out to more farmland. The path on the right was gravel, and again, it didn't look promising. Up ahead, the paved road seemed to stretch on forever, with nothing in sight but more houses with acres and acres of agriculture between them.

"What are we doing?" Austin asked her.

She looked puzzled, but then pointed towards the gravel road. "This way."

"Are you sure?" he asked.

She nodded. "I memorized the map. I'm positive."

"Is it underground? What exactly are we looking for?" Austin asked, suddenly very weary himself.

He'd been expecting something obvious—a building, a military base… something more than a field of what had likely been full of potatoes.

"There's not going to be a flashing sign alerting us, Austin. It is out here, though, and I'll recognize it when we see it. The cover is a mechanic's shop," she said nonchalantly.

Austin shook his head. "Really?"

She nodded. "Yes, really. It's this way. Not much farther."

Austin took a deep breath, hoping the woman knew what she was talking about. He'd seen the maps and known the computer centers would be hidden, but a mechanic's shop in the middle of a potato field seemed a bit far-fetched.

Sure enough, a sign announcing Mike's Autoshop stood out alongside the road.

They kept walking, slowly approaching the building with its sloped roof, faded blue paint in big block letters indicating that they'd reached the shop. It didn't look promising. One of the windows was boarded over, and the garage on the left looked like it had been abandoned for a lot longer than a few months. There were a few cars in the gravel parking lot, most appearing long broken down.

"I'll check the garage," Ennis said, moving to put his face against the glass.

"It looks abandoned," Wendell said, standing back.

Austin moved to the door and tried the doorknob, only to find it locked. He used his shoulder to slam against it a couple times. The door gave way without a lot of fight. Dust floated around the room, highlighted by the sun streaming in through the open door. Austin waved his hand through the air, clearing it the best he could.

"Where in the world would there be a computer center in this tiny place?" Harlen asked, walking in behind him.

"Underground," Sarah said, moving behind the tall counter.

Ennis moved into what would have been the main area of the shop. There were a couple of plain metal chairs pushed against the wall alongside what appeared to be a mostly empty vending machine.

"Food!" Wendell exclaimed, heading for the machine immediately.

Before anyone could say anything, Wendell had picked up one of the chairs and started attacking the front of the machine. Austin observed, shocked at the man's sudden burst of energy. Meanwhile, Sarah disappeared through a small door that Austin assumed led to the garage.

"Here!" Sarah shouted at the same time Wendell shouted his victory at smashing the front of the vending machine.

Austin headed through the door with only the slightest hesitation, hoping Ennis would save some of whatever was left in the machine as he rushed into the garage. Sarah was working at a round, steel door in the floor. It looked like a sewer drain, but she seemed to know it for something else.

"Let me," Austin said, using his strength to turn the door on her behalf, unlocking it and lifting it away.

"That's it!" she exclaimed.

Seeing the clear opening, Austin suddenly realized their mistake and prayed it wasn't too late for them to make up for it. If NWO soldiers were down there, the ruckus they had made coming in would have revealed their presence now that this door was open, if not before. He should have kept Wendell from making all that noise when he'd had the chance.

"I'll go down first," Sarah said before he could voice his worry, turning and dropping to the ground to put her feet on the ladder.

"Sarah, wait! You don't know what's down there!"

She only looked back at him, shrugged a shoulder, and headed down the ladder. "I hope you'll save me, or if not, kill them all and complete the mission."

He stared after her, shaking his head at her carelessness. "Idiot," he grumbled, knowing there was no way he could hold his gun with any chance of defending her while climbing down the ladder.

So, instead of following her down, he chose to wait, listening for sounds of trouble. Ennis came in and stood beside him, looking into the hole. Sarah had disappeared into the darkness.

"It's clear!" she shouted.

Austin was the first to grab hold of the ladder, quickly climbing down and jumping into the underground bunker lit by soft green lights that had to be battery-powered. The room was empty, though, showing nothing but cords and a couple scattered keyboards.

Ennis was beside him again a minute later. "I take it this isn't it," he said dryly.

Sarah picked up a flat piece of metal. "It was. They've cleared it out. They took everything," she muttered, kicking one of the rolling chairs left behind.

Austin scanned the area that had been a hub for the terrorists now controlling the world. It was a small bunker with tables set up around the room that had once held computer equipment. They were too late.

"Was this recent?" he asked.

"What?" Ennis asked.

"Did they recently clear out or was this abandoned a while ago?" he asked, his stomach sick over the idea that the next two computer centers would be the same.

Sarah ran her finger over one of the smooth metal surfaces. "This happened some time ago. It wasn't recent."

Austin breathed a sigh of relief. "Then they don't know we're coming."

"Maybe. They could have decided to move everything as soon as they figured out Callum knew these locations," she replied.

"Gee, so positive," Ennis said sarcastically.

Austin scanned the room and spotted a large metal cupboard pushed up against a wall. He moved to it, tried to open it, and discovered it was locked. He jerked at the handle hard, but with no luck.

"Come on," he muttered, feeling defeated and needing a win, no matter how small it was.

"Maybe we should try Wendell's trick," Ennis said with a small laugh. "We'll attack it with a chair."

Austin tugged on the handle again. All the frustration he'd been feeling over the last week came to a head, his regret over his decision not to go after Savannah himself suddenly boiling over. He'd been telling himself it was for the greater good. He'd get to the computer center and save the world. Suddenly, that reasoning felt empty, even foolish. He kicked at the door before pounding on it with his fists and then his open hands.

He shouted, kicking and yelling obscenities as he released everything from his system, erupting emotion, the metal cupboard before him acting as the punching bag he desperately needed.

No one tried to stop him as he released his unholy rage. Suddenly, though, the door he'd been yanking on and hitting tilted to the side, finally giving in to his assault. Austin stopped kicking and shouting, and jarred the door open.

And while he couldn't make out the words, the plain black lettering on brown packages told him they'd just unearthed military rations. He stared at the shelves that had been stockpiled with food and supplies.

Ennis put a hand on his shoulder. "Good job."

Austin turned to face him. "Thanks."

"We're not giving up. We knew there was a chance this could happen. We stock up on supplies and we move on," Ennis said, his voice calm and reassuring.

Austin nodded, turning to find Sarah standing against the wall and staring at him like he had two heads. "Sorry," he muttered.

"It's fine. I hope you feel better now," she replied, not moving away from the wall.

He took a deep breath. "I do. This cupboard is loaded. We need to take as much as we can carry." He reached for a box of bullets and smiled. "Nine millimeter," he said, using his fingers to nose out a bullet.

"Thank God. We needed ammo," Ennis said, breathing a sigh of relief.

"Sarah, look around and see if there's a weapons cache," Austin ordered, gesturing around to the abandoned crates littering the room. Most looked like they only held junk, but it was worth checking.

Ennis dropped to his knees and pulled out a brown camo backpack. "Well, look at this!" he exclaimed with a big smile on his face. "They were nice enough to leave us a packed go-bag."

"Frame?" Austin asked.

Ennis stood up, holding the bag in one hand and unzipping it with the other. "Yep, internal."

"Good. Load it. I'll carry it," Austin replied.

"What do you mean, *frame*?" Sarah asked.

"Internal frame backpack. It'll allow us to carry more without feeling the weight quite as much as if we were using a backpack like the one you're wearing," Ennis answered.

"Harlen, can you come down here?" Austin shouted. "Wendell, stay up there and keep watch!"

"Did you find something?" Wendell shouted.

"Yes!" Ennis replied loudly.

Harlen appeared in the bunker a moment later, his face lighting up when he saw the rations that included a couple cases of canned water. He reached for one of the cans, popped the top, and guzzled down the liquid. "That was so good," he said with a long sigh.

Austin smiled. "We'll form an assembly line to get this stuff upstairs."

Ennis climbed up the ladder, waiting near the top while Harlen took the middle spot. Austin stood on the ground while Sarah brought him one case of water at a time. After several minutes, they'd depleted the cupboard and were all making their way back up the ladder. Austin wasn't surprised to see Wendell had made his way through several bags of what had to be stale chips and was now working on a Snickers bar.

He glared at the guy, angry he'd mowed down the food without a worry for the rest of them. Wendell didn't seem to mind a bit, and happily chewed on the candy bar while the rest of them tore into the MREs. The last half-decent meal they'd had had been two days prior. So, yeah, Austin understood Wendell's hunger, but they were all starving. Wendell, though, was all about himself and couldn't care less about the others. Wendell snatched one of the MREs, moving outside to eat it when Austin shot him a dirty look.

"How much can we take?" Sarah asked, slurping down a second can of water.

Austin shook his head. "We have the internal frame pack. I can take about forty pounds, which is about one of those cases of water and some of the MREs along with the gear already in the pack."

"That's too heavy. You're going to be hurting after a few hours," Ennis warned.

"We'll drink at least half that water the first day. I can do it," Austin said.

Ennis shook his head. "You need to keep your pack light or you're going to get tired quicker."

"Ennis, I'm not leaving any of this behind. If we have food and water, we don't have to waste time looking for it. This is too important," he argued.

"Why don't we each carry a couple cans in our pockets along with whatever else we can shove in?" Harlen asked.

"We will," Ennis replied. "And put more MREs in the pack itself since they're lighter. We'll get it all, but we'll do it by sharing the load and being smart about it. You don't have to do all of the heavy-lifting yourself, Austin," he said to his brother, giving him a half-smile.

"There were some coveralls hanging in that garage," Harlen said, jumping up from his spot on the floor and heading off through the door.

"I hope he doesn't think wearing coveralls in the middle of the summer while walking a hundred miles is a good idea," Ennis muttered.

Harlen came back with two sets of blue coveralls that were remarkably clean for a mechanic's shop and dropped them on the floor. "Got your knife?" he asked Austin.

Austin nodded and handed it to him. "What's your plan?"

"I'm going to make some fanny packs," Harlen said with a grin.

"What?" Ennis asked with confusion.

"I'm going to cut off the legs, tie a knot at one end, stuff them with whatever, and there you go. I tie it around my waist and I've got myself a fanny pack," he said with a grin. "I'm thinking I personally might need to use a strip of fabric to serve as an extension of sorts. It's been a long time since I've had a thirty-two-inch waist," he said with a laugh.

"Extension?" Ennis asked.

"I'll cut a strip from the torso and tie it to each end of the pant leg," he explained.

Austin's eyebrows shot up. "Wow. That's a really good idea. Make one for Wendell, too. Anyone who's not carrying a pack should have one."

Harlen nodded, already cutting off the first leg. When he was finished, he tossed the leg to Austin, who tied it off at one end and began shoving in a few cans of water, some water purification tablets, waterproof matches, and a couple of the MREs. He held it up with both hands, testing the weight, and decided he could slide in one of the light sticks and some of the dense food bars that tasted awful but packed a lot of calories.

They stuffed the next leg with supplies before going after the second pair of coveralls to do the same.

"What about the arms?" Ennis asked.

Austin looked at the arms and smiled. "Pillows—or pillow-cases, rather. We stuff them with leaves and other debris to make pillows. It isn't luxury, but anything is better than resting our faces on the cold, hard ground."

Harlen nodded. "Good thinking."

Wendell came back into the office then, wiping his face with the back of his hand as he looked down at the butchered coveralls. "What's that?"

"Your new fanny pack," Austin replied.

Wendell wrinkled his nose. "Whatever. Why don't we stay here tonight? We're ahead of schedule and a roof over our heads would be nice."

Austin shook his head. "Too risky."

"Why is it too risky? We haven't seen anyone for miles. This place has been abandoned," he said, practically pouting.

"Who's to say they won't come back? Maybe they're out there right now. We need to get back to the highway. Malachi will be following it to catch up to us," Austin said.

Wendell rolled his eyes, putting a hand on his hip. "You'd rather sleep on the ground than in here just in case the kid shows up?" he snapped.

Austin jumped to his feet and stalked towards Wendell. "That kid you're referring to is my daughter, along with the young man who went off to find her. So, yes, I'd rather be out there where they'll find me. Feel free to stay here by yourself."

Wendell looked around Austin to where Ennis was sitting on the floor. Austin turned to look and caught Ennis shaking his head. When he looked back at Wendell, the man looked angry, but he would clearly be doing as Ennis said and remaining quiet about it.

"Let's get our new fashion accessories on and get a move on," Harlen said, getting to his feet.

Ennis stood up, as well, holding out the fanny pack for Wendell to take. His much smaller frame could probably have done without the extender, but they kept it on anyway. Wendell grumped and complained about how heavy it was, but the others ignored him, putting on their own gear. Austin bounced up and down on his legs, checking the feel of the pack on his back, adjusting the hip belt to tighten it. He didn't want it rubbing and chafing him. He knew it was a risk to wear the heavy pack so close to his body, which would already be sweating, but he was convinced he could handle it. He'd give his skin time to air out and dry as often as possible to avoid chafing over his back that could lead to an open wound and, ultimately, a life-threatening infection with no antibiotics on hand.

"Everyone ready?" he asked.

With that, they set out, following along the old road that Sarah was convinced would intersect with the highway. There was a cool breeze from the west with the scent of fresh, moist air. Austin closed his eyes for a brief second, savoring the freshness of the breeze blowing across the Snake River.

"We should do—"

"Don't move!"

Austin spun around to find a group of five men armed with ARs pointed directly at them. He groaned with anger and disgust.

"We're on our way out of town," Austin told them.

The man in the front of the group, in his mid-thirties and of average build, shook his head. "Yes, you are on your way out of town, but we'll be taking that off your back."

Austin thought about the supplies they had only just managed to get their hands on. It wasn't right. He was sick of taking one step forward only to take two steps back.

"We need something to survive on," Ennis begged them.

"You'll find more. Hand it over."

Austin's gun was tucked under his t-shirt. There was no way he'd be able to reach it before one of the rifle shots hit him. Wendell untied his own makeshift pack and dropped it to the ground.

"You, now," one of the men said, pointing at Ennis.

Ennis grumbled, shaking his head as he took off the pack and dropped it to the ground in front of him. Sarah was standing a few feet from Austin. She looked at him, her eyes wide.

"All I have is a laptop computer," Sarah said, holding up her hands.

The men holding guns on them laughed. "Why are you carrying around a brick?" one demanded.

She shrugged. "It has sentimental value."

"Computers don't work anymore," the leader spat out.

She nodded. "I know, but I hope one day they will. It has pictures of my children on the hard drive. It's all I have left of them," she said, sniffling as she exaggerated emotion.

The men looked at one another. "You can keep your stupid computer, but we'll be taking everything else. We're not taking your word for it, though," he told her, gesturing her to open up the backpack. Once she did so, he stepped forward and looked inside, pawing around the equipment inside. Austin said a silent prayer of thanks when the man stepped back, apparently not having recognized the value of either the messenger apparatus or the solar battery.

Austin undid the front snap of his own pack before sliding it off his arms. He put it on the ground and took a step back, looking at Sarah and silently telling her to do the same. He heard the other packs hit the road and waited for the men to decide what they would do next.

"You've got our gear, so are we free to go?" Austin asked.

The men exchanged looks. "You're free to go. Happy hunting," the leader said with a laugh. "Walk backwards until we tell you to stop."

Austin nodded and took a few tentative steps backwards, stopping to look behind him and then moving again. It was a little surprising that the men hadn't searched their bodies, but he wasn't going to make a fuss and risk someone being shot or them losing their weapons. He was confident they'd find more supplies. Harlen's idea to load their pockets with as much as they could fit was a good thing. Austin had his knife, his gun, and a variety of gear, plus a few of the crappy protein bars. They had all tucked some away in their pockets, in fact.

The thieves finally moved forward, picking up their gear while keeping their guns trained on Austin and the others.

"You can run away now!" one of the men shouted, bursting into laughter.

Austin shook his head, angry, but he knew when it was smarter to retreat than fight. They were outgunned.

"Well, now what are we going to do?" Wendell grumbled.

"We keep walking. Nothing changes," Austin snapped, turning and stomping down the paved road.

"We could go after them," Ennis suggested.

"It's stupid to try. We keep moving. We have enough to get by. Before they interrupted me, I was going to say we could do a little fishing in the river, but I don't want to stop here after that encounter. I want to put some distance between us and them in case they decide they want the laptop or they want to do a more thorough search of our persons," Austin said.

They were quiet as they crossed the road, heading to the wide highway that would put them on the path to their next destination.

21

When Austin awoke early on the morning following the robbery, the first thing he thought of was the fact that Malachi hadn't brought Savannah back. Every day that she wasn't with him filled him with a gnawing worry that he couldn't shake. He'd vowed to never let himself get separated from her again during the long trek across the country, and here he'd gone and done it anyway. It made him furious with himself, and he couldn't help but wonder if she was hurt somewhere. Was she waiting for him to save her? What if Zander had found her?

He sat up to find Harlen standing a few feet away, watching the sunrise. The man turned to smile at him, calm as ever. "Good morning."

"Good morning," Austin grunted, getting to his feet and dusting off the dirt and debris clinging to him after sleeping on the ground.

"You were thrashing about quite a bit the last hour or so," Harlen said.

Austin took a deep breath. "Sleeping isn't easy."

"I imagine you're worried about your daughter."

"I am."

"I know you're not a big believer in a higher power, but I think it helps to have something or someone to believe in. You have to believe she's okay. You two have managed to overcome some pretty tough circumstances, and I believe you'll do it again," he offered, his rich voice washing over Austin and actually calming him a bit.

"Thanks, Harlen. I hope you're right."

"I think we should probably get a move on, though. Better to walk in the early morning when it's cooler," Harlen suggested.

Austin nodded, and the two of them moved around to wake the others. As they stirred, moaning and stretching, Wendell began complaining already. "The sun's not even all the way up," he whined.

"Which means it's still cool. I figure you'll have fewer hours to complain if we move when it's cool outside versus in the heat of the day," Austin snapped.

"Austin," Ennis warned.

They each took care of their morning business and rehydrated from a nearby stream, using their purification tablets, plastic bottles they'd found, and the small collapsible cup Harlen kept stashed in his back pocket. Then, it was time to hit the road. They had another hundred and twenty miles to go to reach Twin Falls. That was at least a five-day walk.

As they traveled, they each ate one of the mealy protein bars. Austin had to force himself to gulp the thing down, the taste lingering in his mouth long after he'd swallowed the last bite. He heard a crinkling noise and looked around. Wendell was behind them, bringing up the rear.

"What's that?" he asked, noticing something shiny in Wendell's hands.

"Gum," he replied nonchalantly.

They all stopped and turned to him. "You have gum?" Ennis practically shouted.

Wendell shrugged. "I got it out of the vending machine."

Austin looked at Ennis, warning him to deal with his friend before he did. Ennis stepped forward, quietly whispering to Wendell. When he turned back around, he had a pack of gum in his hand.

"Would anyone like a piece of gum?" he asked with a forced smile.

"Yes!" they all said, each one of them apparently anxious to erase the taste of the protein bars.

The pack was emptied, and Ennis turned around and handed it back to Wendell, who looked ready to scream. He snatched the empty pack up and tossed it on the road.

"Littering isn't cool," Austin said with a grin before turning around and continuing down the highway, which was already blanketed with trash. It appeared that no one cared about picking up after themselves. That, combined with the wind, meant that trash had been blown all over the place. If and when the power was restored and society was returned to some sense of normalcy, it was going to take a long time to clean up the world.

They'd been walking along the highway in silence, each of them lost in their own thoughts, when Harlen pointed ahead. "What is that?" he asked.

Austin peered in the general direction and spotted a sign made from cardboard and spray paint announcing that Tent City was just a little farther up the road, and that all were welcome.

"Tent City?" Ennis commented.

"You think it's a government run refugee camp?" Harlen asked excitedly.

"I don't know, but I'd be interested in finding out," Austin said.

"What if it's a trap?" Ennis asked, which was what Austin had also been wondering.

"Keep everything hidden deep in your pockets. Sarah, give me the USB. If they take the laptop, I don't want them getting that driver," Austin said, walking up to her and helping her take off the pack.

She'd insisted on carrying the backpack with the laptop inside. He could see she was hesitant, but he didn't care. It was his responsibility. He grabbed it, folded the plastic bag it was stored in as small as it would go, and shoved it deep inside his front pocket.

"Keep your eyes and ears open," Ennis warned the group as they came upon another homemade sign.

In the distance, they caught their first glimpse of the so-called tent city. Tents were set up in all colors, shapes, and sizes in a flat field. Everything was flat and barren. There was nothing around it—nothing but barren, dry land.

A dirt road led from where a sign had been staked into the ground with an arrow pointing towards the tents. Austin didn't get a dangerous vibe from the area. In fact, he could hear kids playing, which was a sound that was so foreign to his ears that he had to stop and take pause. They all did.

"Kids?" Ennis whispered.

"Happy kids," Harlen replied with a smile.

That had to be a good sign, and Austin couldn't help being anxious to see what Tent City was all about. They passed a group of women using rakes and shovels in an area with rich, brown soil. There were healthy green potato plants thriving, and what looked like peppers and tomatoes nearby.

"A garden. An actual garden," Ennis said, clearly impressed.

The women smiled and waved as their own group continued towards what could only be described as the hub of the city. A man wearing khaki shorts and a golf shirt emerged from behind a table set up right off the path.

"Good afternoon, friends!" he greeted them with a friendly smile.

Austin stepped forward. "Good afternoon."

"Are you travelers passing through or are you folks looking for a place to call home?" he asked.

Austin looked at the others. "We're passing through."

The man nodded. "I see. What is it I can do for you?"

Austin cleared his throat, hating to ask for handouts. "Think we could do some trading?"

"For?" the man asked.

"We have a few things that we'd like to trade for some food if you can spare it," he said.

The man smiled. "Let me get the boss. She handles all the trade deals."

The man disappeared inside a large tent set up about twenty feet away. It was twice as big as the others and set apart from the other, smaller tents that sat clustered together. Clearly, the boss didn't want to mix with the little people, Austin mused.

A woman who reminded him a lot of a young Whoopi Goldberg emerged from the tent. She had a megawatt smile that would have disarmed anyone. Her long black hair was in braids pulled up into a high ponytail, and she strolled towards them with confidence to spare, extending her hand to shake Austin's first, and then each of the others'.

"I'm Lilly Gamblin and I guess you could call me the mayor of this fine city," she said proudly.

"I'm Austin; that's Wendell, Harlen, Ennis, and Sarah," Austin said.

"You want to trade?" she asked, not wasting any time.

Austin nodded. "We don't have a lot, but we'd love to get a cooking vessel or some food. We were robbed of all our supplies yesterday, and we have a long journey ahead of us."

She smiled. "Of course, we can trade!"

"Thank you," Ennis said, stepping forward. "That sure would be helpful."

"Why don't you come this way and we can talk over a glass of water," she suggested, strolling towards another tent that looked much smaller than her own.

A man walked by then, and something about him was awful familiar to Austin. He stopped, staring at the man's back, and waited for him to turn around. He disappeared inside a tent before Austin could figure out why he'd looked familiar.

An older woman ducked out of the tent they were headed towards. She looked worn and tired. Austin glanced at what she was carrying clutched in her hands and saw several MREs that looked exactly like the ones they'd been robbed of the day before.

"Ennis," he hissed, grabbing his brother's arm.

"What is it?" Ennis asked.

Austin pointed to the woman who was scurrying away, her back to them. "She had the same MREs we had yesterday."

Ennis shrugged. "They're pretty common. I had a couple cases at the house, as well."

Lilly disappeared inside the tent, telling them to wait outside for her. Austin could hear low voices coming from inside. Clearly, the trade tent was a busy one. When a man in his mid-forties emerged from the tent, his eyes met Austin's only briefly before quickly looking away. He had something tucked under his arm and two cans in his hand.

Austin's eyes dropped to the MREs and then went back to the man who'd turned his body, as if to shield the food from him. Austin shoved his brother hard. "Another one."

"What?" Ennis growled, spinning around to glare at him.

"That man just walked out with more MREs and two cans of water—the exact kind we had yesterday," he hissed.

"Come in, come in," Lilly said, holding the tent flap open and gesturing for them to go inside.

Austin was the last one in, and that's when he knew his suspicions were correct. The supplies, even the pack with the internal frame, were all laid out on display against one side of the tent wall.

Lilly was trading away the goods that had been stolen from them the day before.

22

Amanda trudged along the highway paying attention to every sound. After the incident with the NWO soldier, she remained on high alert. That Humvee had been headed in the same direction they were going, which made her even more convinced they were on the right track. That was good and bad, of course. Great, because she was determined to get to the missiles and knock the NWO on their butts. It also meant she was going to have to fight to make it happen. The NWO wasn't going to go down easy.

"Think we'll find anything?" Mike asked, nodding at a sign that indicated they were two miles from the next town.

Amanda surveyed the area, seeing nothing that suggested they were approaching a metropolis. Maybe a roofline here and there, but nothing exciting. Nothing that held any promise of food. Their rations would only last them another day or two, though, so they had to find more food. She'd been debating whether to save the rations for the end of their journey, but knew the others would never go along with it. She wasn't sure that even she had the kind of willpower it would take not to eat the little food they had when they were absolutely starving. And what was the point of storing up energy for the end-fight if they'd have so little energy that they couldn't reach the fight to begin with?

"I don't know. We should probably get off the main road. We'll try and find a way around without attracting a lot of attention. I don't want to fight. We have to save our strength," she muttered.

"I agree," Mike said.

"We need to refill our water bottles," Gretchen said from behind her and Mike.

"Okay, we'll do that. We'll need to start a fire to purify the water," Amanda said, more to herself than anyone else as she made a mental list of what needed to happen. "We'll have two people on water duty and the rest of us will divide into two groups and check for any useful supplies."

There was a quiet murmur as the others all agreed. It was a hot day, and they'd been walking most of it. Amanda knew they were all exhausted. She guessed they were close to the halfway point of their journey, which wasn't all that encouraging. She'd known the journey was going to be long and hard, but knowing it and getting through it were two very different things.

"There's a couple houses over there," Ezra said, pointing to the east.

Amanda's eyes scanned the area, looking for signs that the homes were being guarded. They'd learned the hard way more than once that, just because a house looked empty, that didn't mean it *was* empty. The occupants were too often lying in wait, ready to defend their little corner of the world.

"I think we keep going into town. I don't want to waste time searching houses that are too far off the road," she replied.

They kept moving down the two-lane highway, seeing a gas station on the right and a propane store on the left. An old restaurant with windows that had been boarded up was the only other business on the main drag through the small town.

"I think this was a ghost town even before the fall," Gretchen said as they slowed their pace.

A gurgling stream ran parallel with the highway starting about twenty feet away. Amanda made note of it, thinking they should make camp while it was still in sight for the night as an easy source of water. They'd be able to purify as much as they need and re-stock without issue.

They came to an intersection and peered in each direction. Left and right looked to lead into small housing areas, and straight ahead was the highway that would continue on in the direction of Cheyenne. The place felt deserted.

"Let's do some brief scouting. Everyone, be careful. It looks empty, but they could be hiding," Amanda warned. "We'll meet back here."

"Do we split into two groups?" Jordan asked.

"Yes. Jordan, you take Gretchen, Ezra, and Drew. Tonya and Mike, you're with me," Amanda said.

Everyone moved into their respective groups, Amanda leading her team to the left while the others went to the right. A breeze swept through the area, blowing scraps of trash across the highway. The whole scene had the feel of a very old Western. They'd seen a few places like this on their way east. Towns abandoned altogether, or spots where people had mostly been killed or chased off, with only a few lonely survivors trying to make it.

It was all part of the NWO's plan. They were killing off small-town America. The people were being driven into the cities to strengthen the NWO or else forced to band together to fight back. She remembered her journey west with Austin. There'd been a lot more people and a lot more fighting. Things had changed even in the short time since. It didn't take long before starvation, sickness, and death brought people to their knees and right to the doors of the NWO. It was a sad situation. If the darkness persisted much longer, there'd be even fewer groups of survivors. Soon enough, small towns would be completely empty as the remaining holdouts looked for shelter out of the NWO's reach—if there was such a place.

"I don't think anyone is here," Tonya whispered as they walked inside a modest, older home with its front door left wide open.

"I agree," Amanda said, checking the kitchen cupboards for food and supplies. She could hear Mike in the living room, overturning furniture. People got very creative with their hiding places, they had learned.

The trio searched several more homes, finding nothing of value that could be useful to them on their journey. Back outside, Amanda looked down the road, noticing several tall, fluffy trees in the front yard of a two-story house at the end. It was clearly the nicest house in town.

"Looks promising," Mike said from beside her.

"It does. Let's go," she said.

They approached slowly, experience telling them that a house like this one would be where the remaining townspeople would choose to live. Why wouldn't they, after all? Why live in a shack when there was a beautiful home sitting empty and up for the taking?

Amanda took the first step that led onto the covered porch of the house, which looked to have been built sometime in the early 1900s. It was the kind of house she loved—with that old, southern charm in every detail, right down to the pillars on either side of the front door that was about halfway open.

"Hello?" she called out, not wanting to startle anyone into shooting her.

"Be right there!" a male voice replied immediately.

Amanda froze, her foot resting on the second step. She looked behind her, staring at Mike's shocked expression. She hadn't expected anyone to actually answer her, let alone with a casual tone. Tonya stood at the bottom of the stairs, her eyes wide enough to make the fear she felt more than clear.

"Shh," Amanda whispered, using her head to gesture both Mike and Tonya to the side of the porch where there were green shrubs to use as cover.

A man appeared in the open doorway then. He was wiping his hands on a dish towel, his eyes weary and pronounced with heavy, dark circles under them. He wasn't a large man— maybe five-eight, thin, and not at all threatening. He wore a red-checkered apron that one might have expected to see on a woman baking pies in a country kitchen.

"Hello," he said, his voice matching the exhausted look on his face. "Are you sick?"

Amanda slowly shook her head, her hand resting on the butt of the gun tucked into her waistband. "No. Are you sick?"

He smirked, putting a hand on his hip. "Do I look sick? Never mind, don't answer that. What can I do for you? I need to get back to my patients."

"Your patients?" Amanda echoed, taking a step up the stairs.

"Yes, my patients. My name is Dr. Robin Ashworth. I'm treating a group of people who've been sickened with what I suspect is typhoid."

Amanda involuntarily flinched, leaning back and away from the doctor as if that would keep her from catching a disease that wasn't spread through the air. "Typhoid?" she echoed, her voice shrill as her mind conjured up images of African villages with dying children.

"Yes. I need to get back. I don't have anything to offer. The few supplies I have must go to the sickest," he said, turning and disappearing inside the door.

Amanda turned back, looking down the steps. "I think it's clear. I'm going inside," she said to the unseen Mike and Tonya.

Mike emerged from the bushes surrounding the front of the porch. "We'll come with you. You never know what you're walking into."

She gave a quick nod before pushing open the front door a little wider. The smell of sickness washed over her, rife with the familiar smell of vomit and human feces. She covered her face with her bent arm, following the light at the end of the dark hall. She gasped when they walked into the bright living room, all of its windows opened to let in sun and fresh air. The smell of sickness overpowered even the air coming in through the windows.

There were at least twenty people of various ages lying on makeshift beds on the floor, plus one on the couch and several on folding cots that had been set up near the windows. There were garbage cans all around the room, flies buzzing over them. It was a horrific sight that belonged somewhere in the medieval ages, not in a world with modern medicine and sterile hospitals.

The doctor turned when he saw her. "You shouldn't be in here. It isn't safe."

"I won't touch anything," she assured him.

"What do you need?" he asked with exasperation.

"You're sure it's typhoid?" she asked.

"The rash on the chest tells me it is, combined with their other symptoms," he said, pulling on a pair of exam gloves and touching the forehead of a young woman who looked ghastly pale lying on a narrow cot.

"How many?" she asked.

He let out a long sigh. "Since it started, I've lost eight children, four elderly, and one middle-aged man. Before the day is over, I expect to lose another two. I've gone through all the antibiotics I had. I don't have any more IVs and I'm at a loss for what to do next. I can't help them."

"I'm so sorry. Do you know the source?" she asked.

He shook his head. "It could be the water. Most of the people living here have been using the stream to get their water because it's close and easy; I doubt many were even bothering to boil it, to tell you the truth. It could have been one of the dishes that was served at a community meal a few weeks ago after a particularly successful hunt, too. I have no idea."

"The stream?" Tonya gasped from behind Amanda.

Amanda spun around. "You guys should go. We can't risk getting infected."

"We have to warn Gretchen and the others," Tonya said, panic in her voice.

Amanda nodded. "Tell her not to touch anything. Anything here could be contaminated."

"There are more of you?" the doctor asked.

"Yes, we're traveling through and stopped to look for supplies," Amanda explained.

"You don't want to stay here and you certainly don't want to eat or drink anything from here. These people were sick for days. They could have spread it around. I don't know how many are out there. The population was small to begin with, but this isn't all of them."

"Are you from here?" Amanda asked.

He offered a small smile. "Yes and no. I moved here two years ago. I had a small practice. It was a nice, quiet town. When the darkness hit, a lot of people packed up and moved, hoping to find success closer to one of the cities. There were probably only about fifty of us left when this happened, and I fear that, by the time this typhoid has run its course, there will be very few survivors."

Amanda shook her head at the horror of it, looking at the ailing victims of a bacterial infection that could have been prevented with proper sanitation. All it took was one infected person to touch another person's food, eating utensils, or use the bathroom too close to a water source, and something like this would spread like wildfire without good handwashing and sanitation… things that were extremely difficult without running water.

"I'm so sorry. Are you taking care of all of these people on your own?" she asked gently.

The doctor shrugged a shoulder. "I'm it. I'm all they have."

"You're exhausted. You're going to get sick if you don't get some rest," she said.

"I don't have a choice, do I? If I stop moving, they all die. They'll lie in their own vomit and feces and the situation will only be that much worse," he reasoned.

"I'll help. I'll stay for a while. Go take a nap, eat, rest," she insisted.

She thought he was going to reject her offer, but he suddenly nodded, suggesting that his personal exhaustion might have been even worse than she'd guessed. "Okay. Thank you. This is Sienna," he said, moving to a young woman who couldn't have been more than twenty. "She can tell you names. I have gloves here, but I'm out of clean trash bags."

"Hi," the girl said, her voice weak as she lifted her head from her pillow.

"Hi, Sienna. How are you feeling?" Amanda asked.

Sienna giggled softly. "Like I've been hit by a truck."

"Sienna and her family were some of the first to show symptoms. They were given antibiotics," the doctor said.

Sienna looked away, tears in her eyes. "I'm the only one that made it," she said in a raspy voice.

Amanda's eyes went to Robin's as he continued, "Her twin brothers were only four, and her little sister was six. Their little bodies weren't strong enough," he explained, his voice flat.

"My grandma died yesterday," Sienna said. "She was all I had left."

"I'm so sorry," Amanda said, longing to reach out and comfort the girl but afraid to risk it.

"I expect Sienna to make a full recovery. She's through the worst of it, but still very weak. She needs to stay in bed," Robin added, his eyes on the girl to emphasize how serious he was.

Amanda could see from the exchange that the young woman was struggling to follow the doctor's orders. "I'll make sure she does," Amanda promised. "Now, go get some rest."

"How many of you are there?" Robin asked first.

"Seven."

"Our resources are limited out here," he said with a grimace.

"We won't take anything. I'll stay long enough to give you a reprieve and then we'll be on our way," she said.

"Thank you. I'll just be upstairs in the master bedroom," he said, walking away with his shoulders slumped forward.

Amanda turned back to Sienna, who was watching her wearily. "Why are you helping us? You know you could get sick."

Amanda forced a smile, knowing the girl was right. This was a risk, but she felt she had no choice. "Because I see a man fighting hard to keep people alive and I can't let him do it alone. Besides, I could use a break from walking and the heat. My whole group can. We'll stay for a while and then we'll be on our way," she told the girl, who had laid her head back against the pillows.

"Where are you going?" Sienna asked, her voice growing weaker.

"We're headed east," Amanda said.

Sienna turned her head to look at her. "That's vague."

Amanda smiled. "We don't really know."

Sienna studied her a bit longer before closing her eyes. With that, Amanda got up and let the girl rest. She put on a pair of gloves and slowly moved around the room, checking on one victim and then another. An older man, probably in his late sixties, was hovering on death's door. His breathing was shallow, his lips a faint blue and his skin ashen. She knew the complications from the bacterial infection were vast.

She continued to make rounds around the room, doing her best to avoid contact with any bodily fluids. One middle-aged man had an intensely high fever. He was violently shaking and appeared to be hallucinating. There was nothing she could do for him, either—except get him clean water. She stood, removed her gloves, and deposited them in a trash bin before walking outside to find the rest of the group gathered in the yard.

"Are we leaving? I don't like this place," Drew said.

"I want you to go to every house, to find pots and pans and build a fire. We've got to get these people some clean water. The doctor can't do it all. Grab every piece of clean linen you can find. I need to clean these people up or it's only going to keep spreading," she ordered, going into Airman mode.

"Is that safe?" Gretchen asked. "Shouldn't we just keep going?"

"As long as we practice good sanitation, we'll be okay, and we have some time to spare. These people need us desperately. Gretchen, do you have any magical remedies that can help with this situation? The doctor has gone through all of his antibiotics. Some of these people are in bad shape and won't make it if they don't get medicine."

Gretchen appeared thoughtful. "The only thing that comes to mind is garlic, possibly raw honey, but I wouldn't know where to look for either."

Amanda sighed with disappointment. "Then water it is. Use pots with handles. Don't put your hands in the water in case it is contaminated."

Gretchen grimaced. "We'll have to be careful. From this point on, don't eat anything without washing your hands thoroughly first. We have that soap that we took. Everyone make sure to use it. Boil everything."

"What about the people around here? Are they going to shoot us?" Jordan asked.

Amanda chewed her lower lip. "I don't think so. There aren't many left alive. The ones who are alive seem to be right here with the doctor. So, just be smart, be careful, and hurry, please."

Everyone nodded and scattered to do her bidding. She knew it was risky to expose herself to the bacteria being harbored inside the house, but the need to help was strong. They could boil enough water for the doctor to use for his own personal hygiene and to try and get fluids into those stricken down. It was all they could do. The rest was out of her hands, but they could spare the time, and there was no way she could just leave these people to die when a few hours of time might make a real difference for them.

23

Austin looked at the other members of his group, watching their faces as they realized it was their own stuff being hawked back to them. Ennis shook his head in what looked to be a mix of disgust and embarrassment, and then Austin's gaze went back to the woman standing over the goods and waiting for them to tell her what they wanted.

"Do you see something you like?" she asked with a wide smile.

Austin looked her in the eyes, nodding at her with a tight smile. "I sure do. I see quite a few things I like. In fact—"

"In fact, we're going to need a few minutes to discuss what we need the most," Ennis said, cutting him off.

Austin glared at him. "Yeah. Right," he grumbled, getting his brother's subtle message not to reveal they'd recognized the goods.

"Don't take too long, boys; these things are going fast," she warned.

Austin opened his mouth to say something in return, but Ennis stopped him again by shoving him hard in the shoulder. Then his brother led the way out of the tent, bypassing the line of customers ready to trade for the things that had been stolen from them. It was hard to be mad at the refugees, of course. They were hungry and doing what they had to for their families. He understood that, but couldn't accept the big picture of what he saw happening.

Ennis walked about thirty feet away, moving behind a row of small tents. The others joined him. Austin had his back to the large tent that was being used as a trading post. "What? What's your plan?" Austin asked his brother.

Ennis used his chin to gesture towards a woman and two kids walking between the rows of tents. They were dirty and looked like they hadn't eaten in days. "What kind of refugee camp demands the refugees give up the little they have to get basic needs met?" Ennis asked.

The others looked around, watching the people mill about, none of them looking all that healthy.

"A for-profit camp," Sarah said.

"Their fearless leader looks well-fed and has clean clothes. Her huge tent could house several families," Harlen growled.

"She's taking advantage of their desperation. They're being forced to give up things they probably fought hard to gain. I wouldn't be surprised if she or some of the men who robbed us robbed each and every one of these people, forcing them to come into her safe haven," Austin said.

"There are some bad people in this world, but anyone who would take food out of the mouths of little kids is a special kind of evil," Harlen said.

Wendell shrugged, holding up his hands. "What are we supposed to do? I think we should just go. We'll find more stuff."

"Will we?" Austin snapped.

"We always do," Wendell shot back.

Austin glared at him. "And what about all these people who will die if they don't start getting some real nourishment? Should we leave them?"

Wendell looked undisturbed. "You yourself said we can't save them all. So, what else are we supposed to do?"

"We can save these people," Austin argued.

Ennis looked at their small group, then back at the tent city. "We don't have to save them. They can save themselves. We'll talk to them, tell them what she's doing, and offer to help them rise up. There are more of them."

"That's risky," Austin said with a grimace.

"I don't think it is. Let's split up, talk to as many as we can, and find out what's going on here," Ennis suggested.

Austin thought for a moment, and then relented. "Okay. We don't have long, though. I don't want to sit around here biding our time. I don't trust that woman."

"I agree," Harlen chimed in.

"Everyone's been friendly—maybe a little reserved, but I think we can talk to them," Ennis said.

"Fine, let's do this," Austin said, turning to move back towards the main roadway dividing the two rows of tents on either side of it.

They spread out, knocking on tent flaps and talking with people. Austin walked down the road, farther away from the trading tent. He got the idea there was a class difference here, the farther he walked. The tents were in disrepair, with some of the inhabitants using duct tape to hold the doors closed. Others had tarps taped over obvious holes. Almost as soon as he began knocking at tent flaps, speaking to the residents, he saw that many people there had been waiting for someone to speak up and say how unfair things were—nobody had wanted to get the ball rolling, it was true, but all of them knew this wasn't right on some level. As he went tent by tent, he saw more and more people coming out into the lane after speaking to him and the others in his group. And they were speaking to each other, too.

Moving on, Austin got to some of the more run-down tents, where he doubted they did a great deal to keep the heat and the elements out. A dirty little boy, maybe three, was sitting in front of one of them, staring into the distance with sunken eyes.

Austin dropped to a squat in front of him. "Hey buddy," he greeted him gently.

The boy looked at him with a blank stare.

"I bet you're hungry," he said, reaching into his pocket and pulling out one of the remaining protein bars he had.

The boy looked at the offered bar for only a moment before snatching it from Austin's hands. He took a big bite, his little teeth tearing off a big chunk.

"Slow down," Austin said with a laugh.

"What are you doing?" A young, thin woman with brown, stringy hair had emerged from the tent.

"I gave him a protein bar," Austin said easily.

Her eyes dropped to the bar her son was greedily chomping on. Austin could see her own hunger and how hard it was to watch her child eat while she starved.

"Thank you," she whispered.

"How long have you been here?" he asked.

She shrugged. "A few weeks, maybe longer. We saw the signs and hoped to find food and shelter. I guess I'm glad we got a tent."

"Can you tell me how it works here?"

"What do you mean?" she asked.

"I mean, is there no food?"

"There's food, but I don't have anything to trade. I don't have any skills, nothing. I'm going to have to move soon. Lilly has been kind and let me stay longer than she normally allows, but I have to go," she said, her voice trembling with what Austin guessed to be fear.

"I thought this was a refugee camp," he said.

"It is, but we all have to pay our own way," she said matter-of-factly. "Lilly is a fair but firm leader."

He nodded in understanding. "You pay through work or other goods?"

"Yes. Some of the other people go out on scavenging trips to get things to use for trade, but I don't have anyone to watch Henry. I don't trust the people here—not enough to watch my baby, anyway. Besides, the scavenging is dangerous. Sometimes they don't come back at all, and other times they get robbed and go through all that work for nothing," she explained. "I guess it didn't used to be this way, but Lilly realized there were too many people coming into the city. She took over to create a better way of doing things. No freeloaders," she murmured.

Austin had to clench his teeth to keep from cursing. He knew Lilly and her goons were behind the robberies and probably killed anyone who fought back. He couldn't sit back and let the young woman and her baby get kicked out; this was clearly all they had.

"What's your name?" he asked.

"Cara."

"Cara, my name is Austin. My friends and I are talking with some of the other residents. We want to help you take this tent city back, along with all the supplies that are being hoarded. Lilly is stealing from people and selling it back. She's not kind or generous. There are enough of you here that you can fight back," he said. "Take back the city. You're stronger together."

She shook her head, her eyes wide. "I don't know how to fight. I came here to get away from the fighting. I just want to live in peace," she whispered.

"I understand that, but sometimes you have to make a stand. If you don't stand up for yourself now, it's only going to get worse. Think of your son. He needs you to be strong for him. He needs to have a safe place to sleep and food to eat. You're his mama. That's up to you. If there is anything you have to do, this is it. You have safety here, I get it, and that means you can't leave. You can't allow her to make you leave if you have nowhere to go. Does she own this tent?" he asked.

Cara shrugged a shoulder. "I don't think so."

"Does she own the land?"

"No."

"Then she has no control over who stays and who goes. Don't give her that control. Rise up. Join the others and fight back. There's food in that tent. I bet there's food and blankets and lots of other things you need in Lilly's tent and the tents of her men," he said, trying to make the woman understand there were options.

He looked down the road towards the main tents and saw others standing in the road. He smiled as he watched Ennis clap a hand on a man's shoulder. It was working. Ennis had been right. They were pulling together a small army. Even if Austin and his group couldn't change the world, he could at least take satisfaction in knowing they had made one small, positive change in the lives of others.

"I don't know how to fight," Cara whispered.

"You don't have to fight," he said, turning back to her. "You have to stand with the rest of the people. Look, they're coming together. Are you going to stand with them or are you going to keep letting this woman use you and take food out of the mouth of your son?"

And, with that last comment, he saw determination coming into Cara's eyes. She watched her son licking at the wrapper of the protein bar, and then reached down and grabbed her little boy's hand. With nothing more spoken, they began the march down the lane, joining in with the others coming out of their tents as they marched together.

"Good job," Austin said to Ennis.

"They're rising up. This is going to be good, and I don't think we're going to have to do much of anything," Ennis said with a proud grin.

"Lilly Gamblin!" a tall man in the front of the group shouted.

Austin moved to the edge of the group, ready to witness the revolt and provide additional muscle if needed. He hadn't just convinced Cara to rise up only to have her get kicked down again.

Lilly emerged from her big tent, her mouth working at something. She scanned the crowd, putting both hands on her hips and calling out for her goons. "What's going on, Gabriel?" she asked with a forced smile.

"We want you to leave. You came in here and took over, and we're tired of it. You didn't start this place and we don't need you trying to run it. Go. Take your buddies and get out of here!" Gabriel shouted.

Lilly grinned, her gleaming white smile appearing venomous. "I'm the mayor of this little city, Gabriel, and I'm not going anywhere."

"You are not the mayor. You're officially ousted. Leave now!" his voice boomed.

There was a rumble through the crowd, and without anyone giving an order, they began to move forward as a unit. Austin walked with them. He had his eyes on the man who'd been the one to rob them. He was looking forward to a little revenge.

There were at least sixty people marching on Lilly and her five men now. Even if they made it to their guns, they wouldn't be able to shoot them all. He loved the look of fear he was witnessing in Lilly's eyes. She had sucked off this group long enough.

The first rock was hurled through the air, narrowly missing Lilly's head.

Soon, there were more rocks being lobbed at the tyrants that had kept these people down. The angry shouts and accusations were being flung just as violently as the rocks and anything else the group could find.

Austin stepped forward. "I'd suggest you all leave," he called, standing less than ten feet from Lilly.

"You did this!" she snarled, putting her hand up to ward off an empty box being thrown at her.

He shrugged. "I can't take all the credit. Leave now or these people will kill you, all of you," he said, looking at the others.

"What's to say we won't come back here and kill them all?" Lilly spat.

"Nothing, except I think it might be a little harder than that. You've angered a lot of people. They don't like you. You've left them to starve. You've robbed from them and then turned around and sold it back to them. I think that, if you're smart, you'll get as far from here as you can!" he shouted out, working to be heard over the advancing crowd.

Lilly glared back at him before turning to one of the men. "Grab all you can and we'll come back for the rest."

Gabriel pushed forward, standing directly in front of Lilly. "No. Everything is ours. You leave with the clothes on your back and nothing more."

The look of shock on her face made Austin smile. She must have realized her tenuous position, though, because a moment later she turned to walk away, her men crowding around her as they followed. Gabriel and about ten other men pressed in behind them, pushing them to the outer edge of the camp and then forming a human fence across the road.

Ennis walked over to Austin, grinning from ear to ear. "I think we can grab our stuff and get out of here. We've done our good deed for the day."

"You did do good, really good," Austin said with a laugh.

"See, you should listen to me now and again. I do have some good ideas."

"You have a lot of good ideas," Wendell said, coming to stand beside them both.

"This is all sweet and cozy, but we have a mission. We're not here to save the world," Sarah said in her usual all-business voice.

Austin looked around at the people congratulating each other and nodding their way in thanks. They'd done all they could for these folks, and more than most would have done. "She's right," Austin agreed. "We need to get our supplies and go."

24

Wendell was so tired of being tired. His feet hurt, and he could feel a blister on his pinky-toe. He'd told the others about it that morning, but they didn't care. None of them cared. They were so dead-set on the idea that they were going to save the world, it made him sick. They were fools. All of them were fools. He was the only one who had the good sense to know when to quit. He wasn't quitting on life, either —he was just quitting their game. They were playing for the losing team, and he was sick of being on the losing team.

He rolled to his side. Even the darkness barely gave them any privacy. That was something else he was sick of. He was sick of seeing them all night and all day. Sick of listening to Harlen snore every night. Wendell wasn't meant for this kind of life. He was meant to sleep in a comfortable bed, in a house or a luxury apartment where he'd have his own space.

Things had to change. He'd been in this weird state of limbo for too long. Sometimes, drastic measures were needed, and that's what he was about to do; he was taking drastic measures. He waited a little longer, knowing Ennis was on watch. Wendell planned on getting up and taking over for him soon. He'd already planned what he would say. He was going to tell him he couldn't sleep and would take over watch early. That should earn him some brownie points, too.

He rubbed his eyes, then mussed his hair before getting up and walking through the dark towards the tree where Ennis was keeping watch.

"Hey," he whispered.

"Oh crap! You scared me!" Ennis muttered.

"Sorry. I couldn't sleep. I'll take over watch," he said, trying to sound generous.

"Are you sure? I still have another hour or so; plus, Austin has next watch," Ennis said.

"I know, but I'm up and we might as well let him sleep while he can. I'll wake him in a couple hours," Wendell offered.

"Fine. I'm not going to argue. I'm beat. We kicked butt this time. We made it a whole day early. That's impressive. Way to hang in there, Wendy," Ennis said, slapping a hand against Wendell's arm.

"Yeah, thanks," he grumbled.

Wendell settled in against the tree, his eyes scanning the darkness. He hadn't been lying—he was wired and couldn't sleep.

Nerves were making his belly feel funny, so that he had to consciously breathe deep and force himself to calm down. He couldn't look like a wimp. He had to appear strong and like a man who was to be feared.

He waited a little longer before he made his move, taking a few tentative steps away from the others. If anyone noticed him walking away, he'd say he was going to the bathroom. When no one said anything or attempted to stop him, he kept going. When he put some distance between him and the others, he picked up the pace, heading towards the meeting place. He emerged onto the roadway glancing left and right before stepping into the open.

"Don't move!" he heard a man shout.

Wendell froze, automatically putting his hands into the air. "I'm not armed."

"Don't move."

Wendell stayed where he was. A man wearing a black jump-suit emerged from the shadows, approaching him slowly before patting him down. Wendell knew there was at least one other person waiting in the shadows with a gun on him, and more likely several others.

"Clear!" the man shouted.

Zander emerged from the shadows, stepping into the roadway and strolling towards Wendell. Wendell gulped down the lump of fear in his throat. Zander was a scary dude. He knew he was walking a dangerous line, but this felt like his only chance.

"Zander," he greeted him, trying to sound cool and unbothered.

Zander looked him up and down. "You? You're the one leaving me notes?"

Wendell cleared his throat. "Yes, I am. I think we can help each other."

"How could you possibly help me?" Zander sneered.

"I've told you where to find Austin. I think that's a huge help," he stated, finding his voice. "I can take you back to him right now."

Zander made a big show of looking around. "Did you bring the USB?"

Wendell had been afraid that's what Zander would want. He hadn't been able to get his hands on it. Austin had the thing locked down tight when Sarah wasn't using it. They guarded it with their lives.

"I didn't, but I think we can work out an agreeable deal," Wendell offered.

"Why would I need to work out anything with you? I could kill you right here and be done with it," Zander said with an evil smile.

Wendell wouldn't let him see how afraid he was. "Because I'm the man on the inside. I know the plan."

"I don't need a man on the inside. I need Austin dead and the USB back in my hands," Zander retorted.

Wendell shook his head. "I can help you by telling you what they're doing."

"Why would I care? I kill Austin Merryman, and what they're doing doesn't matter."

Wendell gulped down the lump of fear in his throat. "You can kill Austin, but that won't stop them. They've split up," he said, feeling like he was onto something. "If this group doesn't succeed, there's another out there working on the plan. You need me to know how to take all of them down."

Zander examined him, his eyes narrowed, and then he leaned into his face, glaring at him before he spoke. "What are they doing?"

Wendell knew he was taking a risk, but he had to try. He was putting his life on the line and wanted to be compensated. "We'll need to work out a deal first."

Zander stared at him, his dead eyes creeping Wendell out a little. He might have overplayed his hand, he realized a moment too late.

"What kind of a deal?" Zander finally asked.

Wendell breathed a sigh of relief. "I want a job in the NWO. I want the perks. I want an apartment and food to eat," he said, rattling off his list of demands.

Zander smirked. "Is that it?"

"No. I want a guarantee that my friend Ennis won't be hurt. He'll be left alone to do what he wants."

Zander still observed him, a grin on his face flickering for only an instant before he turned to one soldier and then another as if to gauge their reactions. Then he looked back to Wendell, raising one eyebrow. "And is there anything *else* you want?"

"No, that's it. Food and shelter."

"We could probably arrange that. Now, tell me what they're doing with that USB."

That was it, then. He had to trust him and run with it. Wendell had long realized he wasn't going to get a written contract; he just had to hope Zander was a man of his word and wouldn't go back on what he'd agreed to. "They're going to launch missiles at the satellites that are holding nuclear warheads."

He couldn't read the expression on Zander's face, and didn't know if it was excitement or incredulity he saw there. Either way, it wasn't a look that made him comfortable. Zander was a bad, bad man.

Zander burst into laughter. "Shoot down satellites holding nuclear warheads? Wow. Ambitious. Is that really the information you're trying to use for trade?"

"Yes. I'm serious. We've walked for days, weeks, trying to get to the computers that are controlling the satellites," Wendell squealed.

That seemed to give Zander pause. "What's on that USB?"

Wendell finally had his attention. "Lots of stuff. Including codes. Launch codes. They're going to launch missiles at those satellites."

"When?"

"Soon. We're checking the computer center tomorrow morning. If it has what we need, we move forward with our mission. If the computers aren't there or functioning, we're going on to Boise, where Sarah, I mean Dr. Bastani, thinks there has to be a functioning computer center being used by the NWO."

Zander looked at him as if he was trying to gauge whether he was telling the truth or not. Wendell stared back, not backing down. Something about the look on his face told Wendell that Austin and Sarah were onto something. For a very brief moment, he wondered if he'd screwed up. What if their plan could work? What if they could have managed to defeat the NWO and return the country to its former glory? Wendell felt sick, but quickly pushed it aside. If Austin was right, Wendell would win. And if Zander defeated Austin, Wendell would still come out on top.

"I have a better idea," Zander said with a smile.

Wendell felt a shiver of cold dread run down his spine. Zander was an evil human being. Wendell knew for certain he was making the right choice by getting on the winning side now before everything blew up—literally—but that didn't make dealing with the devil any less heart-stopping.

"I'm game," Wendell said, hoping it wouldn't involve him getting killed.

"You and your buddies go ahead and check out the next computer center, which won't do you any good, and then, when you get to Boise, I'll have a little surprise there waiting for them."

"Oh?" Wendell replied, his voice much higher than usual.

Zander grinned. "Yes, I'll see you there, and you'll get what you want if you get your group there and keep your friend alive. I want to be the one to kill him, and I want him to see my face when I do it."

"But not me, right? You won't kill me?" Wendell confirmed.

Zander shrugged. "Do as I ask and, of course, I won't kill you. I don't kill those who do me good service, and it seems like you're falling into that category."

Wendell nodded, reassured. "Okay. I'll see you then," he said, anxious to get away from the man.

The guy had evil energy. It practically oozed from his pores. Wendell turned and started to walk back in the direction he'd come from, hoping they didn't decide to put a bullet in his back and just kill Austin and the group now. He'd thought that would be the plan, or that they'd at least take them into custody now, so he no longer felt like he was walking on firm ground. Nevertheless, he'd played his hand, and he certainly had Zander's attention.

Just as he thought he was in the clear, a soldier caught up to him and grabbed hold of his arm as if he were a prisoner instead of a conspirator.

"What?" Wendell demanded.

"Hold on. Zander wants to make sure you know what to do when you get your friends to Boise," the soldier said flatly.

It took a moment, and then Wendell grinned. He was in.

25

Amanda looked at Robin, happy to see he looked better than he had yesterday when they'd first met. She knew she was pushing it by sticking around another day, but she couldn't bring herself to abandon him and his many patients. He was in need, and they were in a position to help.

"It certainly smells better in here," Robin said with a faint smile, looking around his makeshift hospital space.

Amanda chuckled. "Barely, but that's better than nothing."

"Thank you for all you've done here. It is a tremendous help," he said.

"You mentioned there were antibiotics in the next town?" she asked.

He examined her expression, apparently surprised she'd bring it up, and then nodded. "Yes. At least, there were. There's a large hospital there, and up until a month ago, the supplies were being fairly managed by a group of individuals who'd taken charge of the building. They were rationing out supplies and medicine, but I haven't been able to send anyone to try and get some for us. I've barely been able to keep it together here."

"We'll go," Amanda told him, having been thinking about doing so ever since he'd mentioned it. How could they not?

"You will?" Robin asked excitedly.

"Yes. I need to talk to the others, but I think they'll agree. We are on a deadline and really don't have a lot of time, but we can hurry, and we have the time to spare. We'll get there and get back, and then we'll be on our way."

Robin gently grabbed her upper arm and pulled her out of the living room and into the hall. "Amanda, you should take some of the antibiotics, as well, you and the others. Your exposure risk is high."

"What about you?" she asked.

"I took some in the beginning. We'll see how much is available. If there's enough, I'll take another round just to be safe," he said. "But with all your group is doing, you should make sure you and your people get the first doses."

She smiled, appreciating how good and fair this doctor was, and feeling all the more glad they could help. "Good. How far is the hospital exactly?" she asked.

"About five miles."

She grimaced, calculating the time it would take to get there and adding it to the time they had spent already; she hadn't expected it to be quite so far, and realized she was really cutting it close. They had something like a three-day cushion, but they were eating that up quickly. "We've got to go today, then."

"Be careful," he warned her.

"We will," she replied, already walking down the hall.

The others were outside sitting on the lawn, all of them exhausted after having worked through much of the night, boiling water and doing what they could to sterilize the house along with a few of the other houses where the recovered would be returning to live once they could leave the hospital.

"What's going on?" Gretchen asked.

"We've got a new mission," she said, her tone grim.

"What is it?" Jordan asked.

"We've got to get him those antibiotics. These people won't make it without it," she said. "And, honestly, it will be good for us to. We'll get a round of antibiotics just in case we were exposed while searching this area or traveling, and hopefully have some medical supplies to carry us on our way."

They all looked at each other before looking back at her. "Where?"

"It's about five miles north," she said, grimacing as she saw the looks of dread on their faces.

"Amanda," Jordan protested.

"I know, I know, but we've invested this much time into helping them out. We can do this. Plus, remember we might need those antibiotics, as well," she pointed out more quietly.

Jordan got to his feet and patted Amanda's shoulder as if to reassure her that he was on board. "Then we should go now. In our current condition, it'll take us most of the day to get there and back. Do we know if they're friendly? Is this going to be a battle?"

"Robin doesn't think we'll have any problems. We'll evaluate when we get there. He gave me a note with his signature to pass along to the guard at the hospital. It should be enough to get us what we need," she said. "From the sounds of things, the people running the hospital have been pretty fair and rational; it's just a question of whether or not they've still got enough medicine to go around."

"Let's move then. We ain't got all day," Drew said, getting to his feet, as well.

The rest of them followed suit, quietly discussing the town's situation. Smart or not, they all knew they were doing the right thing, and that meant something to them.

But they'd barely gone two miles before they encountered their first hostile. "Get down!" Ezra shouted when the crack of a rifle reverberated through the area.

Amanda was already on the ground, rolling into the wet grass and weeds, still damp from the brief thunderstorm that had rolled through the area overnight. Tonya's feet were in her face as she rolled. She was breathing fast, weeds and tiny bits of grass sticking to her face.

"Where is it coming from?" Amanda hissed.

"Up ahead. I think they're behind that big truck," Ezra whispered from his position about ten feet in front of her.

"I'm coming up there. Can you get a visual?" she asked.

"No," he said.

Amanda used her elbows to drag herself across the bumpy ground, angling her body to get a better view under the truck. She stared at the pavement, waiting to see a shadow. Ezra handed her the rifle. Everyone knew she was the better shot.

She took the weapon and rested the butt against her shoulder as she looked for signs of life behind the truck. None of them moved, all of them waiting.

"There," Ezra hissed from beside her.

She saw it, too. She would have preferred a head shot, but beggars couldn't be choosers. She took the shot, hitting her target just below the knee. At the scream, she winced, knowing it had to be an excruciating injury. The man's rifle hit the pavement a second before he did, writhing and screaming in pain. Amanda took another shot and put the man out of his misery.

"Don't move, not yet," she ordered.

They waited to see if there was another shooter waiting in the wings. Ezra pulled off the hat he'd made from the kids' clothes. He tossed it into the air. When it wasn't shot at, Amanda sighed with relief, giving the rifle back to Ezra to carry. She pulled the handgun from her waistband and got to her feet.

"Can we get up?" Gretchen asked from behind her.

"I think it's safe," Amanda said, though there was some measure of doubt in her voice. She'd thought it had been safe before they'd been fired on.

"I thought this was supposed to be an easy mission," Drew grumbled.

Amanda scoffed. "So did I. We'll just be a little more cautious."

It was only another mile before they ran into more trouble. This time, they were ready, and managed to avoid the confrontation by quietly taking a wide berth around the area where a group of men seemingly guarded the road.

They could hear gunfire in the distance now, and Amanda pulled everyone behind a bus. "This is some rough territory. Before we go any further, are you all on board with this?" she asked.

"Do we have a choice?" Drew mumbled. "We might already be sick. We need those meds as much as those other people do."

"We do have a choice," Amanda said.

"I say we go. We'll avoid that part of the city," Jordan replied.

"Where's the hospital?" Drew asked.

Amanda grimaced. "It's on the north side of town."

He groaned. "Where all the gunfire is coming from."

"Yes," Amanda confirmed.

She waited, giving them a few minutes to come to their own decisions. She was set on going in, and she couldn't do it alone with any hope of success, but she wouldn't pressure them to go with her.

"We go. We aren't giving up that easy," Drew muttered.

"Then let's go," she said, and started moving again. She hated being so exposed, though. There weren't any trees or any cover in general beyond the scattered sagebrush and defunct vehicles. Still, they kept moving, all of them looking left and right, ready to shoot anything that moved.

There seemed to be a lull the closer they got to the town—which had had a population of forty-two thousand, according to the sign they passed on the way in. It would have once been a pretty place to live, Amanda reasoned. There were lots of trees and a large park with a huge playground. And the big blue H alongside the four-lane road through the heart of the city told her they were on the right path.

"Good evening," she said, smiling to a group of adults sitting outside a barber shop.

There were some grunts in response. It felt very normal—something she would have expected to see before the EMP.

"Doesn't seem so bad now that we're here," Drew grumbled.

"Just keep your heads up," Amanda warned.

The hospital came into view. It was four stories tall and covered a large area, but it was nothing like Robin had described. There were no guards that she saw, and in fact it looked like a war zone. If there had been a guard, he was long gone.

"This isn't good," Gretchen said, defeat in her voice.

A group of teens on skateboards came through the open hospital doors, laughing and cursing as one kicked down a trashcan they passed.

Amanda felt like she'd been the one kicked. "We should check and see if there's anything left," she muttered.

"Really? Do we dare waste our time?" Jordan asked.

"We have to check," she replied. "After coming this far, it doesn't make sense not to."

They moved through the doors the teens had just come out of. The state of the waiting room was awful. It had been vandalized with spray paint, disgusting words sprayed on the walls and the floors. Chairs had been sliced open and dumped over.

"Why?" Tonya gasped. "Why would anyone do this?"

Amanda shook her head as they moved through the double doors that led into the exam and trauma rooms. Everything had been cleared out. The cabinet doors were either ripped off and hanging or gone altogether.

"This is unbelievable. We're not going to find anything here," Drew said.

Amanda thought he was right, but they had to look. "There should be a locked medicine cabinet here in the ER."

"Over here!" Jordan called out.

Amanda took a step in his direction, glass crunching underfoot. She looked down and saw that it littered the floor. The glass for the medicine locker had been shattered, and it was completely empty. "Alright then," she whispered.

An elderly dark-skinned man wearing a blue denim shirt tucked into blue jeans ambled down the hall in their direction then, scowling at them. "There's nothing here. Get out of here!" he shouted.

"We're looking for antibiotics," Amanda said.

He laughed. "You ain't going to find anything here. The tweakers took the good stuff and the antibiotics were gone a couple weeks ago."

He walked closer, and Amanda noticed he had on a nametag. "Carl, did you work here?" she asked, not getting the feeling that he offered any threat. She saw no weapon on him, and her group was well-armed enough to stop him from trying anything if he did have some weapon hidden.

He slowly nodded, eyeing their group. "I did. I was helping man this place until a few weeks ago when we got overrun. It's a shame, a real shame. We was trying to help people, but they came in here and shot everyone or chased them off—all but me, anyhow. I'm too stubborn to leave, but they took everything."

Amanda sighed. "I'm sorry."

"Nothing sorry can do to fix it. There's no more medicine," he said with real sadness.

"Now what?" Drew asked.

"I don't know," Amanda mumbled.

"What made you think there'd still be supplies here? I hear lots of other places are helluvalot worse off than this," Carl commented.

"We met a doctor; he's taking care of some really sick people the next town over. He gave us a note outlining what we needed, thinking this place was still in good shape," Amanda explained.

"Dr. Ashworth?" Carl asked.

Amanda smiled. "Yes, Dr. Ashworth. He's treating the entire town for typhoid. A lot have died, and he's afraid they'll lose more if he can't get the medicine they need."

Carl hung his head, shaking it slowly. "What a shame. All of this is so pointless. And I know it's only a matter of time before they come here and kill me, too. I'm tired of fighting. I'm done."

She hated to hear the sound of defeat in his voice, but could understand why he felt that way. He was an old man. He didn't look all that healthy, and would be no match for people who thought there might be something worth stealing there.

"We could take you back to Dr. Ashworth if you'd like," Tonya said, stepping forward.

Carl smiled at her. "Thank you, but my place is here. I've lived here my whole life; worked in this hospital for fifty years. This is where I'm going to die."

It was a grim prediction, but very likely. "Are there any other clinics or facilities in the city where we might find some antibiotics?" Amanda asked.

Carl looked thoughtful for a second. "You know what, I've got an idea. Follow me," he said, turning and shuffling down the hall, taking turns down corridors in the dark with an expertise that could only have come from years of working in the hospital.

He opened a door to show several desks scattered around the room with tall filing cabinets pushed against a back wall. He walked to one of the cabinets and opened a drawer, pulling out a stack of papers and putting it on the desk.

"What's that?" Amanda asked.

"Few people know there's a warehouse in town—a medical supply warehouse. Looks just like a normal business building, so you'd never know it if you weren't told. I know the address is on some of these invoices," he said.

Amanda smiled, resisting the urge to yell in excitement. "That would be amazing."

"Here it is—this place, right here. They don't advertise what they are, but I've been around long enough to know people. I know they've got all kinds of stuff in that place, assuming it hasn't been looted already," he added. "It's rough in that part of town, though. I don't know if you'll be able to get in there."

"We'll check. Thank you, Carl. Are you sure you don't want to go to Dr. Ashworth's? I know he'd love the company, and he could use all the able bodies he can get right now," Amanda said.

Carl looked tired. "I'm okay here. I've got a nice warm bed, and I can't bring myself to leave. I still have a few friends around, too."

Amanda understood his reluctance to leave. The fear of the unknown was hard to deal with.

"Good luck," she told him simply before he handed her the address and they turned to head out of the hospital.

26

Malachi watched Savannah sleep with Andy tucked against her in the small space of the tent. The little boy hadn't said much in the last two weeks. He did talk to Savannah, but his sentences were stilted. The kid had been extremely traumatized, and Malachi felt completely inadequate to help him. Savannah had expressed to him that she felt the same way. They were kids themselves, not all that much older than Andy. They didn't have witty anecdotes to impart or years of wisdom to help them know what to say or do. All they could do was talk to him… when he was willing.

Savannah stirred in her sleep, her eyes opening and looking directly at Malachi. "Hi," she said with a smile.

"Hi."

"How long have you been awake?"

He shrugged. "Not long. I've been thinking."

"About?"

"We've been moving too slow. I think we need to pick up the pace and head straight to Boise."

"What's in Boise?" she asked.

"Your dad's final destination, where we're supposed to head if catching up seems unrealistic. It's been two weeks, Savannah. Two weeks of wandering. It's time to follow the plan," he murmured.

"It's not my plan!"

"You're right. It wasn't. But it is now. It's time to go."

She looked away, first into the tent's ceiling and then at Andy, before speaking. "I'm sorry. I know running away was stupid."

"Hey, it's okay. We're past that now. Or, rather, your dad is probably still going to be furious, but I'm okay," he said with a laugh.

She groaned. "That's not all that comforting."

"Sorry."

"Are we going home today?" Andy asked, waking up slowly.

He asked the same thing every morning. Malachi wasn't sure if it was because he was confused or if he really thought there was a home to go to. He imagined it must be difficult for a little boy to understand his original home was gone. Almost all homes were gone.

"We're going to ride the horses some more today," Savannah said, stroking the boy's hair.

Andy grimaced. "Again."

"Yes, again. Pretty soon we're going to meet my dad and Malachi's mom. They'll be so happy to meet you," Savannah told him. "And then we'll find a home before you know it," she said, though Malachi could hear the lie in her voice—both of them, anymore, had a pretty hard time believing in the idea of a permanent or real home.

Andy didn't look convinced, but he'd proven to be a real trouper. He got up and rubbed his eyes before they all crawled out of the tent to peer around the meadow they had made camp in the night before. "I'm ready," he said bravely.

It didn't take long to take care of morning rituals and get the horses tacked up. They had so little to pack up, moving on happened quickly.

Savannah helped Andy onto Raven's back and handed him a bottle of water. Andy drank a few sips before handing it back. Climbing up behind him, she gathered the reins. "Ready," Savannah said with a sigh.

Malachi mounted Charlie, giving him a light kick once he'd settled, and together the horses ambled out of the meadow and onto the road nearby. "I think we have to move faster and longer today," Malachi said.

"I know," was Savannah's reply.

He squeezed Charlie's sides, getting him to pick up the pace, and Raven followed, moving faster as they made their way over the flat pavement. It was dry, barren land. He'd struggled to find them food with no time and little to hunt for.

"Did you guys eat a lot of fast food when you were on the road?" Savannah asked Malachi.

This was something they'd been doing the last few days, talking about the days before the EMP and what their lives had been like.

"No. Not really. Sometimes it would be a real luxury if we got to stop for a burger, but my parents preferred to go to grocery stores. My mom always made our lunches and, at night, we either had the potlucks or something my mom would cook. What about you?" he asked.

"We ate out—a lot. I got really tired of it towards the end of our year on the road, but right now I would kill for a Big Mac," she said and laughed.

"And a Slurpee. That was something we did have a lot of," he said, practically tasting the icy drink on his lips.

"Ice. I miss ice," Savannah chimed in. "I wonder if we'll ever have ice again," she said with a sigh.

"Your dad thinks so. It's why he's doing all this. He really loves you, Savannah, and he's willing to do whatever it takes to make sure you have a normal future," Malachi said.

"I don't know if 'normal' is realistic," she replied.

They passed a driveway, not bothering to venture down it. They had learned the hard way that it was too risky. They'd been met with more guns than Malachi cared to count. Despite the fact that they were three kids in need of food, people preferred to shoot first and ask questions later—except that they didn't ask questions. They just ordered them to go away. Thankfully, they'd been able to hold on to the horses, which had been surprising enough in itself, but none of the regular folks they'd met along the way were interested in more mouths to feed. Not while they were busy protecting what little they had.

"I'm hungry," Andy whined.

"I know, buddy," Malachi said, hating to see the boy starving.

"We need to hunt or fish," Savannah said.

"Tonight. We'll find water and we'll do some fishing," he stated, feeling like he was the man in charge and not entirely liking the responsibility of keeping a little kid and a girl alive. It was a lot to handle, and he wasn't doing a great job.

"I think we're nearing another town," Savannah said, her voice hesitant.

The last town they'd been through had not been kind. "We'll go around if you want," Malachi offered.

She shook her head. "No, it takes too long to do it that way. We can do it."

The houses were a little closer together as they moved west, heading into another small town. Malachi saw a grocery store, one of the huge ones, to his left. It was too tempting to resist.

"Do we dare?" he asked.

Savannah was staring at the massive building, cars scattered around the parking lot. "Malachi, it's going to be empty."

"But what if there's something small left, something we could use?"

She grimaced, but finally gave a slight nod. "Okay."

"I'll go in. You stay here with Andy and the horses," he said.

"But what if you run into trouble?"

"Then run. Get on the horses and ride hard," he ordered.

She scoffed. "Like I'm going to leave you. We should all go in."

"We can't take horses in a grocery store!"

She burst into laughter. "Why not? Who's going to stop us?"

He thought about it then, and realized there were no rules. Rules had gone away when the power had gone out. Indeed, there was nothing stopping them from taking the horses into the grocery store. "Alright then. Andy, we're going to find you something to eat!"

Savannah scowled at him. "Don't get his hopes up."

"I will get down on my hands and knees and look under every shelf. We'll find something," he insisted.

The horses' hooves made a resounding clippity-clopping as they crossed the paved parking lot. The store appeared empty, but Malachi knew looks could be deceiving. Andy hugged Raven's neck as they passed through the double-doors that had been pried open.

"Holy cow!" Savannah exclaimed.

Malachi's eyes went wide as he looked at the disaster. There were boxes, garbage, and even money strewn about the store. The shelves were empty, absolutely cleared out as far as they could see. Yet, Malachi wasn't going to give up.

"We go down every aisle, kick over every box, and then we'll go in back and check the stock," he said confidently.

Andy made a gesture, indicating he wanted off the horse. Malachi reached up and helped him down. The little boy darted towards the end of an aisle and picked up a plush stuffed animal. He held it close, hugging it to him and murmuring incoherently. Savannah and Malachi exchanged a look as they watched the little boy.

"I guess it was worth it to come in here," Savannah whispered.

Malachi agreed, walking towards Andy and scanning the shelves. The only thing they were finding was a lot of trash. He wasn't going to give up, though. He wanted to provide, and kept praying as they meandered up and down the aisles, excitedly picking up boxes and then tossing them to the ground.

"Oat cakes," Malachi said, pointing to a bag that had been left on a top shelf in the very back.

"It's food. We can add some water if they're really stale."

Malachi grabbed one of the empty boxes and used it to pull the bag forward. It wasn't a lot, but it gave him hope. Andy was walking alongside them, clutching the plush toy that Malachi was sure was some kind of horse. It was black with a patch of white on the nose and vaguely resembled Raven.

They moved into the condiment aisle, found a bottle of mustard to add to their stash, and kept walking. "I'll check the back. You two stay right here," Malachi said.

Savannah was holding her nose. "It stinks really bad," she grumbled.

Malachi looked at the dead refrigeration units that lined the entire back wall. Milk, cheese, and other refrigerated products had been picked through, but a lot had been left to rot. The products put off a sour, putrid smell that turned his stomach, but he ignored it.

"I'll hurry," he said, pushing open the wide swinging doors and moving back into the huge store room.

"Is it bad?" Savannah called out.

"It looks like it did out there," he replied, his eyes scanning the dark space. He didn't see or hear anyone. "It's clear. Go ahead and come back."

The doors pushed open, flooding the area with faint light. Savannah grabbed a few empty boxes and some of the spoiled containers from the dairy section to put in front of the doors, propping them open to offer more light. Together, they did another sweep of the area, finding an open case of pickles that was half-full. The jars were heavy, but Malachi insisted they take them. The jars would prove useful to carry water once the pickles were gone.

"Look," Savannah called out, pointing to several boxes.

Not food, but cheap little grocery store toys. They grabbed a few for Andy before moving around the area. They managed to score salad croutons and seasonings, but nothing else.

"This is better than nothing," Malachi said as they walked out of the grocery store.

"Andy's happy," Savannah said, looking up and smiling at the boy who still clutched his new stuffed animal close to his chest.

"That's a huge plus," Malachi agreed.

They walked back to the road, each of them gnawing on a stale oat cake, jars of pickles weighing down the saddlebags. Savannah was already planning to make a mustard and pickle sandwich with the oat cakes when they settled in for the night. Malachi wasn't quite as thrilled by the thought of that, but the idea of eating a sandwich was exciting.

"Do you hear that?" Savannah asked, stopping and cocking her head to the side. "Someone is shouting for help!"

"It's a woman!" Malachi said, his natural instinct pulling him to help the unseen voice.

"It's coming from over there." Savannah pointed ahead.

They walked faster, Raven and Charlie led behind them. They could hear the screams of a woman mingled with men's voices. Malachi had no idea what they were walking into, but it sounded like a desperate situation.

"I hear water," he said, picking up his pace.

There was the sound of splashing, and men hollering at one another to help someone. Malachi looked back at Savannah, silently asking her permission to rush into the situation. She nodded and he took off, pushing through the trees.

A woman was thrashing around in water that didn't look all that deep, but she obviously didn't know how to swim. She was crying out for help and heading deeper into the lake. There were three men, as well, one of them following her deeper into the lake while the other two stood on the bank, shouting at him to get her.

"I can help," Malachi shouted.

The men turned to look at him, surprise on their faces. The man in the water didn't look happy to see Malachi. "I can't reach her," he grumbled.

Malachi kicked off his shoes and socks, hating the idea of getting wet, though it was a hot day and it would cool him off. He walked into the water splashing and holding his arms up as he passed the first man, who had stopped his pursuit of the woman. Malachi ignored him and kept moving.

"I'm going to help you," he told the woman who was sliding under the water and then coming up, her arms flailing wildly.

"Get away!" she screamed.

"I'm going to help you back to shore. You have to stop splashing," Malachi said, his voice calm as he moved towards her.

"Don't touch me!" she gurgled, her head dipping below the water when he reached for her arm.

"Malachi! Be careful!" Savannah shouted from the bank.

He turned to look at her and saw that the man in the water was climbing onto the rocky shore, the other two already heading up the small incline. He was on his own.

"I'm going to put my arm around your waist, okay?" he said to the woman again.

She looked at him, her brown eyes wild and her long brown hair clinging to her face. "Don't hurt me," she whimpered.

"I'm not going to hurt you!" he insisted, wondering what she was doing out here if she couldn't swim. Had she been trying to drown herself or what?

He reached for her and then pulled her forward. He could no longer touch the rocky floor of the lake, which meant he was going to have to pull her and hope she didn't tug him under. She seemed to be calming down, though, and wasn't fighting him.

"Please, don't hurt me. Let me go," she begged.

He felt the ground under his bare feet and used it to propel himself forward. The woman under his arm had gone almost limp, her fight gone.

"That's Savannah," he said, talking to her and trying to keep her calm.

The woman stared at Savannah and Andy. Malachi was convinced he could overpower her if she got any wild ideas. She dropped to her knees and crawled the rest of the way out of the water. She was on her hands and knees soon enough, sucking in large gulps of air and coughing between breaths.

"Are you okay?" Savannah asked her in a gentle tone.

The woman shot up, getting to her feet and looking back and forth between them. "Are you with them?" she asked.

Malachi shook his head, instinctively taking a step back and holding up his hands. The woman looked to be in her thirties. She was small, very thin, and didn't look like she'd been eating well at all. She had fear in her eyes, and her movements were jerky. She looked like a scared, wild animal, truth be told, and Malachi didn't want to be too close.

"We're not with anyone. We heard your shouts for help and came to investigate," he said.

Her eyes darted back and forth. "I'm leaving. Leave me alone!" she shrieked.

"We're not going to hurt you," Savannah assured her.

"They were going to kill me!" the woman shouted.

"What?" Malachi gasped, looking over his shoulder to make sure the men were truly gone.

"They tried to, to, you know," the woman whispered, looking at Andy. "They tried to attack me. I kicked one of them really hard and then I ran. I ran right into the lake even though I don't know how to swim. They told me they were going to drown me!"

"I'm sorry. I promise, we're not with them. Can we walk you somewhere?" Savannah offered.

"No! Stay away! Don't follow me!" she shouted.

Malachi looked up at Andy. He was sitting on Raven's back, staring at the woman. "That's fine. Go. You're scaring the boy."

The woman looked up at Andy, her features softening as she offered him a slight smile. "Thank you for helping me," she whispered, and then she rushed past Malachi, going in the opposite direction of the men.

Savannah stared at Malachi, apparently shell-shocked. "We need to get out of here," she whispered, looking around.

She was right. He dropped to the ground and quickly pulled on his socks and shoes. The day was warm enough that he would dry quickly. He hoped his jeans dried before they had time to chafe. He couldn't afford to be dealing with raw skin. His own sweat would keep the skin wet and that could lead to infection. He wasn't about to walk in his underwear, though, so he'd just have to hope for the best.

27

Amanda's stomach was revolting against the putrid air. The smell of fire and rot remained strong as they moved through the city. It was making all of them nauseated. She pulled her shirt a little higher, resting it on the bridge of her nose. It did little to block the smell. She would have killed for a little Vick's vapor rub to smear under her nose. She remembered working on a stray dog that had gotten an infected leg wound, the skin around it going necrotic. The wound had smelled very much like what they were smelling now.

"I think we're close," she said in a low voice, as if that would help conceal their presence as they walked down the sidewalk.

Ezra was walking alongside her, the rifle slung over his shoulder and his own shirt pulled over his face. "I hope so. This smell, it's too much. I don't even want to know what it is."

"I'm guessing poop is the strongest odor," Mike offered.

Amanda shuddered, knowing the liquid running down the storm drain was likely human waste. The smell emanating from it had the distinct odor of urine.

"Death," Gretchen said in a somber tone. "We're smelling death."

"And garbage. I feel like we're wading through a landfill," Tonya complained.

Amanda knew they were all suffering. It was the filthiest city they had been in yet. It was like everyone living in the area had given up on common decency. No one cared enough to bury the dead or dig latrines. It was the worst representation of social breakdown she had ever witnessed, and she hoped never to encounter it again.

"There." Amanda pointed to a street sign. "We turn left here and go down another block and we'll be there."

"Where is everyone?" Jordan asked from the back of the group. "Why haven't we seen anyone?"

"They're probably lying low. It's hot and I doubt there's much to find," Amanda said, her eyes scanning the windows above them.

She felt it, too. The city had been very lively at one point. It was a little hard to believe they were the only ones roaming about, as if everyone was lying in wait, ready to attack. The feeling had her on edge, all of her senses on high alert as they continued down the sidewalk. She had a mission, though, and that's what she was focusing on, drowning out the smells and the sights of trash and death scattered all around them.

"Sniper!" Jordan called out at the same time a shot rang out.

Mike kicked open the door to a small Hallmark store. They rushed in, listening as two more shots were fired.

"I think that came from above us," Amanda whispered.

"Like in the upstairs of this building!" Gretchen hissed.

"Stay flat against the wall and move. I don't know that they were even shooting at us. It didn't feel like it, but be careful; we have to keep going," she ordered.

She took the first step outside, pressing her body flat against the brick wall. The ledge separating the two floors was about six inches wide—not a lot of shielding, but enough to block them from view from directly above. All was quiet as the others came out, following her lead.

Her eyes moved around the area constantly, looking for any threat. If she'd been wrong and the shooter was across the street in one of the buildings, they were easy targets, lined up against the wall like they were waiting for a firing squad. She came to the edge of the building and knew it was time to cross the street, exposing them entirely.

There was a large rock in front of her; she squatted and picked it up before sliding up against the wall again and tossing the rock into the intersection. Nothing happened. Amanda turned to look at the people trusting her to keep them alive. She drew in a deep breath, held up three fingers, and silently counted down.

They sprinted across the street to the building that looked like they could be the business offices of a CPA firm. Just the sight of it suggested it was unlikely anyone would have guessed it to be a medical warehouse.

"Around back," Amanda whispered.

They jogged around the massive three-story building until they found a roll-up door and a regular door about ten feet away from the corner. That's where she ran to. It was locked, of course.

"Now what?" Ezra asked.

Amanda took a deep breath, trying to think. It was a steel door with no handle on the outside. She slapped her palm against the door, angry that everything was so difficult. Then, to her surprise, the door opened a few inches. Her eyes went wide as she stepped back, gesturing for the others to get back.

Ezra pulled the gun off his shoulder while she reached for her own.

"We don't want any trouble," she started.

"What do you need?" a very large, husky man demanded, stepping into the open doorway.

"Uh, we, uh, we're looking for some antibiotics," she said quietly, a little intimidated by the man.

"Why would you come here?" he asked.

Amanda couldn't get a good read on him. His size was definitely that of an NFL linebacker, but his demeanor was that of a large teddy bear. He didn't appear mean, either—intimidating, yes, but not outwardly cruel or violent. The Glock in his hand added to the intimidation factor, though.

"We know this place is a medical warehouse," she said, doing her best not to sound accusing. "A man at the hospital told us."

Gretchen and Tonya stepped forward, standing next to Amanda. "There are sick kids," Tonya told him simply. "A town, not far from here, they've been hit with typhoid. There's a doctor doing everything he can to save them, but he's losing the battle. He needs antibiotics. They're good, peaceful people," the woman pled, her voice soft and with a sense of truthfulness that came from years of preaching to sinners.

The man looked from Tonya to Gretchen, who was looking at him with a serene smile on her face. "How many of you?" he asked.

Amanda jerked her head around their small group. "This is it. Seven total. We're not part of the town, but we feel like we have to help them. I don't know if you've been out there, but it's bad. Good people are hard to find these days, but these are really good people who need help. We feel obligated to help."

The man looked like he was really struggling.

"Please," Mike added.

That seemed to be the turning point. Seeing a grown man beg for help was the very thing they'd needed to convince this big guy they were telling the truth.

"Come inside," he said.

Amanda knew there was still a risk the man could get them inside and shoot them, but it was a risk they had to take. There was a candle burning, casting very limited light in the area. The man picked it up and moved to open another door. Muted light beckoned them. She followed him through with her hand at her side, ready to move for her gun if the guy tried anything.

He opened another door to what appeared to be a large employee break room. There was a small window that provided some light. Amanda looked around, taking in the tidiness of the room. There was a stack of candy bars and vending machine finds on the counter next to a coffee machine.

"Are you here alone?" Amanda asked.

The man eyed her carefully and she realized her question hadn't come out right. "Yes," he answered.

"Have you been here for long?" she pressed.

"I'm the security guard. I was hired over a year ago. I worked the graveyard shift. When things went dark, I came over to check on things and found everyone had fled. I decided to keep guard, knowing the value of what's really in this building," he explained.

"I'm Amanda," she said, hoping to put the man at ease.

"Hank Dry," he said, reaching out to shake her hand.

They made the introductions before Amanda broached the topic of getting the meds. "Hank, Dr. Ashworth is waiting for us. Things are really dire. We have to get back as soon as possible."

"We'll have to look through boxes to find what you need. I don't know how they organized this stuff, and the scanner doesn't work," he said. "Do you know the names of the medicines?"

"Dr. Ashworth wrote down a few things for us to ask for," she said.

"I'll show you where things are stored," he said, walking out of the breakroom and leading them down a hall.

He used a key to unlock a door that opened to a massive storage room with high ceilings. It looked like a warehouse from the inside, which was a stark contradiction of the outside of the building.

"Everyone, spread out. Anything that ends with a 'cillin' or 'cycline' is what we're going for. We don't want to be greedy, but we need enough to treat all those people," Amanda instructed.

"And ourselves," Mike muttered.

"Yes—us, too," she replied.

Hank helped them search. After they opened each box, he made sure they closed it back up and put it back on the shelf in its proper place. Amanda appreciated his attention to detail and the fact that he still cared about his job. She guessed he needed something to care about, the way things were going.

"Why did you stay?" Ezra asked him as they searched boxes next to each other.

Hank shrugged one of his beefy shoulders. "I didn't have anywhere to go and I thought it was a temporary power outage. Then, it kept going. But I made a commitment and I intended to keep it. Plus, I was kind of hoping that, when things did settle down and return to normal, my boss would give me a bonus for keeping the merchandise safe," he said with a grin. "Guess we're past that point now, but it is what it is."

"Good thinking at the time," Ezra said with a small laugh.

"Hank, this city isn't safe. You're not going to be able to stay here much longer," Amanda said gently.

"I don't have anywhere to go," he replied.

"I bet Dr. Ashworth and the others would be happy to have you," she offered.

There was a shout then, and then a hoot of excitement further down the row where Mike and Gretchen were digging through boxes. "Jackpot!" Gretchen squealed. "We found it!"

Everyone stopped what they were doing and rushed over to check out the white plastic bottles the others had found. Amanda confirmed the labels herself and nodded, smiling. "Load up. I think you're in the right area. Let's check the other boxes. We might need to try a number of different antibiotics in case the first doesn't work."

Everyone worked with renewed energy as they pulled boxes down, loading as much as they could into their pockets and using large triangle-size gauze pads to make carrying bags that could be looped through their belt loops. It wasn't exactly incognito, but they had to take as much as they could. They shoved a variety of other medical supplies into their backpacks. Amanda wanted to give Dr. Ashworth everything he needed while keeping a few things for themselves.

"I wish we could take all of this," Mike muttered.

"Me, too," Amanda agreed. "It won't be long before this is all taken or destroyed."

"I've spent months guarding this stuff, not even knowing what all of it was. I wish there was a way we could distribute it to those who need it," Hank said, looking around the room.

"It's very dangerous out there," Ezra told him.

"I'll go with you," Hank announced.

Amanda stopped what she was doing. "Good. I think you and Robin, the doctor, will do great together. I know he'll appreciate all the help he can get."

"You're not staying?" Hank asked.

"No, we're passing through. We're kind of behind our schedule—to meet friends," she quickly added.

"Oh," Hank said, sounding a little disappointed.

"I think we might see each other again, though. Who knows, we might be back to take refuge from the storm raging all across the country," she said.

Tonya looked at her, understanding in her eyes. They had talked about their mission and what it meant if they failed. Assuming they survived at all, they would need somewhere to live. They couldn't keep traveling. It was no way to live. After this mission, at least they'd have some others to call friends.

"I think we have enough. Let's get out of here," Ezra said.

Amanda was in agreement, as were the others. Being in the city was terrifying, danger sitting at every turn. Now that they were carrying life-saving medicine, the stakes were raised.

"It's going to be dark soon. I want to be out of here before the sun fades," Jordan said.

They moved out of the building, Hank taking them down some back alleys that would normally have been more dangerous than the busy streets, but not any longer. They were the safer option now. With his guidance, they made it out of the city before dark. Remembering the trouble they'd encountered earlier, they took a wide berth back to the two-lane road that had brought them into the city.

As the sun faded and the heat finally let up, Amanda felt herself relax a little. The smells of the city finally subsided, allowing them to draw in fresh air.

"That was the worst we've seen," Ezra commented.

"I think we've got a glimpse of what the future looks like if we don't change things," Gretchen said.

"I think you're right, which only makes me want to try harder," Amanda said quietly, more determined than ever.

Walking down a dark road with few trees and nothing but flat land stretching out in all directions was a little eerie. Amanda felt exposed, and it made the hairs on her arms stand up. She didn't like it, and couldn't wait until they rejoined Austin and the others. He made her feel safe in an unsafe world.

28

Austin and Ennis got up before the sun broke the horizon, Wendell watching them walk out of camp. He was anxious, nearly desperate to have some time away from the brothers. They were close to Boise and the next meet-up with Zander. Wendell knew Zander was planning something for them when they got to Boise. Austin searching for the other computer centers was just the delay Zander needed to get ready to take out Austin, intent as he was on making a big show of killing him and the others. Wendell understood the impulse, after all Austin had put him through—it was a way for Zander to flex his muscles and exact revenge. Personally, Wendell didn't care how or where it happened. He only wanted to make sure he wasn't mixed up in the chaos. He felt no guilt that they would all be dead soon—only annoyance and anxiety over the fact that he'd thought his dealings with both Austin and Zander would be done by now.

At the same time, he felt he had to get the details of their information from Sarah or he'd have nothing to trade on. He had no doubt in his mind that Zander would kill him if he didn't think he was valuable. Wendell had already shown his hand by telling him about Austin and Sarah's plan, so he had to get more information to ensure his value to the NWO.

With the brothers out of sight, Wendell got up, used the bathroom, and waited a little longer before he made just enough noise to wake up Sarah and Harlen. He already had a plan to get rid of Harlen and give himself some time alone with Sarah. She didn't talk much, but he was determined to make her talk to him.

"Did they leave?" Harlen asked, getting to his feet and stretching his back.

"Yes. And Ennis said you know where the stream is. He asked if you could fill the water bottles before we move out," Wendell said easily.

Harlen gave him an examining look. "I thought we filled them last night?"

Wendell picked up two of the empty bottles. "They're empty," he replied.

Harlen looked suspicious, but Wendell pretended innocence. He'd dumped the water out before they'd woken up, but it was all part of his plan.

"Alright," Harlen said, picking up the empties and walking away.

Sarah was sitting up now, rubbing her eyes as she turned on the laptop.

"Back at it, huh?" Wendell asked before moving to sit beside her.

She gave him a look. "I need to make sure I have the information correct before we go in there."

"You're doing an amazing job. I'm so glad I'm on your side," he said, smiling wide.

"I've done nothing yet."

"You've done everything. All of this is because of you. We're about to shut down a terror organization and it's all because of your ability to decrypt those codes," he said.

That seemed to hit the mark. "I do have superior knowledge of such things. It's why they wanted me. It's why I always stayed two steps ahead of them."

"You knew about their plan before?" he questioned.

She grimaced. "I had an idea. Callum is the one who really knew."

"I can't imagine how difficult it must be to have all the information. You know, you can talk to me. We can share the burden of carrying the information," he offered.

"What do you mean?"

Wendell grimaced and made a big show of sighing. "I hate to say it, but any one of us could be captured or killed. It's not wise for only one of us to know all the information. It makes sense for several of us to have the knowledge needed to shut this thing down."

That seemed to get her attention. "You're right. Austin knows some things, and Amanda has the necessary information, but if one of them is killed—" she let her voice trail off.

"You can tell me anything. I don't talk to anyone. I'm kind of a loner if you haven't noticed," he said, shrugging as if he didn't care either way.

"Austin knows the codes and I know the codes," she said, her closed-off body language revealing that she'd become a little uncomfortable.

"Sarah, you have to know there's a very high risk that Austin will be killed on sight if the NWO finds him. And you... of course, they'll want you. You're a valuable commodity. Where does that leave the rest of us? How can we save the world if the only two people in the world that can stop this thing have been shut down?" he reasoned.

She stared at the screen in front of her, filled with various files. He could tell he was making headway. She was thinking about it.

"I don't know... these codes aren't to be bandied about," she said, her voice full of hesitancy.

"Sarah, I'm one of you. I'm risking my life to do this. I've been putting my life on the line for months to try and keep Austin and his daughter alive. We're all in this together. I've proven myself time and again. I don't want all of this to be for naught," he added, doing his best to keep his voice calm, reasonable. "I think we need to have a back-up plan. I'm the perfect option. No one sees me as a threat. No one thinks I'm capable of doing anything at all. I'm the dark horse," he said, the words ringing true to his own ear as he spoke them.

It was a compelling argument and he knew it. She had to see why it was important to share the information with him.

"Why don't we talk to Austin about this when he gets back?" she said.

Wendell fought back an urge to growl. "We can't tell Austin. We can't tell anyone. Can you imagine what would happen if one of them was captured and tortured? They'd tell them I had the information. Then I would be killed along with you and Austin. Then what? No one would be left to do what needs to get done to save our world," he said.

Sarah chewed her bottom lip. "No one pays much attention to you," she agreed.

He ignored the anger that threatened to bubble to the surface with her statement. "No, they don't. I'm not one of the big tough guys and I'm not the most outspoken. I'm hiding in plain sight."

She turned to look at him. "You are. That's exactly what you're doing. You've joined up with these people because you don't have the skills to survive on your own. You stay quiet, keep your head down, and no one notices you're there, hanging onto their coattails."

He clenched his teeth. He didn't particularly care for her bluntness or her assessment. "I guess you could look at it that way."

That seemed to sell her. "Fine, I'll tell you the codes. You'll need some other information, as well, just in case I'm killed."

He made a cross over his chest with his fingertip. "I won't say a word."

She rambled off a slew of information, all of which he committed to memory, knowing his very life depended on him knowing the codes. It was all he had. She had been right about one thing: he couldn't survive on his own. He was clinging to Austin's coattails now, but he planned on jumping to Zander's coattails at the first chance he got.

"You're making a wise decision," he said.

Harlen walked back into camp just then, looking from Wendell to Sarah. Wendell smiled at him and got to his feet. "I'll get a fire started and get the water purified. Today is going to be a big day."

He was almost giddy with the idea of sleeping in a real bed and eating real food as soon as tomorrow night, or possibly even that night. He'd earned it. He had put in the time and energy, and deserved all the luxuries coming his way.

29

Austin could feel the excitement humming through the group as they passed a sign announcing they were entering Boise. Their destination wasn't much further, though he expected it wouldn't be an easy path. They expected there to be the usual turf wars and people like Lilly Gamblin running the streets. They'd been dealing with it for months and knew the drill.

"What if—" Ennis started, before Austin held up his hand and shook his head.

"Don't say it. We need a little good luck and positivity right now. I refuse to believe we're going to strike out again," Austin said firmly.

He heard a choking sound then and turned to look at Wendell. The guy had been acting strange since he and Ennis had come back from hunting earlier that morning. He didn't like it. Wendell looked like the proverbial cat who'd eaten the canary.

"The computer center is on the edge of the south side of town. We don't need to risk it by going into the city," Sarah said.

"Are you sure? I thought you said it was on the north side?" Austin asked.

"I was wrong. I studied the map some more and I'm confident it's on the south side," she replied.

Austin was at her mercy; they all were. The city sprawled out before them looked daunting. He wanted it to be on the south side, though, as it would make his life a lot easier. The remnants of buildings that had been burned to the ground stood like massive tombstones on either side of the street. He could still smell fires and the scent of burning plastic.

This was nothing new, of course. It had been the norm as they'd traveled the country. Cities were always the worst, full of hostiles and death.

Walking through Boise, they passed body after body lying in the midst of more destruction than any of them could have wrapped their minds around just months before. The city was in shambles, and anyone alive was hiding out. Slowly, Austin began to think they might pass through the city and reach the computer center without getting into any skirmishes. He didn't let his guard down, but it was turning into a quiet day.

"Why do they stay?" Harlen asked, shaking his head when they passed several bodies lying shot down in the middle of the street. "Why stay?" he asked again.

"Because they had nowhere else to go. Where could they go?" Ennis replied. "They die in the place they know or they die in the wilderness. I'm sure there were a lot of resources in the beginning, and honestly, it would have made sense at that point for some of them. Unfortunately, too many people fighting for the same thing is always going to end up with the weak being killed off."

"I can't wait for this to be over. I'm so sick of the death. It's all so pointless. They could have lived together peacefully. They could have banded together and fought back," Harlen said.

"I think the propaganda being spread drove them to fight one another. Can you imagine what it would have been like for them?" Austin asked, not expecting an answer. "I think we're all pretty lucky we were where we were when it happened, and lucky to have found each other on top of that."

Ennis smiled at him. "That's very upbeat of you."

Austin shrugged. "I'm feeling upbeat. I know this is it. We're going to do this. I refuse to fail."

There was another choking sound from Wendell. Austin shot him a glare.

"We're close," Sarah announced, her eyes scanning the area. "It's in an Italian restaurant."

"What?" Austin asked.

"It's an underground bunker. They had to have a front. These bunkers are all over the country posing as simple businesses," she answered.

"Is that it?" Ennis asked, pointing ahead to a broken, faded sign. 'Anthony's Italian' was barely legible on the sign.

"It is! Let's hurry!" Sarah said.

Austin's heart kicked up a beat. He had to believe they'd find success on this, their third try. He couldn't fail. He refused to fail, thinking of Savannah somewhere out there. He wanted to give her hope and a future she could look forward to.

"I'll go in first," Ennis said. "Cover me."

Austin pulled his gun from his waistband, his eyes moving as he scanned the front of the building. Ennis pulled open the door and Austin moved behind him, ready to shoot if a threat emerged. The restaurant appeared empty, though, with only a few tables scattered about with dingy tablecloths draped over them.

Together, they moved towards the door that would likely lead to the kitchen. Austin imagined the bunker entrance would be hidden in the cooler or maybe under a prep table. Ennis pushed open the kitchen door then... and they came face to face with Zander, other members of the NWO scattered in the room beyond him. Austin cursed. Ennis didn't move, staring at the man's cold, dead eyes.

"Well, well, well," Zander said with an evil grin.

Austin quickly evaluated the situation. He was still in the dining area. To his left were several tables that could provide minimal cover.

It was Harlen's voice that cut through the silent stand-off, his deep baritone projected at Zander. "Don't move."

Zander laughed at him, looking straight at Austin. "You might want to tell your man you are outgunned and outmanned."

Austin stared at him, doing his best to use telepathy to talk to Ennis. It had worked with Savannah. He hoped his brotherly bond was just as powerful.

"Why don't we sit down and talk about what it is you want?" Austin suggested casually.

"I want you dead," Zander replied dryly.

Austin smiled, slowly shaking his head. "I don't think so. I think you want the information I have."

"Oh, I want that, too, but I don't think you're the only one who can give it to me."

"I have the USB," Austin pointed out. "Or rather, I know where it is. No one else does."

"That's true," Ennis replied.

"You don't need the drive, Zander, you have me," Wendell said, his voice cutting through loud and clear behind him.

"Ah, there's my little buddy. You've done good," Zander said with a small laugh.

The heat of the realization slammed into Austin. Zander meeting them at the computer center wasn't a coincidence. All he had suspected had been real. Wendell was a traitor.

"You weasel," Austin hissed even as he heard his brother cursing under his breath.

"See, Austin, I don't need you. My buddy here has everything I need."

"Your buddy doesn't have what you want. I'm the only one who has that," Austin shot back angrily.

Ennis very, very subtly moved to the side, just an inch or two. To anyone else, it looked like he was just shifting his weight, but Austin recognized it as a sign to initiate an escape.

"Let's—" Zander started to say something, but Ennis used that moment to throw his body against Zander, giving Austin the split second he needed to draw his gun and fire at Zander.

His shot missed, but Zander and Ennis scuffling in the doorway was an effective plug to keep the soldiers lined up in the kitchen from spilling into the dining room. Ennis slammed his fist into the other man's gut, fighting for his life in hand-to-hand combat. Austin knew there was no way they could win a true gun battle in the close quarters, and jumped to push a table towards the door.

"Ennis, back!" he ordered.

Ennis jumped backwards, leaving Zander on the ground and bloodied from Ennis's thrashing. Before the men behind him could push through or do more than take aim, the two brothers pushed the table in front of the door, turning it so the width of the table lay across the door as shots fired into the other side. They pushed two more tables in front of it before rushing outside and away from Zander and his men.

Harlen aimed his gun at one soldier who'd apparently been sent to stand guard, but he froze instead of pulling the trigger. Austin took the shot for him, dropping the man where he stood. Sarah looked terrified, huddling against the outside restaurant wall. Wendell was nowhere to be found.

"We have to go, now!" Austin shouted.

Sarah stared at him, terror paralyzing her. He sprang forward, grabbing her arm at the same second that a flood of NWO soldiers came around the corner.

Ennis started shooting, holding them back as Sarah stumbled to her feet and Austin pulled her along until she was running beside him, and only then did he begin turning to fire at the soldiers as he ran. Harlen and Ennis were shooting at select targets, being strategic with the minimal ammunition they had. Austin ran after his brother, running more than two blocks before he stopped to look behind them. They hadn't been followed, which was strange.

"Oh no," he mumbled, realizing Sarah wasn't with them.

"Where is she?" Harlen gasped, struggling to draw air after their escape.

"Where is she?" Austin screamed at Wendell, who'd for some reason joined in their fleeing the scene, having hid only long enough to escape immediate fighting.

Wendell looked wild-eyed. "He tried to shoot me," he whined, grabbing his arm. Blood trickled down his forearm.

Austin glared at him, hating him more with each second. "Where is she?" he hissed.

"I don't know. He shot me!"

"I don't care!" Austin shouted, getting closer to the other man's face and fighting the urge to shoot him now himself.

"He grabbed her. I tried to pull her with me and he shot me!" he wailed again.

"We have to go back!" Austin said, already moving towards the restaurant.

"We can't," Ennis said, reaching for his arm and pulling him to a stop. "We can't go in there; the three of us are no match for them, not like this."

Austin spun around, his eyes on Wendell as he took long strides towards him. He stopped in front of the shorter man, his chest bumping against his chin. "What did you do?" he demanded.

Wendell shook his head. "I didn't know they'd take her. He was supposed to take me!"

"Why would he take you? You don't have what he needs—she does!" Austin shouted, furious he'd been so stupid as to let Wendell get the upper hand.

Wendell looked scared. "I do. I have the codes."

"What?" Ennis and Austin said at the same time.

Wendell gulped and looked at Ennis. "Sarah gave me the codes. It was supposed to be my bargaining chip. Zander was supposed to take me with him. We were going to stop everything."

Ennis exhaled a whoosh of breath. "How long have you been working with him?"

"Not long," Wendell whispered.

Austin faced his brother, ignoring the traitor in their midst for a moment. "He told them where we would be."

Ennis looked like he'd be sick. "Why? Why would you do that to us? We've been nothing but good to you," he said, staring at Wendell.

"I'm going to kill him," Austin said, steel-voiced. "I'm absolutely going to kill him."

"No!" Wendell screeched. "You can't!"

"I can. What else have you told him?" Austin asked, grabbing Wendell's injured arm.

Wendell whimpered in pain, trying to pull away and making Austin squeeze tighter. "I told him the plan. I told him Amanda would be in Cheyenne to launch the missiles."

Austin cursed, and then jerked at his arm so that he screamed and his eyes went even wider. "Does he have Savannah?" he asked, his voice tight as he forced the words out.

Wendell looked from Ennis back to Austin. "I don't know. I don't think so. He never said anything to me."

"You've been talking to him?" Ennis questioned, the hurt and betrayal evident in his voice.

"He has to die," Austin said firmly.

Ennis reached up and put a hand on Austin's shoulder. "You can't kill him."

"Why not? He's no good to us. I never want to see his face again!"

"You can't kill him because you would never be able to live with yourself for killing such a pitiful man," Ennis said.

Austin froze, and then stared at the man in front of him, hating everything he saw. The beady eyes, the pointed nose, and the man's disgusting personality in general. He was a weasel.

"You can't kill me. I know what Zander's plan is," Wendell blurted out.

Austin scoffed. "We all know what his plan is. He's going to go after Amanda and stop her before she can launch those missiles."

Wendell was shaking his head. "But I can help. I can pretend to feed him information. He trusts me!"

"Is that why he shot you?" Austin asked dryly.

That seemed to make the man pause. "I was in the way. I shouldn't have been in the way."

"You seem to be in the way everywhere you go," Austin snapped.

"This isn't helping," Harlen said, finally getting over his shock and stepping in.

"He's right," Ennis agreed. "We can use Wendell to feed Zander misinformation."

Austin only looked at his brother, wondering if he'd been hit in the head. "He's playing you—us. He'll say anything to stay alive. He'll tell Zander what we're doing and betray us, again. You can't trust him, Ennis. He's a rat, a stinking rat that needs to be put down."

"Wendell, you know Austin will kill you, and slowly, right?" Ennis demanded, looking at the man cringing before them.

Wendell nodded. "I swear, I won't betray you again. I was afraid he'd kill me. He found me in the woods and threatened to kill all of you if I didn't tell him what we were doing," he squeaked out.

Austin knew he was lying. "I don't believe you."

"It's all we have, Austin. Do you want to get Sarah back? Do you want to do what we set out to do?" Ennis asked him.

"I know where the bunker is," Wendell blurted out. "It's not at the restaurant."

That got Austin's attention. "Where is it?"

Wendell seemed bolstered by Austin's interest in his information. "I'll show you. That means you need me alive."

"I could just beat you until you told me," Austin replied easily.

"Austin," Ennis warned.

"Guys, we need to get out of here in case they come after us," Harlen said.

Austin looked down the road in the direction they'd last seen the soldiers. "They don't want us. They got Sarah and they think they got everything they needed," he sneered, looking back at Wendell. "They didn't, Wendell. They didn't get it all."

Austin fought the urge to touch the USB in his front pocket, carefully wrapped inside a sealed bag and stuffed inside the remaining protein bar he'd been carrying for over a week. Sarah had been suspicious early on, afraid something like this could happen. Thinking of it, he brushed against the messenger tucked in his other pocket. Over and over, he'd been tempted to turn it on to message Amanda, but he knew she wouldn't get any messages until she turned hers on. They needed a plan to stop Zander before he got to Amanda.

Wendell was not to be trusted, though. He and Sarah had talked about that fact several times. He had to believe Sarah had given Wendell false codes.

"Harlen, watch him; keep your gun on him. If he moves or blinks, shoot him," Ennis ordered before grabbing Austin's arm and pulling him away.

They crossed the street, moving into the tall grass. Austin kept his eyes on Wendell the whole time, not trusting him to not try to run or overpower Harlen. Harlen was a big guy, but he was also inherently kind and would struggle to shoot a man at point blank range.

"Austin, you can't kill him. I know you want to—and trust me, I want to, as well—I can't believe he did this to us, but we aren't like that. We don't kill people unless we have to. It will weigh on you for the rest of your days," Ennis said.

"He betrayed us. He sold us out. He sold out Amanda. Zander probably has a contingent of men already after her. They'll kill her, Ennis," Austin growled, feeling his fists clenching involuntarily at the thought of it.

"Give her some credit. She's proven herself to be a worthy opponent. She isn't going to go down without a fight, and we all know how important this mission is," Ennis said, forcing him to look into his eyes.

Austin faced his older brother with the weight of everything that had happened making him rethink everything. "Is it worth it?" he demanded suddenly. "Is the mission really worth all of us dying? I should have gone after Savannah. I left my daughter with the idea I was going to save the world. I was arrogant, and now it might all be for nothing. I might die. You might die. All of us will probably die by Zander's hand and our mission will have been a waste of time and life. We could have found somewhere to lie low. We could have found that island you talked about. We could have run away and left all of this to someone else to fix. Isn't that what our military and our government are supposed to do? Why are we doing this? We both know we don't have a shot at actually succeeding," he said, his words falling heavy on his heart.

Ennis grinned darkly at him, and then shook his head. "Austin, you are arrogant. You always have been, but that's what makes you who you are. You have never given up. You have never listened to people when they told you it was too dangerous, or you shouldn't go into a war zone to get a story. You did it because you were compelled to and that's what you are doing now. You don't quit. This mission is absolutely a Hail Mary, yeah, but there's the slightest chance we can pull it off. You've convinced me of that, and you can't give up on this now. You can't. If you do, you will never be able to live with yourself," Ennis stated simply. "We've got a chance to make all of this worth the fight. We need to take it."

Austin let the words sink in. He knew his brother was right. If he was forced to retreat to some hideaway and live out the rest of his days, he'd never be able to rest easy. He would always think back to the moment he'd quit. He couldn't walk away— not yet, at least. It wasn't in his DNA.

"What do we do?" he asked his big brother. "We both know Wendell disappeared while we were running, and then he was with us again. What if he was talking to Zander or his men during that time? What if he's still working with them, on something new?"

"It doesn't matter, Austin. Our plan is the same, and we're not going to let Wendell bring it down. We get to that computer center and give Amanda the best shot at success of shooting down those satellites," he said, a small smile playing on his lips.

"You make it sound so easy," Austin muttered.

"I said you couldn't kill Wendell, but I didn't say you couldn't knock him around a bit until he gives you the location of the bunker the NWO is hiding out in," he said with a wink.

Austin nodded, staring at Wendell across the road. He loathed the man, but suspected he did know more than he'd already told them, regardless of when he'd learned it. Just looking at him turned his stomach. "I think we should check the restaurant first. Wendell could be trying to throw us off."

"I agree. Let's go. I don't want Sarah in his hands for long. We saw what his men did to Nash."

Austin felt a pang of guilt, followed by grief at the reminder of Nash's death. He'd dragged Sarah into this mess kicking and screaming, and he was going to do whatever he needed to get her out of it.

30

It was early the morning after Amanda and her crew had delivered the antibiotics to Robin. She estimated they were about a day behind schedule, which worried her. They'd been too exhausted to travel anymore last night. She felt too exhausted to travel now, but they had to move. They had to make up for lost time. The thought of running part of the way did not appeal to her. In fact, she realized it could be dangerous to do so in the high heat. She was only grateful the humidity was relatively nonexistent—that at least offered some small consolation to her tired body.

They had crashed out in one of the empty houses in the small town. Hank had been kind enough to offer to stay up with the sick people all night while Robin had gotten a few hours of sleep. Now, Amanda got up and quietly walked out of the house. The fresh morning air helped to waken her senses. She couldn't believe the difference between the small town and the city when it came to cleanliness. A little care went a long way.

There were too many people in the city, and too many of them didn't care about what they were doing. It wouldn't be long before disease ran rampant through all cities.

She took care of personal business before going back into the house to rouse her people. Her wake-up calls weren't met with excitement, but nobody begged for more sleep. All of them knew how important their journey was, so it only took ten minutes before everyone was up and ready to move.

"We've got to move fast, guys," Amanda said as they all waved goodbye to Hank and Robin on their way out of town.

"How fast?" Tonya mumbled.

"I think we might need to actually jog intermittently. We're behind schedule."

She set the pace, her arms swinging as she moved over the highway, envisioning herself eating up the miles. The group kept up with her, though there was a lot of heavy breathing as they walked.

"Truck!" Ezra shouted, moving off the roadway.

Amanda followed him, her eyes moving as she looked up and down the highway in search of what he'd seen. "Where?" she hissed.

Everyone else already lay stretched out on the ground. "Up ahead. It's sitting off to the side of the road a little."

Amanda popped her head back up, identifying the truck that looked like so many of the other vehicles they'd passed along the way. "What about it? Did you see someone?"

"No, but it's off the road, like it was going around the stalled cars. That means it came after the other vehicles stalled," he explained.

She thought back to the Hummer she and Austin had happened upon, and wondered if it was the same situation. There could be more soldiers lying in wait.

"I'll go check it out," Ezra volunteered.

He started walking towards the truck, his rifle aimed outward, ready to shoot the first thing that moved. Amanda watched from behind a small passenger car, waiting to see if he'd be attacked. When Ezra reached the truck, though, he looked in the windows and turned to wave his hand, indicating it was all clear.

She jogged over, inspecting the empty vehicle. "What do you think happened?" she asked.

Ezra opened the driver's side door and jumped inside, turning the key in the ignition. When the truck started, he and Amanda stared at each other, both slack-jawed.

"Did that truck just start?" Mike asked, rushing towards them with the others hot on his heels.

"It's running," Amanda gasped. "Everyone, get in. I don't know who was driving this thing, but we're taking it. Go!" she hollered.

Ezra got behind the wheel, sliding the rifle between the two front seats. Gretchen and Tonya got into the back seat of the quad cab while Amanda took shotgun. The others climbed into the bed of the truck.

"Do you remember how to drive?" Gretchen teased as Ezra seemed to struggle for a few seconds before putting the truck into drive.

"Not a bit," he joked, and then he hit the gas, bumping along the edge of the highway before finding a hole between stalled cars and getting into the left lane.

Amanda sat back, the window down and the wind blowing through her hair. It felt good to be in a moving vehicle. She closed her eyes and let herself relax for a moment as Ezra drove as fast as he could down the highway, slowing down to pass the occasional vehicle in the road. They traveled for an hour before Ezra cursed under his breath.

"What is it?" she asked, her eyes immediately scanning the area for trouble.

"Gas. We're going to run out of gas," he muttered.

She groaned. "Figures. Did anyone see that last sign? How close are we?"

"The sign I saw said eighteen miles to Cheyenne. That couldn't have been more than a few miles back," Tonya answered.

The truck began to sputter, making it clear they'd been running on fumes. "Come on, come on," Ezra quietly begged.

The truck jerked a few times before the engine cut out. Ezra coasted to a stop before putting the transmission in park. They all sat quietly for a few seconds before Amanda opened the truck door. "Let's go. That saved us a lot of time, but we still have a good five to six hours of walking. We'll make camp outside the base and go in first thing tomorrow," she said.

Everyone piled out of the truck before setting off. Amanda looked back at the truck as they moved. It didn't look like it had belonged to the now, but there was no way to know for sure. She hated the idea of stealing someone's vehicle, but it had been for the greater good. They had to get to Cheyenne if there was even a remote chance of returning the world to normal.

The limited water they had was almost gone, though Amanda thought they'd escaped getting sick. They'd each taken another round of the antibiotics to stave off any chance of developing typhoid, which gave Amanda hope they would all be okay, but they needed more water and they needed food. She could only hope they'd find sustenance in Cheyenne, as well as survival. It was early evening when the massive base came into view, its large hangars standing out on the horizon. The surrounding land was barren, showing no signs of life. Part of her had been hopeful they'd arrive to the base and find American forces not just in command, but gathered in force.

"That's it?" Gretchen asked as they stood on a small hill over-looking the area.

"That's it," Amanda said with a nod.

"And we're supposed to walk in there and push buttons to launch missiles, like it's no big deal?" Ezra asked skeptically.

"That's the working plan," Amanda replied.

"Tonight?" Mike asked.

Amanda pulled the messenger out of her pocket. She'd resisted the urge to turn it on time and time again. Sarah had warned her and Austin both about the potential for the battery not holding power, and she really just had to trust there'd be enough juice for her to get the signal from Austin. Without it, they'd be shooting blind and could make things far worse. Resolve firming her spine, she put it back.

"I think we need to do a little surveillance. If our Air Force is in there, we aren't going to get far," she replied.

"If they are in there, why don't we have them take care of it?" Ezra asked.

"If they believe us, you mean. But first we need to know if anyone is in there. This base could be overrun already. We need to see if the NWO has taken over," she said, hoping that wasn't the case.

"I think I see water over there," Gretchen said pointing off to the side of the land they'd come upon.

Everyone looked in the general direction, pleased to see a small lake. "Let's go. We'll get a small fire going and get our water needs taken care of," Amanda said.

They turned off the road, walking through the tall grass towards the lake. There were a few houses scattered about, but all were set back far enough from the road that Amanda felt confident no one would see them as they made their way down to the water.

"I can't resist. I have to get in," Mike said apologetically.

Amanda looked at the water tinged green. It did look very inviting after a long, hot day on the road. "I'll stand watch. Go ahead," she encouraged.

Part of her wanted them to have a little fun on what could very well be their last day on earth. She had no idea what the base held in store for them, but the very idea of walking in there, finding the silos, and entering the launch codes without any problems was a pipe dream. Their only advantage was that the NWO didn't know their plan. They would still be chasing Austin west. She sat down on the bank and watched the men strip down to their underwear and wade into the water. Gretchen and Tonya settled for rolling up their pants legs and wading at the edges.

The men had fun, diving under the water and splashing one another. She watched them, smiling at seeing them act so normally. This was why they were doing what they were doing. This was why they had pushed their bodies beyond endurance. There had to be more good times like this in the future, when they could relax by a lake and frolic in the water. Savannah and future generations deserved to know what it was like to feel safe and have fun. Amanda let herself relax, feeling relatively safe for the moment.

But, as always with good moments in this world, the moment was short-lived. The first sign of trouble floated across the peaceful lake. *Men's voices.* Amanda clapped her hands once, grabbing the attention of the men in the water. Gretchen and Tonya were already out of the lake, hurriedly putting on their socks and shoes.

"Company," Amanda hissed.

The men rushed back to the bank, trying to get out of the water as fast as possible.

"Stop right there!" a male voice rang out.

They stopped on command, their half-naked bodies dripping water as they stared up the slight incline. Amanda turned to look behind her and saw four men, all wearing black and carrying semi-automatic rifles.

"We weren't doing anything," she said, infusing fear into her voice.

"Who are you?" one of the men asked.

"I'm Jessica and these are my friends. We've been crashing in that house over yonder and just thought we'd come out for a swim," she said, trying her best to sound ignorant and innocent at the same time.

"We've been through all those houses. No one is living there," the man replied.

"We only arrived a few days ago. We saw the house was empty and claimed it for our own," Mike said easily. "We didn't know it was spoken for. We'll move on."

The soldiers exchanged looks before one stepped forward, eying Amanda closely. The gun was still sitting in her waistband. She could reach for it, but she'd be shot before she ever got a shot off. Ezra's rifle lay next to his pile of clothes, which the soldier immediately spotted.

"How many weapons do you have?" he growled.

"Just the rifle, sir," Ezra replied, taking another step out of the water.

"Don't move," the soldier ordered, raising his gun and aiming the barrel at Ezra's head.

Ezra's hands went up. "We'll go."

"This area is under our control," the soldier announced proudly.

"I thought this was an Air Force Base," Amanda asked.

The soldier sneered at her. "It's our base now."

"Oh, we didn't know. We came here looking for refuge. We'll move on," Amanda said, using a small voice.

The soldier stared at each of them in turn. The men in their state of undress was actually helping their situation, Amanda realized. If the soldiers would have encountered them thirty minutes before, the situation would have been very different, but as things were, they couldn't have looked more harmless and unthinking.

"You seen anyone else out here? We're looking for a group of people, a woman and a couple guys who would have come from the west, making trouble," the soldier asked.

"We've seen lots of women and lots of men. Most dead," she replied nonchalantly, fear making her nervous.

They were looking for her, it seemed, but how had they known she'd be in the area? Her mind raced as she thought about Austin being captured and tortured for information. She quickly corrected her thinking, however. He would never give up the plan. Though, one of the others might have.

The soldiers seemed satisfied with her answer, and slowly retreated, leaving them with instructions to get out of the area by tomorrow if they didn't want to be removed in body bags. Once they were out of sight, the men quickly dressed, no one talking in case the soldiers remained nearby. Amanda didn't want to look like the woman in charge. She walked over to Ezra, whispered in his ear, and then wrapped her arm around his waist. His arm went around her shoulder as he pulled her into his side.

No one questioned them as they put on a big show, looking like the happiest couple in the world, Ezra carrying himself proudly and taking on the role of the leader of their group. If the NWO soldiers were watching, she hoped they had eliminated all suspicions about their identity. Things were going to be much more difficult now. Getting into the computer center to launch the missiles was going to take some serious planning.

31

Savannah walked alongside Raven, Andy barely keeping his eyes open as the gentle rhythm of the horse's hooves lulled him into contentment. They weren't far from Boise, and all she could think about was seeing her father again. She owed him a huge apology for running off. She knew it was wrong to have done it, but she couldn't change things—and, in her mind, she wondered if maybe she'd been meant to be there to save Andy. There was no doubt in her mind that he wouldn't have survived without her and Malachi finding him, and she figured that had to mean something.

"I think we can be there tomorrow," Malachi announced, walking beside Charlie.

"I wonder why they didn't go to that other base," Savannah mused aloud. "It was closer."

"Amanda and Sarah said the missiles needed were at the Warren base. Your dad did mention it," he answered.

"Oh," she replied, staring across the flat terrain with the freeway seeming to stretch on forever. She was so tired of the flat, dry land with so very few trees to break up the monotony.

"Look!" Malachi pointed to a sign, never seeming to tire of pointing out even the smallest of sights.

Savannah herself was sick of the signs and the history. As it turned out, they really were following the Oregon Trail. There were various signs marking spots along the way. It was like the world's longest, most exhausting history lesson. Reading about the journey was one thing. Actually walking it was entirely different.

There was a large gazebo off the road they were traveling, which seemed odd—why would anyone have bothered planting it in the middle of the southern Idaho desert? Malachi had already veered off-road, taking Charlie with him as he headed in the direction of the structure.

"Come on, Raven," Savannah sighed, too exhausted to tell Malachi they needed to keep going.

"Check it out!" Malachi said again.

Savannah helped Andy down, walking to where Malachi was reading a large board describing what they were seeing.

"That's the city?" she gasped, staring at the buildings sprawled out in the distance.

"It is. That's Boise. We're about ten miles away."

"Look at the river," she said longingly. She would have killed to dive into that cool water, drink gallons of it, and wash her hair all at the same time. They hadn't bathed in a week. There was dirt and sand clinging to her skin and her hair, and even coating her teeth.

"We could stay here tonight and go into the city tomorrow. Your dad is down there somewhere. There's a National Guard base, he said. He was supposed to be in that area," Malachi added excitedly.

"Okay. We can stay here for tonight. It'll be nice to have a solid roof over our heads and something other than the ground to sleep on. That tent gets stuffy. Does that sound good, Andy?" she asked.

The boy slowly nodded, still not talking a lot. Savannah looked around the area. It was filled with weeds and sage-brush. She saw nothing they could forage for dinner, though the river in the distance was beckoning. It was too far for them to get to before nightfall. She could wait one more day, she assured herself.

They sat down on one of the picnic tables under the giant gazebo. It did feel good to rest her feet and get out of the heat of the day. Her eyes stared down at her hands, covered with a layer of dirt she felt convinced would require a full bar of soap to scrub clean. The color of her skin was darker than she had ever seen it, and it wasn't all dirt. She'd gotten a deep tan from the hours spent in the sun every day with no sunscreen. She figured skin cancer was the least of her worries, of course. She wasn't sure she'd live long enough to develop cancer.

Malachi stretched out across one table, closing his eyes. Savannah watched him as he fell into a quick sleep and began snoring, and then her eyes moved over to Andy. The kid was just as dirty as she was. She offered him a small smile. Andy's eyes widened as he stared at her, and in another moment she recognized the look as fear.

"Andy, what's wrong?" she asked, reaching out to take one of his hands in hers. "You're okay," she assured him.

There was the slightest sound from behind her. Malachi bolted upright.

"Don't move!" a woman's voice called out.

Savannah spun around, ignoring the command. A woman wearing camouflage and pointing a rifle at them greeted her from perhaps thirty feet away, and she was getting closer, with other men and women in camouflage further out behind her. The woman's dark brown hair was pulled back in a sleek bun. Savannah guessed her to be in her mid to late forties. She had a hardened, weathered look about her that was intimidating.

Andy whimpered behind her. "He's a little boy and you're scaring him!" Savannah seethed.

"You're all kids! Is this a trap?" the woman barked.

More women and a few men were coming up behind her, hurrying forward now that she'd gotten so close and initiated contact, all of them wearing the same green fatigues. She recognized them as U.S. military, but couldn't determine which branch. "We're not a trap," Savannah said firmly, hoping the people pointing guns at them were actually the good guys.

"What are three kids doing up here? Did Staff Sergeant Harrison send you here?" the woman asked.

Malachi and Savannah looked at each other. "We don't know who that is," Savannah answered.

"We've traveled from Colorado. We're supposed to be rejoining our group in Boise," Malachi explained.

"Your group? What group are you a part of?" the woman asked.

"My dad, his mom, and a few friends. We're not a part of any army or whatever," Savannah quickly added, noticing the way the woman had gone on edge.

"You've come here from Colorado? On your own?" she asked skeptically.

"Yes," Savannah answered firmly, staring into the woman's eyes to try and prove she wasn't lying.

The woman seemed to be evaluating them, sizing them up. "Get them some water," she ordered.

"Thank you. This is Andy. I'm Savannah, and that's Malachi," she said, hoping to put the woman at ease.

"I'm Master Sergeant Beth McAuliffe. Everyone calls me Macbeth. We're with the Air National Guard," she announced.

"You're with the Guard? Does that mean the government's running?" Savannah asked excitedly.

The woman winced. "No. Not technically."

Savannah sighed. "Oh."

"Who is that other person you asked about?" Malachi questioned.

Macbeth let out a long sigh. "She was my right hand until a few weeks ago. We had a difference of opinion. Her tactics are not in line with my own way of doing things. We've sworn to fight for our country and that's exactly what my team and I will keep doing. Harrison has taken a small faction of Airmen and some other people she's recruited. They're holding one of the hangars where the bulk of our supplies has been stored."

Savannah groaned. "More fighting?"

The woman's look softened some, understanding in her eyes. "Is it like that everywhere?"

Savannah nodded, her eyes going to Andy, who was greedily gulping down the water that had been flavored with a packet of electrolytes. "Yes. My dad is hoping he can stop this from getting worse."

"And how does he plan to do that?"

Malachi and Savannah exchanged a look. As much as she wanted to trust the woman, she knew it was foolish to take anyone at face value, but if they couldn't trust the government and a woman like this, who could they trust? Ever? "He's trying to stop the NWO," she said simply.

"You know about the NWO?" Macbeth asked, sounding surprised.

"Oh, we definitely know about them," Malachi muttered.

"You know about them and your dad left you alone?" she demanded, sounding irritated.

Savannah looked down at her hands. "I kind of ran away."

The woman paused, pursing her lips. "I see. And, somehow, your father is planning to take down the NWO? How big is this group? We've been in the area and we haven't seen them. We've seen plenty of the NWO. We think they're going to try and take over the base. Harrison is too stubborn to listen to me. We're stronger together, but she's convinced she can save herself by hiding out on base and guarding it. She won't last," Macbeth said with a hint of sadness.

"My dad has information that can stop them!" Savannah blurted out, earning a look from Malachi.

"Who is your dad?" Airman Cliff asked, having just introduced himself to Andy.

"No one. He just happened to get the information right before everything went dark. We know the NWO has satellites hovering above the earth, armed with nuclear warheads that will be launched should our government make any forward progress in bringing the power grid back up. He came here to shut down the control systems that allow them to move the satellites. Our friends are on their way to Warren Air Force Base to use the launch codes my dad has to launch missiles at the satellites and take them all down," Savannah said, speaking quickly before she changed her mind, her words tripping over one another as she rushed to get it all out before Malachi shut her down.

343

Macbeth's mouth was hanging open. The other men and women crowded under the gazebo looked just as shocked. After several seconds, Macbeth opened her mouth to speak and then shut it again, seeming to collect her thoughts.

"Who is your father?" Macbeth asked again.

"No one you would know. He isn't military. He isn't anyone," Savannah answered. "He was a journalist before things went dark."

"And he's planning to take on the NWO?"

Savannah looked at Malachi before answering. "Yes. We've kind of been chased by them all the way from Tennessee. My dad has a USB stick that they want. I've been captured by them. They burned down the house we were living in and they've murdered several of our friends trying to get the information."

"How big is your father's army—I mean group," the woman corrected herself.

"Five. There were five of them when they left Colorado," Malachi answered.

Airman Cliff scoffed, shaking his head and looking at some of the others. All of them smirked or outright laughed. "Five people are going to take on that army? You say you've seen them; what would make him think he could ever be successful?"

"Because he's the bravest man I know. My uncle is with him and they are not going to go down without a fight. He's probably down there right now, fighting for his life. We have to get there and try to help!" Savannah snapped, her chin going up and her shoulders going back as she defended her father.

Macbeth held up a hand. "You seem to know a lot about what's happening."

"Like she said," Malachi spoke up, stepping forward, "Austin, her dad, has a lot of information. Someone found out what the NWO was going to do and slipped him a USB with the information. That was right before the EMP, but there are files and files on what the plans are, how they were going to distribute propaganda and all that, along with the information about the satellites and the missiles. The guy that got the information worked for the NSA. He gathered the information in hopes Austin could get it to the right people before they could launch their attack. It was too late. That man was killed by the NWO and they've been after Austin ever since. It isn't a joke, ma'am, and I for one firmly believe Austin will do what he has set out to do," Malachi said, his voice full of fight. "That or he'll die trying," he said more quietly.

Macbeth looked from Savannah to Malachi, and then to her people. "We need to talk. Sit tight," she said in a gruff voice.

Savannah watched the group move away about twenty feet. She guessed there to be maybe twenty to thirty of them, with more standing guard near the roadway. The fact that she and Malachi hadn't seen or heard them approaching was testament to their exhaustion. They'd been focused on the view and hadn't been paying attention to what was happening behind them.

"What do you think they're talking about?" Savannah murmured.

"I don't know. Hopefully, it isn't about whether or not to kill us. I'm tired of people trying to kill us all the time," he replied.

Little Andy gasped. "Malachi, really?" Savannah scolded.

"Sorry. Don't worry, Andy. They seem like good people. They gave us water," he said, holding up his bottle of water.

Savannah drank from her own, the somewhat putrid grape flavor making her cringe. She knew she needed the water and the packet of electrolytes that had been dumped in it. And they couldn't be all bad if they were offering them water—she hoped.

Macbeth walked back, a few of the men coming with her while the others stayed back, checking weapons and making various hand signals. Savannah got to her feet again, ready to fight if need be, even though she knew she didn't stand a chance.

"We'll escort you into the city. The computer center you're talking about is at our base. Your father will be ambushed. There were NWO at the main gates. Harrison may have already been overtaken. We have to try and help her, and we will help your father if we can," she promised.

"You're going to help the person who kicked you off base?" Malachi asked.

"I'm sending one of my people in to arrange a meeting. I think she'll be more inclined to join forces if it means combatting the true enemy. One of the things we argued about was her wanting to go after the NWO, while I wanted to lie low and protect the base," she explained.

"Really?" Savannah asked. "You'll back my dad?"

"If he has what you say he has and he has a plan, I'd love to meet him and see how we can help. We're here to serve. It's what we signed up for and it's what we intend to do until there's nothing left. We're committed to our country," she said simply.

"When?" Malachi asked.

"Now. We can't afford to wait," she said, her tone grim.

"What? Why?" Savannah asked, sensing there was something being left unsaid.

"Like I said, the NWO has already been there. Harrison can't hold them back for long," she said.

Savannah had been looking forward to resting, but it wasn't meant to be. "Come on, Andy. Let's get the horses."

"We have some nourishment packs. You kids look like you could use some food," Macbeth offered, a smile on her lips as they moved to the horses.

"Please. Andy hasn't eaten in a couple days," Savannah said.

Macbeth smiled. "I'm guessing that means you two probably haven't eaten in longer than that. We're here. We'll do what we can to keep you safe."

Savannah had to blink back the tears she felt pressing at her eyelids. She was tired, making her more emotional, but it had been too long since someone had taken care of her. She was tired of being strong for Andy. The idea that she could rely on someone else for a while was welcomed, even if it might be for just a short time. "Thank you," she whispered, and then she turned to help Andy onto Raven.

It felt good, safe, to be encompassed by armed soldiers, fighting for the good guys. She could let her guard down. She looked over at Malachi and smiled. He smiled back, and it was a real smile—something she hadn't seen in days.

32

Zander walked along the blacktop, the morning sun already promising it was going to be a scorcher. His men stood in front of one of the hangars at the Air National Guard base outside Boise. This was where he had expected to find Austin. It was empty, deserted as far as his men could see. They had searched the hangars and the barracks already and found the post completely abandoned. He would have killed the men in his army had they run like cowards.

The empty base only proved the point of the NWO. The government had been weak, easily overthrown with the EMP. It was why the NWO had been formed. They needed a strong, controlling force running the world. So much politicking had left the country and several other so-called world powers weak. They'd been hamstrung, and it was time for a superior force to take over. He was a part of that force, and would one day be sitting at the round table with the true leaders of the world.

First, however, he had to put down Austin Merryman. The man threatened to destroy all of his hard work and the sacrifices he had made. He would find him, kill him, and end the man's one-man quest to save the world. He'd thought, by now, that the man and his friends might have come after their doctor, but so far that wasn't the case. Maybe he'd been smart and abandoned her, but if that was the case, it was all the more important that they get her to talk. Austin Merryman would not get away from him again. One way or another, he couldn't depend on their traitor to bring them to the base.

"Good morning, sir," one of the guards greeted him.

"We'll see. Is she still alive?" he asked.

"Yes, sir," the man replied.

If she was alive, that meant she hadn't talked yet, and it was time to turn up the heat. He didn't like not knowing where Merryman was. Zander felt the stagnant air hitting him as he entered the hangar. He smelled blood and the distinct scent of urine. That made him smile. She'd wet herself.

Zander stared down at the woman tied to the chair, her ankles tied to the legs of the chair and her hands behind her back. She was completely immobilized and at his mercy. The good Dr. Bastani wasn't looking so hot. He'd left his men alone with her to extract the information they needed, and she wasn't talking. The less she talked, however, the harsher the persuasion tactics.

"You might as well just tell me where he is. I'm going to find him. You can make it easier for me and I in turn will make it easier for you. Wouldn't you prefer a bullet to the head over this laborious torture?" he asked.

"I don't know where he is," she whispered.

He stared at her cracked and bleeding lips. Both of her eyes were swollen shut and her left cheek had a nasty gash across it. He knew she had to have several broken ribs after the beating she'd taken with the heavy book his men had tossed to the side.

"Where were you supposed to meet him?" he growled.

She tried to open her eyes, her head bobbing backwards as she attempted to look at him. "I wasn't supposed to be separated from him."

"Liar! Merryman would have a contingency plan!"

Zander looked over at the man standing nearby. He gave a brief nod, indicating it was time to inflict more pain. Zander had been furious when he'd discovered that Merryman still had the USB. His men had scoured the area, and the man had all but vanished—he'd slipped from his grip again, and he was all the madder because it had been his own fault for wanting to make a big statement, and take down the man himself, by himself. He'd made another mistake, and he'd be lucky if it didn't really cost him. His best bet was getting this woman to talk.

When his obedient soldier held up a length of two-by-four for Zander's approval, he nodded again. The man swung the board, connecting with Sarah Bastani's knees. She screamed in pain, her body jerking as she cried out. Zander couldn't stop the smile from spreading across his face. He envisioned Austin in the chair. He wanted to make Austin bleed and scream in pain in retribution for the suffering he had caused him.

"I don't know," Sarah whimpered.

"Arm," Zander uttered.

His man swung the board, connecting with the doctor's upper arm. More screams erupted from her mouth. The sounds were strangled, her throat clearly raw from the screaming and lack of fluids.

"No more," she murmured.

"This doesn't stop until you tell me where he is," Zander said, bending over at the waist to get close to her battered face.

The woman spat at him, blood and spittle hitting him in the face. His arm swung out, his hand slapping her cheek hard. Her head tilted to the side, hanging low.

"Alright, Dr. Bastani. I gave you the chance. You know I'm going to find him. You are prolonging your discomfort. I promise I will kill you as soon as you tell me what I want to know. But I will keep you alive until then, and I will let these men hurt you for days. You will not die. You will not escape. No one is coming to save you. Give him up and you can die peacefully," he said.

He wasn't interested in promising her a bunch of things he had no intention of following through with. She was a smart woman, so he figured a more direct approach was the way to go. Apparently, though, she enjoyed the torture.

Fine. He was happy to oblige her with more pain and suffering if that's what she craved. "Take her to the recruiting center," he said to his men before walking out of the hangar.

33

Austin hadn't slept all night. He couldn't stop thinking about Nash, knowing Sarah was likely being put through the same torture. There was nothing she knew that the NWO didn't already know, except for where to find him, but she couldn't tell him that.

He knew Zander would be looking for him. They had managed to find their way into an old, long-abandoned shack on what he suspected was the training field for the airbase. It was riddled with bullet holes, indicating that either the Air National Guard or some trespassers had used the shack for target practice.

He suspected they had taken her onto the base. The problem was, the NWO had claimed it as their own. They had spent the night doing recon, discovering there was a relatively small contingent of men with Zander. After Wendell's little revelation about him giving up Amanda's whereabouts, Austin suspected part of his small army had gone after her. She should already be in Cheyenne—at least, he hoped she was. He held the messenger in his hand, unable to keep from turning it on after everything that had happened. He was relieved to see it remained fully charged, and the blank screen stared back at him. Should he send a message? Sarah had warned him that it could be tracked. Sighing, he turned the device off and put it back in his pocket. It would have to wait.

Ennis came into the shack with Wendell beside him, which was where he'd been glued for the last twelve hours. Austin knew the weasel was afraid of him. He should be, too. Austin was ready to kill him slowly for his betrayal.

"Ready to move?" he asked, glowering at Wendell.

"I am," Ennis replied.

Austin looked at Wendell, stepping forward and going nose to nose with him. "You screw us over and I will make sure you die. Ennis won't be able to save you. Zander won't save you. You. Will. Die."

"I swear, I'm not lying. Zander's in there. I know that's where he's taken her," Wendell said.

"You won't get a gun. I don't trust you not to shoot me in the back," Austin snapped.

"How can I help if I don't have a weapon?" Wendell whined.

Ennis turned to look at him. "You should have thought about that before you set us up. If you want a gun, I suggest you ask your buddy Zander."

Austin grinned, happy to know his brother completely backed him in that regard. Wendell was only alive because he'd told them where to find Zander. The original location for where they'd thought the computer center had been located was inaccurate. It was on the base, in a bunker that was concealed within one of the hangars. Wendell claimed to know which building the center was in, and while Austin wasn't sure he believed him, Gowen Field was too big for them to search the numerous buildings blindly. He had to trust Wendell, and that made him very uncomfortable.

"We're going. Harlen, are you ready for this?" Austin asked the man who had been sitting quietly.

"I'm ready. I don't want to leave her in there another minute," he replied simply.

"Then let's go. We've got darkness on our side. Wendell, you better not be setting us up," Austin hissed.

"I'm not. I know where it is."

"What about Sarah? How are we going to find her?" Ennis asked.

"You're certain he was going to hole up in the recruiting center?" Austin asked Wendell for the third time.

"Yes. I was going to meet him there," he said, somewhat forlornly.

"Well, it looks like you still will," Austin said dryly.

All except Wendell checked their weapons. They had limited ammunition, which meant they had to use stealth. They would never survive a gun battle. Austin refused to lose, however, no matter how the odds might be stacked in Zander's favor; he refused to give up without putting every ounce of strength he had into succeeding in this mission. He'd had his moment of doubt, and Ennis had reminded him of who he was. Now, what mattered was moving forward.

They walked out of the shack, the darkness thick as they started towards the airfield that stretched out for hundreds of acres, surrounded by industrial businesses. None of them spoke as their ears strained to pick up any sounds suggesting they might have been discovered. Austin was skeptical about Wendell's information, but he had no other choice but to at least check it out.

After walking for about fifteen minutes, Austin saw the building where the bunker was supposed to be hidden underground.

"Over there," Wendell said, pointing to small, rectangular, one-story building.

"That's where you think Sarah is being held?" Ennis asked.

"Possibly," Wendell replied, suddenly not willing to commit.

Austin had to weigh his options. If he went after Sarah first, the NWO would certainly know they were there. It would destroy the element of surprise, and they would never make it to the underground computer center.

"I know what you're thinking, and you're right," Ennis said quietly.

"What is he thinking?" Harlen asked.

"We're going to the bunker first. We do what we came here to do and then we go after Sarah," Austin said firmly.

"What? We can't! We have to go to the recruiting center first!" Wendell said, his voice panicked.

Austin stopped walking and moved to stand in front of Wendell, his suspicions reaching higher by the moment. "You seem upset by that. Why?" Austin asked.

Wendell quickly recovered, shaking his head. "I only meant, they're probably torturing her. We have to save her."

"Austin is right. We can't reveal our presence. It's what Sarah would want," Ennis said.

"I agree," Harlen said.

Only Wendell looked upset by the decision, but they only got one chance and it had to be used for the mission. Austin hated the idea of Sarah suffering at Zander's hands, but she would have insisted they get to the computers before they tried to rescue her. And she'd have been right.

"There." Austin pointed to the huge white structure sitting alongside a runway.

The door was hard to miss, even in the dark of night, and they ran for it.

Austin nodded. His heart was pounding; so much was riding on this moment. Harlen reached for the doorknob, testing it to see if it would open. He pulled, and they all exchanged looks of relief. This was the first step.

They encountered no soldiers as they walked along the wall towards the back of the hangar where Wendell claimed the entry to the underground bunker was carefully concealed.

Wendell pointed to a table, seemingly randomly placed against the back wall. "That's it."

"How do you know?" Harlen questioned.

Wendell looked uncomfortable. "Zander told me."

Austin didn't believe they were getting the whole story. "Zander told you the location of the computer center?" he asked skeptically.

"Yes."

Austin spat, and then he shoved the table out of the way, dropping to his knees and feeling along the floor. He found the handle and yanked it open. He knew he should have been quieter, but he was frustrated. He was tired of failing, tired of losing friends. And if Zander had given this information to Wendell, then either this was a trap, or Wendell had really managed to weasel his way into the man's organization, which almost wasn't any better considering that they'd considered him one of their own—to a certain extent—all this time.

"Are we going in?"

"Wendell is," Austin said, getting to his feet.

Wendell gasped. "What?"

"You're going in first. If they're down there waiting for us, I want them to shoot you first," he said nonchalantly.

"I don't have a gun," he hissed.

"Nope, you don't. Good luck," Austin said, slapping him on the shoulder, almost hoping there was a firing squad waiting for him.

"It's dark," he protested.

"Go."

Wendell grumbled under his breath before throwing a leg over the edge and onto the ladder leading underground. The other three stared into the hole, watching Wendell fade into the darkness below.

"I don't see anything!" Wendell shouted, loudly enough to make the rest of them cringe.

"I'll go," Austin said, climbing onto the ladder and praying Wendell wasn't setting him up.

He reached the bottom, finding a faint light in a metal shield hung over a door just ahead of them. He realized they were in a small room, probably no bigger than ten by ten. He called up to Ennis and Harlen, letting them know it was clear to come down.

"What if they're waiting for us?" Ennis whispered.

"We fight," Austin replied. "Wendell, open the door."

They all drew their weapons, expecting a fight. Wendell actually whimpered as he pulled open the wide door. Austin blinked, his eyes adjusting to the light.

"Drop your weapons and put your hands up!" a shout from somewhere inside the room echoed around them.

"I'm unarmed!" Wendell screamed.

Austin didn't hesitate. He wasn't going to give them the jump. His eyes adjusted and he saw an outline of a figure. He dropped to the ground and aimed for where he guessed the head would be just before he pulled the trigger. He heard a sharp intake of breath and then a thump.

Wendell screamed and dropped to his hands and knees, crawling backward. Austin advanced with Ennis on his left and Harlen on his right. A shot rang out then, making his ears ring. He trusted Harlen and Ennis with his life. Another soldier had been hiding behind some boxes, but the fallen soldier had knocked them askew and given Ennis a shot—he took the soldier out before he could decide who to shoot, that indecision costing him his life.

"Clear on this side," Ennis reported.

"I'm clear!" Harlen called out.

"Where are the computers?" Austin asked, not expecting an actual answer.

He scanned the area, realizing belatedly that they weren't in a computer room at all. It was a storeroom. The three of them picked up the dead soldiers' weapons before moving to the shelves, where they found ammunition, grenades, and even several grenade launchers.

"Those guys weren't guarding the room," Austin muttered. "They were probably down here picking up ammo and heard us coming."

"Maybe so, but this is exactly what we need," Ennis breathed as he reached out a hand and gently caressed one of the launchers. "This is a forty millimeter, M203 grenade launcher. I've had my eye on one of these for a long time," he said reverently.

Austin barely glanced at him as he filled his pockets with ammunition. "We need the computers. We're running out of time!"

Harlen was carefully putting grenades into his pants pockets. Austin rugged the tactical vest off of one of the fallen soldiers and put it on his own body, ignoring the blood. Ennis followed suit even as Harlan dug one from a box. With that, each of them began stocking up in seriousness, gathering ammo, grenades, and anything they could carry which might be used against the NWO. And, as they finished, Austin realized Wendell had vanished.

"That little weasel!" Austin hissed.

"I'm sorry. I should have trusted your instincts. He knew this wasn't the right place," Ennis muttered.

"Let's go. We need to check the other hangar. He might have been right about it being in a hangar. Maybe he got the wrong one," Austin said, not really believing it.

They scrambled up the ladder and through the hanger, heading out into the early morning light streaming through a cloudy sky. In the distance, he could see another hangar. They jogged towards it, getting within a hundred feet of it before men poured out of the building, all of them armed and fanning out in front of the hangar, effectively guarding it. Austin darted behind an abandoned Jeep that sat among other vehicles, his brother and Harlen close behind him.

"I guess we know where the real computer center is," Harlen mumbled.

"Got that grenade launcher?" Austin asked his brother.

Ennis grinned, looking a little too happy to be killing people, but Austin understood. This was the NWO they were fighting, and the weapon was an exciting toy for him. Harlen and Austin kept watch over the vehicle, waiting to see if the soldiers would make a move, but the NWO soldiers seemed content to wait for the fight to come to them. Hidden out of sight, Ennis dropped to his knees and quickly loaded the grenade launcher before getting to one knee, holding the weapon, and aiming over the Jeep's hood. Ennis and Harlen separated, aiming the semi-automatic rifles they had lifted from the soldiers in the bunker.

"Now!" Ennis shouted.

There was a crack, and a second later, several soldiers dropped when one of the powerful rounds exploded. Ennis turned, aimed, and fired again. He shot off several rounds, effectively stunning the army, none of whom had expected grenades or automatic weapons. Austin and Harlen jogged forward, spraying the area with two and three-round bursts from the automatic rifles.

Ennis caught up with them, firing his own rifle. The men who were still able to do so looked to be retreating. These soldiers hadn't seen much resistance, and it showed—they weren't near ready to see their friends fall or stand up to automatic weapons, let alone grenades and a small force with a real cause to die for.

Leading the way, Austin ran across the wide runway, heading for the building where Wendell had told them Sarah could be held. He believed nothing the man had said, however. He'd chosen his side.

"Let's get in there," Austin said, firing a few more rounds at the retreating soldiers.

They rushed inside the massive hangar, finding a jet of some type parked inside, useless after the EMP. Austin looked for another obvious entrance to an underground bunker. Nothing announced itself.

"Let's check the back," Ennis ordered, running the length of the hangar.

Unlike the first bunker, there was nothing there. No doors in the floor, and not even any furniture that might have hid one. "It isn't here," Ennis declared after they'd searched the full length of the building.

"The recruiting center!" Austin shouted, already running towards the door. And those soldiers who'd run had gone in the opposite direction, he now realized—heading away from the danger and the heart of the fight.

He heard Harlen and Ennis behind him, but didn't turn to check on their progress. Austin was furious with himself. He'd been played. Wendell had known he would go for the computer center first. It had been a red herring, meant to throw him off. He was going to shoot him when he saw him.

The recruiting center looked abandoned, and there was nowhere to take cover. If soldiers were waiting, they'd see them coming. There was little he could do about that, though. He wasn't going to give up. He kicked open the door to the recruiting center, finding that the lobby empty. There were two closed doors on the right and another one along the back wall.

His gut told him that the back door was the way to go. He pointed. Ennis and Harlen nodded, all three of them aimed forward. Austin walked to the door, turned the handle, and pushed it open. It looked like a typical stock room, with lots of leaflets and paperwork along with various items used for recruiting, but it was a shelf about a foot away from the wall that was the giveaway.

Ennis jerked his head to indicate he understood and followed Austin. He pulled the shelf forward several feet, revealing a secret door. Excitement pumped through Austin's veins. It had to be the entrance to the bunker. He pushed the door open, darkness greeting them once again. Unlike with the other bunker, the entrance into this one was through a low door. Austin didn't hesitate, instead jogging downward, following the tunnel as it led underground.

Gunfire greeted him, slamming into the walls and the ground in front of him. A ricochet slammed into his chest, but the bullet was effectively stopped by the Kevlar vest he had picked up off one of the soldiers. The round only knocked him backwards into Ennis, who kept him from falling all the way to the ground. He quickly reached under the vest, touching the tender area with his fingertips to check for blood. The Kevlar had done its job. He had no doubt in his mind that Wendell had alerted the NWO forces they were coming. They'd been lying in wait, essentially trapped. They'd walked right into it, though there hadn't been much choice, he felt even now.

"What do we do?" Ennis asked.

Austin hated to say it, but they had to retreat. They had to draw them out and fight them on more even ground. "Go back —we'll bring them to us."

Ennis turned and ran back up the steep incline to the exit. Austin looked behind him to see if they were being followed, and it was only when he slammed into his brother's back that he realized where the real trap was.

"Oh, I've missed you," he heard Zander say.

Austin groaned. They'd come so far, he couldn't believe it was all over. And yet, again, he stood next to his brother, facing the man he'd come to hate more than any person he had ever met in his life. Pure evil stared back at him.

34

Amanda's heart raced thinking about how deeply she was trusting these people she'd trained to be her small army. It wasn't a lot to go on, but it was all she had. They had no weapons—not really—which meant they had to rely on stealth alone. They had to try to break into the missile launch facility, hope no one was still manning the launch systems, and enter the codes Sarah had given Amanda. Then, they had to wait for the signal from Austin, hoping against hope that Austin had been able to disable the satellite control systems. That was a lot of hope and a lot of luck, all needing to go in their favor if they were to succeed. Or, at least, that's how it felt.

"Keep your eyes open," she whispered.

It was the early morning, and sunlight highlighted the base sprawled out before them. They faced a daunting task, and that was all the more clear as she looked at the building they figured to house the launch facility… to the extent that she started to second-guess herself. For a breath, she froze, but apparently it was visible enough to those who'd come to know her so well.

"We can do this," Ezra said in a low voice.

She let out her breath in surprise, and then offered him a half-smile. "Thanks. Do I look terrified?"

He chuckled. "No, you don't."

"Good, I'm hiding it well, then."

"Heads up!" Mike shouted, the warning coming just a few seconds before shots rang out.

Gunfire rained down on them as Amanda dropped to her stomach, Ezra right beside her.

"He's hit," Gretchen cried out, her hand reaching out and touching Mike's shoulder. "Mike! Mike!"

Amanda looked to her left, clasping a hand to her mouth when she saw Jordan's lifeless body lying in an awkward pose.

"Who's hit?" she called out quietly.

"I'm good," Gretchen replied. "Mike's dead," she added, a sob tearing through her voice.

"I'm okay," Ezra said, his voice devoid of emotion.

"Tonya?" Amanda asked, a second before more gunfire rang out. Amanda closed her eyes as she took stock of their situation, praying that the God the revivalists worshipped was up there watching over them.

The gunfire stopped as quickly as it had started. She knew the tactic. They weren't necessarily aiming to kill; they were spraying them with bullets to keep them pinned down until they could capture them. But being captured meant they would face Nash's fate.

"I'm okay, I'm okay." Tonya was crying.

"I'm hit, but I don't think it's bad," Drew said in obvious pain.

Amanda propped her chin on the dirt, her eyes scanning the area. There was a metal outbuilding not far from where they lay. If they could get there, they could gain some cover. Another building stood about ten feet away from the first. They could leapfrog. The idea blossomed in her mind. "We get to that building," she said, pointing.

"Is it the NWO shooting at us?" Ezra asked.

"It has to be. They were sent here to guard the base," she replied with disgust.

"I don't think I can walk," Drew groaned.

Amanda nodded, biting her lip. "I'll get to the shed. Give me the rifle," she ordered Ezra. They traded weapons, him taking her handgun.

"What are you going to do?" Tonya whispered.

"I'm going to the shed so that I can provide some cover while the rest of you get over there. Ezra, help Drew. Drew, I'm sorry, it's probably going to hurt, but we have to get you over there. Maybe I'll be lucky and find another weapon," she joked.

"Be careful," Ezra said as she began to belly-crawl across the hard, dry ground, rocks scraping over her arms and belly.

She kept moving, dropping flat to the ground when sporadic gunfire erupted. It felt like forever before she managed to get to the corner of the shed. She got to her knees, scrambling to the door and reaching up to tug it open. The door gave way, creaking open as she crawled inside. The shed was dark, making it difficult for her to see clearly, but she could see the outline of something large. She got to her feet, wiping off the pebbles and chunks of dirt stuck to her elbows before reaching out to feel what it was.

"Oh please, please work," she whispered, running to the driver's side of the Humvee parked inside the garage.

She had to hope it was one of the NWO's vehicles that had been sheltered from the EMP. The keys were in the ignition—its cover had been how rundown the shed looked; the NWO's forces never would have expected this shed to be searched for supplies. It was almost too easy. She hesitated, wondering for a moment if it was a trap. If she turned the key, it could set off a bomb. More gunfire erupted. She didn't have a choice. She would die in a quick boom or die out there with her friends.

She squeezed her eyes closed and turned the key. The sound of an engine filled her ears and she screamed in excitement. "Yes!"

The gunfire wasn't stopping, so she didn't have time to get out and open the doors. She'd seen it in the movies—she just hoped it worked in real life. She put her foot on the brake, put the massive vehicle into drive, and hoped for the best, slamming her foot onto the accelerator. The Humvee lurched forward, ramming the thin metal doors so that they burst open. She raced towards where she'd left her friends, doing her best to keep the rig between where the gunfire was coming from and the surviving members of her team.

She hit the brakes, dirt flying up as Ezra yanked open the rear passenger door. Tonya and Gretchen jumped into the back. Drew maneuvered himself into the back door, Gretchen reaching out to help him inside. The gunfire was getting closer.

"Hurry!" she shouted.

Ezra slammed the back door and hopped into the front. Amanda hit the gas immediately, the vehicle's back end sliding as she fought to regain control of the vehicle.

"Rifle?" Ezra asked.

She jerked her head towards the back. Ezra turned in his seat, grabbed the rifle, and rolled the window down before he started shooting. Gretchen did the same in the backseat, using the handgun to shoot as they passed soldiers who were now scattering.

"Hold on!" Amanda shouted, veering to the right and heading directly at a group of soldiers. They tried to run, but she hit the gas, speeding towards them and knocking a few over like bowling pins. Bodies flew as the heavy vehicle slammed into them, bumping past like some technological monster.

Tonya screamed, ducking down low as Amanda drove over bodies, then doubling back to race towards the base. She blocked out the images of what she'd just done, ignoring the blood on the windshield and speeding over the bumpy ground until they were at the launch facility. There, she put the Humvee in park and rested her head against the steering wheel.

Her hands were shaking and her heart pounding. She couldn't fall apart yet, though. Her mission wasn't over. "Everyone okay?" she asked.

"We're good. Let's get in there before the survivors make it over here," Ezra said, jumping out of the vehicle.

Amanda nodded, opening the door and getting out to stand on shaking legs. Tonya and Gretchen helped Drew inside the building.

"It's going to be through that steel door, and that door isn't going to be easy to get past," she said, pointing to the white door ahead of them.

Before they could worry about how to open the door, however, it opened, a gun barrel poking out that was then followed by an Airman in fatigues.

"I'm going to ask you to leave. We don't have food or water. There's nothing for you here," the young man said in a controlled voice.

Amanda studied the uniform for a moment, recognizing it as the real thing. "I'm Amanda Patterson, former Airman First Class. I'm not here for water or food," she told the man, praying he'd believe her. "We're here because we know who's been behind the EMP and how they're operating, and we know how to stop them. We need to launch your missiles at satellites that are going to keep us in this perpetual state of darkness if we don't."

The guy didn't look convinced. "Right, because that sounds completely legit," he replied with an eyebrow raised.

Amanda sighed. "Look, I know it sounds far-fetched, but can we convince you inside the bunker? There's an army of men out there that are intent on killing us, and we've traveled a long distance to get here. Please, we've come a long way to try and do this for a reason."

The man looked at each of them. "Give me your weapons first. Put them on the ground and kick them over here. I'm not alone in here. If you try anything, you will be shot and killed."

Amanda's head bobbed up and down. "I get it. We won't try anything."

They pushed the few guns they had over and the Airman kicked them out of the way. "Keep your hands up."

Amanda went first, entering a narrow hallway. The others crowded in behind her. They were met by another Airman and led down underground. "In there," the second man ordered.

They were pushed inside a very small lounge. They kept their hands in the air, doing their best to appear non-threatening.

"Explain," the first man ordered, keeping his gun trained on them.

"There are satellites currently in space which have nuclear warheads that could cause another EMP. We can't fix what's wrong already, but we can ensure it can't happen again, at least not by the controlling force," Amanda explained. "We have every reason to believe that the NWO has plans to counteract any measures the government is taking to get the grid back up, and that they're prepared to trigger another EMP at the worst moment possible if we don't take action first."

The two Airmen exchanged a look. "We can't launch those missiles without direct orders."

"I have the launch codes," Amanda said simply. "I think the President and all your other bosses will understand when they learn why you launched them. This could change everything. We have a chance to get back to normal once again," Amanda begged them.

The men exchanged a look. "We need to talk it over. Stay in here and don't move."

The door slammed behind them. Amanda looked at her friends, seeing their grief and pain. Drew had already lowered himself to the floor, and Gretchen was doing her best to tend to his leg. Amanda closed her eyes and sent up another silent prayer, begging for the men to see the right path forward. If they didn't, she would have to force them—and kill them if she had to.

35

Austin took a split second to evaluate his options. He wasn't going down without a fight. He lunged, pushing Ennis out of the way and throwing himself at Zander, propelling the man into the plate-glass windows facing the runway. Zander's body slammed against the window, giving him leverage to push back. The force of his weight nearly toppled Austin to the ground, but he managed to stay up, taking a swing and slamming his fist into Zander's jaw. The sound of bone hitting bone, followed by a grunt from Zander, gave Austin the adrenaline rush he needed to keep fighting.

He was about to swing again when Zander brought up a knee, connecting with Austin's stomach and driving the breath from his lungs with a loud whooshing sound. Austin's instinct was to bend over to protect his stomach, but just stopped himself from doing it—he knew that's what Zander wanted. A knee to the face would take him down. He pushed past the pain and shoved hard, putting some space between himself and Zander before lunging at him again, swinging with his right and then his left fist, landing on Zander's jaw and eye socket.

Austin felt like he was getting the upper hand in the fight and began punching in earnest, his hands and wrists growing numb as he unleashed months of anger on his nemesis. His strength began to wane, though, his punches becoming weaker, giving Zander the opportunity he needed to push him away.

Austin stood a few feet away struggling to draw in air as he stared at Zander's bloodied face. It felt good to see the damage. He wanted to make him bleed more. He grinned, his own split lip causing him to wince in pain. Then, as if in slow motion, Zander reached behind him and produced a knife, holding it in his hand as if he was ready to throw it at him. Austin stared at the blade, calculating the damage it would do when it plunged into his body—and then he heard something behind him.

"Down!" Ennis shouted.

Austin tried to duck, but Zander saw the danger and lunged towards Austin, wrapping his arm around Austin's neck before he had a chance to move away.

"Get back!" Zander shouted.

Austin pulled with all of his strength, kicking back and jerking himself out of Zander's arms. The knife blade sliced his arm as he moved. Another soldier appeared and slammed into Ennis's back, the blow knocking him forward.

"Get them!" Zander screamed, lunging at Austin with the knife.

Austin kicked high, knocking it from Zander's hands and rushing at him again, slamming his body into the glass. Zander shoved hard, putting some space between them and allowing him to throw a punch that landed on Austin's chin. Several gunshots erupted from somewhere to his right. Austin looked towards the new threat and saw that Ennis and Harlen were engaged in a gun battle. He couldn't help. Zander was his focus.

The two men continued to fight, punching and kicking as they tried to tackle one another to the ground, both knowing that would likely be the end, depending on who ended up on top. Their struggle took them back into the doorway that led down to the bunker, and Austin fought with all he had, his body growing more tired with every blow. The sound of gunfire continued to rage. As long as there was gunfire, he had to believe Ennis was still fighting.

Zander delivered a powerful kick, throwing Austin through the door and into the massive bunker. He found himself on a catwalk of sorts with a steel grate under him, giving him a view of the computer center below. He jumped to his feet, knowing the stakes were raised. The narrow catwalk with the waist-high railing wasn't a great place to fight. He could feel the structure shake as he lunged forward, knocking Zander to the steel surface.

The man was smaller than himself, but he was a fighter. He jumped to his feet, swinging out and connecting with Austin's jaw. The blow sent him reeling into the railing, his tall frame bending backwards as the rail caught his back. Zander was on him in a flash. Austin pushed against Zander, nearly knocking himself over the railing with the force. It gave him the space he needed to get away from his tenuous position. He was about to throw another punch when he was hit from behind. The blow knocked him to his knees and made his head spin. He fought to keep from passing out, slowly turning to see his attacker and Wendell standing there, a look of pride on the small man's face as he smiled. There was a steel pipe in his hand.

"Wendell?" Austin murmured, trying to understand what was happening.

"Thanks," Zander sneered. "I knew you'd come in handy eventually."

"I told you I was on your side!" Wendell assured him, smiling at Austin and then Zander.

Austin felt sickened to see Wendell's outright betrayal coming around as a deciding force again. He didn't have long to dwell on it, however. Zander kicked him hard in the ribs, knocking him to his side and making him gasp for air. Wendell took that as his cue to imitate the move and kicked him from behind, the toe of his boot hitting him in the kidneys. It was blow after blow as the two men kicked him in his torso and head. Austin curled into a fetal position, trying to protect his body and doing his best to shield his head with his arms. He knew he was going to die, and at the hands and feet of not just Zander, but Wendell, as well, which made it all the worse.

A single gunshot stopped the violent kicks to his body. He opened his eyes and rolled to the side, attempting to crawl away. His body throbbed all over, and he could feel blood trickling down the side of his face, likely from the blow to the back of his head. He recognized Ennis's boots and looked up. He was thrilled to see his brother—until he saw the red patch on his stomach. He'd been injured and was bleeding badly. Wendell lay dead now, a gunshot wound to his head. Austin struggled to stand up. Ennis held the gun on Zander, his face a sickly pale, his hand shaking with the effort. Austin saw how dangerously weak his brother was, but he wasn't in much better shape himself.

"Shoot him!" Austin ordered, his voice barely above a whisper as he fought to recover from the beating he'd just taken.

Before Ennis could pull the trigger, Zander dove at him, but he tripped over Austin's foot and fell into Ennis rather than delivering the hard tackle he'd intended. He heard his brother grunt, Zander cursing, and then the two of them slammed into the railing.

"Die!" his brother shouted as the two flipped over the railing, Zander's body on top of Ennis's.

A gunshot rang out, followed by Zander's shout of pain a split second before a sickening thud echoed up through the room.

Austin screamed, using the rail to pull himself up as he looked over the edge to verify what he had heard.

"No!" he shouted, staring down at his brother's broken body. A pool of blood was forming around him. His eyes were staring up at him, but seeing nothing. He was dead. Zander wasn't moving, either. His neck was grossly twisted. Austin hoped he was alive and suffering. Zander deserved to suffer dearly for the pain he had caused over the last few months. The victory over Zander was bitter, though. His heart ached at staring into his brother's lifeless eyes, even as he vowed to make sure his death wouldn't be in vain.

He gingerly pulled himself to his feet. His head was spinning, and there was a stitch in his back that had him doubled over. He hobbled along the catwalk, making his way back to the tunnel that led to the center. He had to find Sarah. He hoped she was still alive. He needed her to do her thing with the computers below. In moments, the sound of gunfire had him pressing his body against the wall.

Just because he'd won the battle, that didn't mean he had won the war. He wanted to sink to his knees and sob, but he couldn't. He had to keep going. He carefully poked his head out the door and saw a soldier down, his gun lying beside him. Austin grabbed it, prepared to take out as many of Zander's men as he could.

And then he looked out the window, and he froze. "What the —" he muttered, staring at men and women in desert fatigues shooting at the men wearing black jumpsuits.

Had the cavalry finally arrived? He watched the gun battle for a few seconds more before remembering he had to get to Sarah. He rushed towards one office door, forcing it open and finding the space empty before opening a second door. There, he found her, bloodied and bruised and looking like she was barely breathing.

"Sarah?" he whispered.

"I'm here," she said, clearly not seeing him.

"Sarah, it's Austin," he said, crouching behind her and quickly untying her arms before moving to untie her ankles.

"Austin?" She sounded confused.

"Zander's dead. I'm here. The computer center is cleared out. The United States military is here. They're killing them," he said.

"We have to hurry. I'm afraid I'm going to lose consciousness again," she muttered, her voice weak but still holding that all-business attitude.

"Can you walk?" he asked.

She shook her head, moaning at the movement. "My legs are broken."

His eyes widened as he realized she had to be in shock. Two broken legs had to have her in excruciating pain. His own injuries prevented him from carrying her, though. He looked to the desk and quickly grabbed the office chair, wheeling it to where she was barely staying upright in the chair. He very carefully moved her into the wheeled chair and pushed her towards the bunker.

"Hang on. We'll get you help," he assured her as he pushed her down the long tunnel that led underground.

They made it to the computer center and he turned the chair carefully, walking backwards down the ramp to the ground floor to prevent her from being dumped out. She sucked in a breath when she saw the two bodies lying on the floor.

"I'm so sorry," she whispered.

"So am I. There'll be time for that later. Can you tell me what to do?" he asked anxiously.

"Push me up to that terminal. I can see out of my right eye. I'll need you to put my hands on the keyboard," she said, her voice weak.

He very gently lifted her hands, her wince of pain making him wish he could kill Zander all over again. He watched in amazement as her fingers moved over the keyboard. She was a remarkable woman. She paused once, seeming to slowly draw in a breath before continuing what she was doing.

"You're doing great," he encouraged her.

"Like you would know," she quipped breathlessly.

He grinned from behind her, happy she still had her very dry sense of humor intact. She tapped away before her hands stopped moving.

"Sarah?" he questioned.

"It's done."

"It's done?"

"Yes. Let's hope Amanda has managed to do her part," she breathed out. "I'm tired," she mumbled, "so tired, and it's done..." her voice trailed off, and then her head slumped forward slightly.

"Sarah?"

She didn't answer. He carefully turned the chair. Sarah's head dropped forward, her body slack. He gulped before carefully extending his fingers to her neck. He detected a pulse—faint, but it was there.

Pulling the sat. messenger out, he typed in the message: *Ready here. Launch now.* He wanted to say so much more, but the shorter the message, the more likely it would get through clearly and not overtax either device's battery. And, really, what more was there to say? He clicked send, waiting and watching as the cursor blinked back at him for what felt like forever before indicating the message had been sent. Blowing out a breath, he left Sarah in the computer center and made his way back up the tunnel to check on the firefight. He needed to see if the coast was clear before he attempted to get her—or himself—help.

"Dad!" he heard a familiar voice cry out.

At first, he thought maybe he was dead. But he turned his head toward the voice anyway, and saw Savannah racing towards him. Malachi was right behind her, accompanied by a woman who looked very much like a military commander.

Savannah threw her arms around him, squeezing him, hurting him and infusing him with strength at the same time. He hugged her close, tears streaming down his face. She pulled away, her hands going to his face. "Oh God, you're hurt."

"I'm okay. I'm fine," he assured her, catching his breath and telling himself that this was real—this was happening. He had his daughter back.

Malachi stepped forward, a smile on his face. "I told you I could do it."

He chuckled, the action jarring his ribs as he tightened his hold on his daughter. "Yes, you did. Thank you, Malachi."

"Dad, this is Macbeth. She brought her unit to help you guys. Where is everyone?" she asked, suddenly realizing it was just him.

"Savannah," he began, and then he choked on his brother's name.

"Uncle Ennis?" she whispered, tears in her eyes.

He slowly shook his head. Her hand clasped over her mouth, tears filling her eyes. "Oh no."

"Was Harlen out there?" he asked.

"I didn't see him," Malachi answered.

Austin closed his eyes briefly before shaking off the pain. His brother had sacrificed his life to save Austin. It was going to be one of those things that stuck with him for as long as he lived. He could grieve later, he reminded himself.

"Sir, it's good to meet you. Your daughter filled me in on what you guys plan to do. Was your mission successful?"

"Yes. Well, this side of it. Now we have to wait."

Savannah was quietly sobbing. A little boy stepped forward and grabbed her hand. "It'll be okay," he soothed her.

Austin looked at Malachi for answers, wondering how in the world they had ended up with this child as a companion.

"This is Andy. He and Savannah kind of found each other. He's with us now," he said firmly.

Austin looked at the little boy and offered a smile. "Hi Andy. I'm Austin."

The boy hid partially behind Savannah's body. Austin didn't know the story, but imagined it wasn't something that could be explained away in the next few minutes.

"I need to get back to the bunker and check on Sarah," he said. "She needs medical attention, and we need to see if Harlen made it through the fight—last I saw him, he and Ennis were firing on NWO soldiers."

"I have a medic. He can check you out," Macbeth said, and with an extra-calm voice that suggested she thought he might be in shock. Austin wasn't sure she was wrong, but that didn't change anything.

"He needs to check out Sarah first; she's in rougher shape than me."

36

Amanda paced the small room, anxious to follow through with her mission. For the last hour, while they'd waited on the airmen, she'd paced restlessly back and forth staring at the messenger and willing Austin to send her the go. She wouldn't turn it on to check yet, as she didn't want to waste battery and had to wait on these men anyway, but without a message, she had no way of knowing if Austin had succeeded. It was a shot in the dark. The door opened, and all of them turned to stare at the two men who had brought in a third, this one with graying hair and a set to his face that suggested many years of service. She looked to his sleeve, saw the extra stripes, and knew he was the one in charge.

"I'm Amanda Peterson," she said, stepping forward.

"General Silas. The men tell me you want to launch our missiles and you have the codes to do so?" he said, his voice gruff.

She nodded. "Yes, sir."

"That, and the story they've related to me, sounds rather insane," he told her flatly.

"Yes, sir, I know it does, sir, but I swear to you, this is real. Very real, in fact, and every minute we waste talking about the merits of our plan could be aiding the NWO."

She quickly filled him in on what the plan was, showing him the sat. messenger and stressing the importance of timing. At first, she didn't think he believed her. The man had a stone-cold look on his face, his arms folded over his chest as she spoke. When she was through, his expression hadn't changed. There was no indication of which way he was leaning. It wasn't until he'd mulled it over for several excruciating minutes that he finally nodded.

"We'll take you downstairs. We have a first aid kit for your man, as well," he said, looking to Drew.

"Thank you," she gasped, fighting back emotions.

"I've heard it's bad out there," the lieutenant general commented.

"It is. It's terrible, and if the NWO is allowed to continue, there will be nothing left. It's dangerous and deadly," she said, looking him directly in the eyes.

"I understand. We've had minimal contact, all through Morse code. It's a little hard to explain details in that fashion," he quipped dryly.

"Is the government still functioning?" she asked.

The man cringed. "We're at bare bones. We get some Morse code and we've picked up some transmissions over our one working satellite, but I can't tell you who's where and what's happening. We could have used some of those messengers like you have," he told her, eyeing it.

"We got two off of an NWO soldier. We're assuming that's how some of them have been communicating," she said, relieved to finally be talking to someone on their side.

"Do you have the target coordinates?" the general asked.

"Yes, sir."

He stared at her, obviously waiting for her to tell him.

"Um, my friends were supposed to somehow transmit them via the computer link at their end, setting up the launch, and then let me know we're a go by using this," she explained, holding the messenger up again. With that, she finally turned the messenger on, holding her breath as she did so. And, while it turned on, no message popped up. She let out her breath. "But I haven't heard from them yet," she said, more quietly.

While one of the men attended to Drew under Gretchen and Tonya's watchful eye, Ezra and Amanda followed the general into the launch center.

"Sir, we've received a transmission from Boise," a young woman announced. "The airmen we've been in contact with are on the other end, but it sounds like we have communication from the other half of this woman's group, who are now with Airmen at a base the NWO were holding."

Amanda almost vomited with relief when she offered the general their all-important launch codes. The other group had made contact, the mission was out of her hands, and Austin was alive. He'd done what he'd set out to do. Amanda looked to the general, waiting for him to order the launch. In her hand, she still held the messenger, which had given her hope up to this point. Whether it was broken or not, she didn't know, or maybe something had happened to Austin's, but that no longer mattered.

"Let's do this," the general said in a stern voice.

Amanda and Ezra watched quietly as codes and sequences were called out. They checked and rechecked codes, entering them on a keyboard and verifying their information until a green light bloomed on the screen.

"Sir, we're ready," the young woman sitting at the terminal said.

"You're sure about this?" the general asked Amanda.

Amanda took a second to think about it, and then, suddenly, her messenger beeped and she looked down at the incoming message. A smile lit her face as she confirmed, "Yes, I'm sure."

"If we launch those missiles and shoot down our own satellites, we could be further crippling our country," he warned her.

"Yes, sir, I understand that, but those satellites are not in the government's control. At any time, the NWO could launch those missiles, and there's a good chance they'd be using those satellites to induce another EMP and counteract any efforts the government is currently undertaking to get things back under control and the grid up and running. Those are nuclear warheads, am I correct?" she asked, going off of what Sarah had told her.

"Yes."

"If the NWO is in control of those warheads, the entire world is at risk. I've met several of them. They would not hesitate to use those weapons to destroy the planet. They are martyrs—suicide bombers, if you will," she said. "With them controlling those satellites and those warheads, we are all in danger."

He nodded, turning back to face the screens. "Launch the missiles," he ordered.

Amanda and Ezra stood shoulder to shoulder, watching the computer screen as it showed the missiles shooting into the sky. Within what felt like seconds, the monitors showed the trajectories and destinations of each missile. And then another caught her eye.

"What's wrong with that one? Is it broken?" she asked.

The general smiled, shaking his head. "Not broke at all. Those are the coordinates."

"Where is it going?" she asked, worried someone had missed a number.

"New Mexico," one of the young men at the computer announced.

Amanda gasped. "No! They're supposed to be going into space!"

"Those are the right coordinates," the man replied.

Ezra and Amanda exchanged a look of horror. "What did we do?" she moaned.

"Pull up our map, tell me where that thing is headed," General Silas ordered.

There was a lot of tapping on the keyboards, and then an image came onto one of the display screens. "Sir, it's Alamogordo, New Mexico. White Sands."

General Silas hissed through his teeth. "That's Holloman."

Amanda was shaking her head. "Air Force? We just bombed our own Air Force base?" she asked, her mouth going dry.

"We lost that base a couple days before the EMP," he told her.

"What? How? Why wasn't it in the news?"

"It wasn't known to us that the base had been lost until hours before the EMP. The NWO had infiltrated the command system. They were hiding right under our noses and none of us were the wiser. They took over the base, killed those that tried to fight back, and ran the rest of them off. We had just begun hostage negotiations when everything happened. They used a similar maneuver to initiate a coordinated attack across the country. They launched warheads that detonated in the atmosphere all across the country and over other nations around the world. We were helpless to do anything. The damage had been done. I think this is swift justice. The NWO are going to be toast in about thirty seconds. That's their central command, and we're hitting it." A grim smile played across his lips.

"We've taken out the NWO headquarters?" Amanda asked with disbelief.

"Yes. In about thirty seconds, the base and the NWO operations will be destroyed. We'll radio the remaining commands and let them know it's time to make a move on the NWO positioned around the country. We'll take them out in full," he said confidently.

Amanda had no reason not to believe him. It made perfect sense. "She never mentioned that little tidbit. I wonder if that's what she found on the USB?" Amanda murmured, more to herself than anyone.

"Who?" General Silas asked.

Ezra and Amanda exchanged a look. "It's a really long story."

"Why don't we go get something to eat and you can tell me all about it. I'd like to know how a few average citizens managed to save the world," he said, heading out of the room.

Amanda chuckled. "I don't know if you can describe Austin or Sarah or even Ennis as average, but we did it."

37

Austin carried his cup of coffee out onto the covered porch of the cabin he called home in the Sawtooth Mountain range, about thirty miles northeast of Boise. It was late afternoon and the sun had begun sliding into the hills, casting the landscape in beautiful warm hues. He loved this area. He loved the mountains. It made him feel closer to his brother. Ennis would have loved the cabin. Sitting down, Austin stared out at the vast acreage surrounding him, filled with tall pines and the sounds of a gurgling stream just beyond this property. It was early fall, and the birch trees intermingled with the pines had changed color, creating a gorgeous, fiery landscape.

He put his coffee on the small table next to his chair and picked up the notebook he'd been using to write down his thoughts. He was thinking about writing a book one day, and wanted to remember every detail. It had been three months since they'd launched the missiles and effectively decimated the NWO with the blow to their headquarters and their plans. Now, the country was enmeshed in a slow rebuilding process.

Power was being brought back to the major cities, with hospitals the first to be restored, but it would be a long time before the rural areas would be fully powered. Manufacturing factories were focused on producing the transformers and various electrical equipment needed to restore the power grid. Austin imagined it would be a year or more before they would have television, computers, or a fraction of the technology they'd been used to relying on before the EMP.

His thoughts went to Ennis as he considered the months ahead. They always went to Ennis. He and his big brother had never been all that close in life, but the couple months they'd had together as adults had been some of the best of his life. His loss was a hurt that was going to take a long time to heal. He still had a hard time visiting the little memorial he'd built in the backyard as a tribute to Ennis, Nash, Sarah, and all the others who'd lost their lives in the fight to save the world.

He heard the sound of a horse's hooves coming up the drive along with an irritating squeaky wheel. He was going to have to fix that, he thought to himself. He got to his feet and stepped off the porch, smiling when he saw Amanda sitting atop Raven, the cart being pulled behind her.

"You're back earlier than I expected."

"It was an easy trip," she said, smiling as she dismounted.

He walked to her and put his arms around her before giving her a quick kiss on the lips. "I'm glad you're home."

"I'm glad to be home. And I look forward to the day a trip to the market isn't a full day's journey," she said with a laugh.

"Soon, baby, soon," Austin assured her, running his hand over her hair.

"I scored some good stuff. There's a full grocery store set to open soon. The government is shipping in supplies from their various warehouse stashes all across the country. It will be rationed, but hopefully will be a nice bonus to what we can harvest from the forest. We'll be okay," she told him.

"I think, after what we went through, we'll definitely be okay. This winter will be a cakewalk compared to the three months on the road," he said.

"I got you something," she whispered to him.

"Oh, really?"

She was beaming as she grabbed his hand and pulled him towards the cart. There, she unfastened the tarp and flipped it up. His mouth fell open. "No way!"

"Yep. It's an old-school typewriter. I bet you thought you'd never have to use one of these giant bricks," she said with a laugh.

He reached out and ran his hand over the round black keys. He had fond memories of his mother sitting at their kitchen table and writing letters on a typewriter very similar to the one Amanda had picked up for him. "This is awesome. Thank you," he said, giving her another kiss.

"You're welcome. It's really Mrs. Gray you should be thanking. Everyone thinks of you as a hero. We were chatting at the market. She asked about you. I told her you wanted to write a book one day. She offered the typewriter she had stashed in her back room," Amanda said with a smile, "complete with ribbon and everything she said you'd need to get using it."

"That's awesome. I'm no hero, though," he added quietly. "I wish everyone would realize that. The ones who died are the heroes. I was selfish. I wanted to live in a safe world again. I did this for myself and us," he said, his voice gruff with emotion, just as it always got when someone called him a hero or tried to thank him for his role in the takedown of the NWO. It was why he rarely left the cabin. He wasn't ready to be showered with praise for doing something that was right. He wasn't ready to talk about his brother or Nash or any of the others, either.

"Where's Savannah?" she asked, looking around.

"Malachi came up for a visit," he said, adding feigned disgust to this tone.

Amanda playfully swatted his arm. "Stop. That boy would walk to the ends of the earth for her. I don't think you could have found a better young man for her. They do love each other, you know—I hope you accept that."

He wrinkled his nose. "I don't know if I'm ready to accept it... but I will let them explore the whole relationship thing," he added quickly, before Amanda could protest. "She's fifteen, but I know after everything she's been through, she's more like a twenty-five-year-old. I won't interfere, but I will be keeping an eye on things. I want her to have as much of a childhood as she can."

Amanda grinned. "You're doing good. You're coaching her and Malachi. I think it was incredibly sweet that he asked you if he could give her a promise ring."

Once again, Austin grimaced. "Like I told him, they can be promised to one another, but I don't want to hear about any marriage plans. I don't care how mature they think they are; they both need time to recover from all they've been through. It's only natural they're drawn to each other, but things might change with time. I'm only asking them both to take some time to make sure they know what they want."

"Drawn to each other like you and I?" she asked, looking up at him.

He grinned, giving her another quick kiss. "I think it's a little different from you and I. We're older, wiser, and far more world-wise. Malachi has been sheltered his entire life. Savannah, well, she's my little girl."

"Yes, she is, but she's not going to be that for long."

Austin had grudgingly accepted that. "No, she won't, but for now, she needs time to recover from everything she's gone through."

"I got something special for Andy. Where is he?" she asked, changing the subject.

"He was playing with his cars in the living room."

Amanda grabbed Austin's hand and walked with him into the three-bedroom cabin, leaving Raven tethered out front for a few moments; she'd get back to her soon and get her back to Charlie. Andy was sitting on the floor, his collection of Hot Wheels spread out over the wood floor. He looked up when he saw Amanda, his face lighting up. Amanda dropped to her knees and presented him with two more Hot Wheels. They were used, but everything they had was used. Surviving and flourishing now meant a lot of scavenging and trading among other survivors.

Trading wasn't just the current form of currency, either. It had become a way for survivors to begin to trust one another again. The military had been sending out small contingents of troops to spread the message about the NWO and their manipulations. They were working hard to restore trust among the survivors, explaining the propaganda and asking for acceptance. It wasn't an easy task, but things were slowly changing for the better.

Austin, unable to stop being the overprotective father, walked into the kitchen, looking out the window into the backyard, to where Savannah and Malachi had been hanging out. They were both seated on the bench he had fashioned from downed trees. Ennis's headstone was about five feet away, with another for Sarah close by. His eyes rested on the headstone, imagining his brother keeping an eye on Savannah from wherever he was.

Savannah looked up and saw him. She smiled and waved. Her eyes were bright and her face was filling out a little more, the signs of the hunger and weariness after their travels almost erased. He walked to the back door and called outside. "Amanda's back. Can you help unload the groceries?" he asked.

"I'll help," Malachi said, jumping up from the bench.

"I think she got a few things for your mom and the others," Austin informed him as Malachi came inside.

"We really appreciate that. She told me to invite you to the service on Sunday. We'd all really love for you to come—and the rest of the family, of course."

"I'll talk with Amanda. I'm sure she'd like to see you all. How is everyone?" he asked.

"Gretchen has been helping some of the townspeople with medicinal herbs and stuff. She's like the town doctor for now. My mom helps her a lot, and Harlen is always with her. I think they like each other. Drew's leg still bothers him, but he's been a real help around the house. Ezra's met a woman, too, and I think it's serious," he said.

"Wow. I've missed a lot," Austin said with a chuckle, knowing he'd been keeping to himself more than the others might have preferred. "I promise we'll get into town to visit soon. I've been working nonstop around here getting ready for the winter," he said, feeling a little guilty for his lack of friendship. He'd retreated to the mountain hideaway like a self-proclaimed hermit, needing time alone and away from reminders of all that had happened.

"It's okay. We understand. I'm just glad I got to come up and stay for a few days. I kind of miss being in the mountains," he said with a laugh.

"Trust me, I think this winter is going to be a real wake-up call. We might be coming down to your house in town for refuge," Austin joked.

"My mom would be happy to have you. We all would," he said.

Tonya and the others had decided to stay together. Because of their "hero" status, they'd been given the pick of the empty houses in town. They'd chosen a larger home on a piece of land they planned to farm. Tonya was going to be picking up where her husband had left off with his ministry. They were excited to be holding services, and, next year, they planned to be able to feed those who were hungry while providing shelter on the farm they were building. It was a noble idea, and Austin had faith they'd make it work.

Austin and Malachi walked around the cabin and began the task of unloading the cart and carrying the goods inside while Savannah caught up with Amanda. It felt good to be establishing a new normal. Austin looked forward to the day when he could flip a switch and have lights, but he was okay with the way things were. Having Amanda in his life, along with Andy and Savannah, was all he needed. It made him feel complete once again. He had a loving family and his heart was full. It was something he had been missing in the year before his world had been turned upside down.

Things had been dark long before the EMP had hit. Now, he was finally walking in the light.

END OF SURVIVE THE CONFLICT

Survive the Chaos, 11 July 2019

Survive the Aftermath, 8 August 2019

Survive the Conflict, 12 September 2019

Do you love post-apocalyptic fiction? Then keep reading for
an exclusive extract from *Dark Retreat.*

THANK YOU

Thank you for purchasing *Survive the Conflict*
(Small Town EMP Book Three)

Get prepared and sign-up to Grace's mailing list and be
notified of her next release:
www.gracehamiltonbooks.com/mailing-list

If you enjoyed this book:

Share it with a friend,
www.GraceHamiltonBooks.com/books

Leave a review at:

ABOUT GRACE HAMILTON

Grace Hamilton is the prepper pen-name for a bad-ass, survivalist momma-bear of four kids, and wife to a wonderful husband. After being stuck in a mountain cabin for six days following a flash flood, she decided she never wanted to feel so powerless or have to send her kids to bed hungry again. Now she lives the prepper lifestyle and knows that if SHTF or TEOTWAWKI happens, she'll be ready to help protect and provide for her family.

Combine this survivalist mentality with a vivid imagination (as well as a slightly unhealthy day dreaming habit) and you get a prepper fiction author. Grace spends her days thinking about the worst possible survival situations that a person could be thrown into, then throwing her characters into these nightmares while trying to figure out "What SHOULD you do in this situation?"

You will find Grace on:

BLURB

Three months after life as she knows it was decimated, Megan
Wolford has only one goal: protect her daughter, Caitlin, at
any cost. When a mysterious illness strikes Caitlin down,
Megan is forced to forage for medical supplies at a remote
lodge. The last thing she wants is help from her fellow

survivors when so many in her life have let her down—but soon she'll find herself with no other option.

Ex-Navy SEAL Wyatt Morris is doing everything he can to hold his family together after the tragic death of his prepper Dad, so when Megan enters their lands, he is mistrustful at first despite feeling drawn to her. He won't turn away an ill child though--no matter how deadly the world has become. But the arrival of another stranger named Kyle soon gives them all a new reason to be suspicious. Wyatt knows he'll have to forge alliances in order to keep his family safe, but trusting the wrong person could be a deadly mistake.

When Megan and Wyatt discover her daughter's illness may be linked to Kyle's arrival, it sets off a race to discover the truth before it's too late to save Caitlin—and the rest of the Morris clan. Can they work together for survival . . . and something more?

Get your copy of ***Dark Retreat (EMP Lodge Book 1)*** *from Amazon*

EXCERPT

Wyatt crept into the house with his pistol leading the way. When they returned home, they found the back door had been busted in. His senses went on high alert at the thought of someone inside. He gestured to his brother, Jack, to stay quiet. They were expecting looters at some point. Wyatt had put the

412

boards over the windows, hoping to deter anyone. They had worked too long and too hard to build this place up and make it into the safe retreat his family needed.

The cabin and all of preps that were concealed in and around it, were a labor of love for him and his father. This was the place they were all going to live out their days when it hit the fan. Unfortunately, things didn't go as planned and now they were forced to improvise.

Jack grabbed his wife's arm. "Take Ryland and hide," he whispered into her ear.

Willow nodded and used her eyes to direct her 12-year-old son to follow her. Jack and Wyatt's mom, Rosie, already knew she was to go with her daughter-in-law and grandson and quietly followed them into the thick trees that surrounded the lodge. Wyatt had created a blind beyond the backyard. This was the designated area for them to hide should intruders show up. The blind created a small space between the rocky hillside and the house. They could stay out of sight while looters did their thing. Wyatt had made it look like the place had already been looted. He had tossed the trash around and littered the area with broken glass to sell the story. Behind the boards, the windows were in tact. He only wanted to appear looted and abandoned. If someone did get in, they wouldn't find anything. Once the would-be bandits realized there was nothing there, they would leave and the family could go back to whatever it was they had been doing.

Wyatt designated himself as the one to enter the cabin, with his younger brother standing guard outside. The door had something blocking it. Not a problem considering Wyatt had the keys to the front door. It seemed silly to carry around keys nowadays, but it was a habit and a locked door could be enough deterrent to keep looters out. He instructed Chase and Albert to stay at the back while he and Jack went to the front. Using hand gestures, he ordered Jack to go upstairs while he searched below.

He walked through the house, not making a sound. His Navy Seal training kicked in and he carefully went about clearing each room. When he walked into his own room, he was stunned by what he found. A woman and child were sleeping in his bed. It felt like a scene out of the Goldilocks fairy tale.

Wyatt took a few seconds to evaluate the situation. The child was clearly not well. Her face was unnaturally pale and the area around her eyes was black. A black-haired woman was curled around the little girl in a protective gesture, even in sleep. He couldn't see much of her features, but he judged her to be in her late 20s or so. He imagined she must be the girl's mother, the resemblance was plain to see.

He heard footsteps behind him and spun around. Jack was approaching. He wasn't exactly stealth.

"Shhh," he said turning to his brother.

It was too late. The woman on the bed had been awoken. She looked mad, scared and fierce all at the same time. She stared at them with wide, brown eyes. There were heavy bags under each of those beautifully shaped almond eyes that were only enhanced by her pale skin. Scratches and bits of dried blood marred what he expected was perfectly smooth skin on her face. Her black hair was a tangled mess with little bits of birch tree seeds and various other foliage mixed in.

Wyatt took in the rest of her appearance. She had clearly had a rough time of it judging by the tears in her khaki pants. Her over-large gray t-shirt was thread bare. Despite her rather roughshod appearance, she was stunning. The shapely arms revealed she was muscular, but not overly so. The woman was not a wilting flower; he could see that just by the look of defiance she was issuing.

Wyatt held up his hands in a universal sign of surrender, "We aren't going to hurt you," he stated slowly and calmly.

She stared at his brother who was still pointing the gun at her. One raised eyebrow was all she needed to do to question his assertion.

"Jack, put the gun away."

Wyatt turned back to the weary woman watching them. "Look, we aren't going to hurt you," he paused, holstering his own weapon. "But, you are in our house, in our beds, so, well, you kinda need to tell us who you are."

His natural instinct was to protect a woman, especially a woman who was clearly on her own. The fact she had a young, sick child with her sealed the deal. He wasn't going to hurt her or kick them out. Call him chivalrous, but he wasn't about to send a woman and child off to fend for themselves. Not in this new world. His dad would never do something so harsh and he wanted to be like the man who gave his life for his family.

The woman opened her mouth, but quickly snapped it shut. It took about 2 seconds for Wyatt to figure out why.

"Who is she?" came a harsh voice from behind Wyatt.

Before he could answer Albert, there was another voice, much more serious. "Did you check her for weapons?"

Wyatt sighed, they weren't making the best first impression.

"Chase, Albert, can we give the woman a chance to introduce herself before we drag her in front of the firing squad." Wyatt winced when he heard the sharp intake of breath from the woman he had just threatened to put in front of a firing squad.

He turned back to apologize. She had stood and was now stalking towards him, with no sign of fear.

She stopped about 6 inches from him, pulled her perfect shoulders back and laid into him.

"My name isn't important. Clearly you neanderthals were never taught common courtesy or human decency. For you to actually threaten a woman and her obviously ill daughter is despicable."

Wyatt took an involuntary step back as she pressed forward. He stepped on Jack's foot, who was also trying to get out of the way of the woman bearing down on them. The room suddenly shrank and the door opening narrowed. She was pissed. That was pretty obvious. The scared look had disappeared and she looked downright furious. Wyatt felt the need to explain himself and his friends.

She didn't give him the chance.

"Don't you worry about checking me for a weapon." She pointed a finger at Chase, "Unlike you, I don't need to wave a gun about to scare people. Does that make you feel more like a man? Does it make you feel powerful?" She guffawed and swung her brown eyes back to Wyatt, "I, unlike you people, don't need a gun. I," she jabbed herself in her chest with her own finger, "don't need weapons to defend myself."

Wyatt knew there was a domino effect happening. Jack, Albert and Chase had all lined up behind him to get into the room. With every step the woman advanced, he was pushing back. If he didn't stop his retreat, they were all going to fall on their butts.

He started to speak again. He wasn't going to let her cut him off. Squaring his shoulders and speaking with as much confidence as he could gather, "I'm sorry. I, we, aren't going to hurt you." Her nostrils flared and he realized he offended her again —somehow. "I mean, we aren't like that. We," he stammered. "I mean, we, I mean, I am not like that. We aren't like that," he said with authority. So much for the confidence he chided himself. He turned into a blubbering idiot.

Her eyes became small slits and he could feel her looking him over. It was unnerving. It was exciting. It was completely brazen, but if he was being honest with himself, he loved it. It had been a few months since he experienced the excitement of meeting an attractive woman who showed any kind of interest in him. This interest may be a little on the negative side, but he could see she was passionate. Passionately hating him, but passion was passion. He grinned.

Once she was finished with a very thorough inspection, she met his eyes again, "We will leave. Tell your little army to back off." She sneered at Jack, "Stand down, big boy. This big, bad lady means you no harm." Wyatt wanted to laugh at the woman who was probably only a little over 5 foot tall. He actually had to bend his head down to look at her. His little brother was just a couple inches shorter than he was. And Chase, well Chase had often been referred to as the Green Giant throughout high school. He had shot up their sophomore year and hadn't stopped growing. Chase had several inches on him.

"You boys. Go take care of the door," grumbled a clearly irritated Rosie. "Wyatt, Jack, you know better," she said pushing them aside so she could get into the room. Wyatt flinched when he heard his mother's tone. He was 34, but it didn't mean his momma didn't scare him at times.

Rosie marched right over to the opposite side of the bed and sat down. She put her hand out to feel the little girl's head. She wasn't the least bit bothered by the woman who was staring her down.

"My name is Rosie Morris. The first two *neanderthals*," she smiled when she said the word. "Those two are my boys. The grumpy old guy in the back is Albert and the one who wants to shoot everybody is Chase."

Wyatt watched his mom break down all the walls the woman had erected around her.

"I'm Megan Wolford," she said in a much calmer demeanor than she spoke to him with. He was only a little offended.

"Ryland and Willow are waiting outside. I imagine Ryland will be thrilled to have another kid to hang out with." While she talked, she had pulled the sheet from the little girl and was looking her over. Jack took that as his cue to leave and quickly shuffled out of the room.

Wyatt decided it was best to leave his mom alone to do what she did best—mother and nurture. He turned and used his head to silently gesture to the rest of his group to leave. They did so and he gently closed the door behind him.

Megan studied the woman carefully examining her daughter. Her natural instinct told her the woman was safe, but the over-protective mother in her wanted the woman to get away from her little girl.

Rosie looked up at Megan as she carefully tucked the sheet back around Caitlin.

"What's her name?" Rosie asked softly.

"Caitlin." Her manners were deeply ingrained and despite what the last three months had been like, she couldn't help but apologize for her initially rude behavior. "I'm sorry about earlier. Your sons had guns on me. It startled me."

Rosie smiled, "Sweetie, I probably would have tossed the lamp at them myself. Don't you worry about it. How long has Caitlin been sick?"

Megan took a deep breath, "She only started acting sick about 2 days ago. She was fine until then."

Rosie nodded her head, "How old is she?"

"Seven, but you would think she was 15 if you hear her talk."

That garnered a chuckle from the rosy-cheeked woman who was small in stature. Megan found it hard to believe she was the mother of the two very large men that had pushed their way into the room earlier. This woman had a gentle nature about her. Megan imagined she probably was the type of lady who baked and knitted before the world fell apart.

"Well, dear," Rosie spoke, interrupting Megan's reverie about days gone by. "Let's go into the kitchen. You can tell me more about her symptoms, we will get you some coffee and we will come up with a way to make her better." She reached out and put a hand on Megan's bent knee. "You are safe here. I promise. Nobody will hurt you."

Megan was hesitant, but what choice did she have? She was out of options. She had heard of a hospital on the state line between Idaho and Washington, but there was no way she could carry Caitlin out the door let alone across the rough terrain.

"I would appreciate anything you can do to help her," Megan told her appreciatively. "I don't know what happened. I don't," Rosie stopped her.

"Let's go get a cup of coffee and we will go over it all from the beginning of her symptoms. I may have something on hand to treat her."

Megan instantly felt guilty. She already knew there was no medicine in the place. She looked down at the floor, trying to avert the woman's eyes.

Rosie had that mother's instinct and smiled. "Not that kind of medicine. I have lots of herbs. I have used herbs to treat the boys and myself for years."

Megan was instantly intrigued. She had of course heard of herbal remedies, but to be honest, in a world where modern medicine was 5 minutes or a phone call away, she had never taken the time to learn about it. Thank God this woman did.

Rosie walked to the door, holding it open, waiting for Megan to follow.

Megan took a second to give Caitlin a kiss on the forehead. "Mommy will be right back, sweetie. I'm going to get you some medicine and we will get you all better soon."

Get your copy of *Dark Retreat (EMP Lodge Book 1) from Amazon*

WANT MORE?

WWW.GRACEHAMILTONBOOKS.COM

Made in the USA
Monee, IL
29 October 2020